More

than

Sometimes

Cal and Teresa
Summer Lake Silver, Book Six

By SJ McCoy

A Sweet n Steamy Romance

Published by Xenion, Inc

Published by Xenion, Inc.
First paperback edition 2021
www.sjmccoy.com

This book is a work of fiction. Names, characters, places, and events are figments of the author's imagination, fictitious, or are used fictitiously. Any resemblance to actual events, locales or persons living or dead is coincidental.

Cover Design by Dana Lamothe of Designs by Dana
Cover photography by Golden Czermak of Furious Photog
Cover Model: Mike Parent

Editor: Kellie Montgomery
Proofreaders: Aileen Blomberg, Traci Atkinson, Marisa Nichols

ISBN: 978-1-946220-77-6

Dedication

For Sam. Sometimes, life really is too short. Few oxo

Chapter One

Cal pushed his chair back away from his desk and folded his hands behind his head. He was pleased with what he'd achieved in his first week. He was starting to get things in order. He nodded to himself. Dan had set this whole outfit up to work well but his focus was elsewhere. Dan was a tech guy, not an operations guy. That was why he'd brought Cal in.

He looked up at the sound of a knock on his office door and had to laugh when he saw Ryan and Manny standing there grinning at him.

"Yes? Can I help you?"

"More like we've come to help you," said Ryan. "You've barely come up for air since you came in here on Monday morning. Now it's Friday afternoon—time to cut loose."

Cal frowned. "It's not even four o'clock."

Dan came to join them and smiled at him. "It's almost four o'clock, though. And since there's no operational need for anyone to be here on the weekends yet, we close up."

Cal raised an eyebrow at him. "That's not—"

Manny came into the office. "There's no point in arguing. I tried that, but I'll warn you now, these guys will only start harping on about how we're supposed to be retired." He shot

1

an evil look at Ryan. "*He'll* start giving you grief about not working full time at our age."

Ryan laughed. "Nah, I wouldn't do that to Cal."

Manny rolled his eyes. "If you start talking about me being even older than him …"

"Nope." Ryan winked at Cal. "I just know that Cal would kick my ass into next week if I gave him even half the grief you let me get away with."

Manny clipped the back of his head. "I've resisted all this time, but if that's what it'll take …"

Dan shook his head at Cal as the two of them watched Manny and Ryan start to wrestle.

"Enough!" Cal had to hide his smile when they both snapped to attention.

Dan laughed. "Damn, you need to teach me how to do that."

Cal shrugged. "It doesn't come easy. It comes from a whole career of having to keep them and a whole team of others just like them in line."

"I don't think that's true," said Ryan. "Even without a lifetime's worth of practice, I'd quake in my boots when I heard you bark out orders in that tone."

Manny smirked at him. "That's only because you quake in your boots at the first sign of trouble."

Ryan raised his fists with a grin, ready to go at it again.

"Can you give it a rest?" said Cal. "For guys who've spent their lives in the field working the kinds of ops you two have, you're more like a pair of little kids."

Dan nodded, but didn't say anything.

Manny blew out a sigh. "You're right. I'm old enough to know better, but this one …" He clipped the back of Ryan's head again. "He brings out the worst in me."

Ryan jabbed his arm with a grin. "You know you love me, really."

Dan turned to Cal. "Do you want to come out for dinner later? I think everyone's meeting up at the Boathouse."

Cal thought about it. Ryan was right that he'd barely come up for air since he'd started work on Monday. He'd stayed here at the office until late each night, only going back to the house to eat, sleep, go to the gym, and shower before returning in the morning. All he wanted to do tonight was repeat the routine, and if finishing early gave him a few extra hours then he should use them to run errands and start putting the house in order. It was only a rental, and he wasn't sure how long he'd stay there, but ...

Manny raised an eyebrow at him. "Don't say no. I've promised Nina that she'll get to meet you tonight."

Cal smiled. He was eager to meet the woman who'd managed to change the intense, take-no-shit special agent he'd known for half a lifetime into this new grinning, play-fighting version of himself, who Cal had to admit he liked even better.

"Come on, boss." Ryan looked more serious now. "I love that I get to work with you again, but I've been looking forward to you being a part of life around here, too." He smiled. "It's a new one for us."

"It is." In all the years Ryan had worked for him at the agency, they'd rarely socialized. There wasn't room for it in that life. And this ... this was supposed to be a new life: his retirement. He needed to remember that and try to learn to chill out more. "Okay. What time?"

"Missy and I are going over there at seven-thirty," said Dan.

Manny nodded. "That's when we said, too. Nina's trying to get her friend to come."

Cal narrowed his eyes. Manny knew better than to try and set him up with a woman.

"Don't look at him like that," said Ryan. "He can't be held responsible for Nina. She's a sweetheart and she wants to see everyone happy. She'll want to set you up with someone who'll take care of you."

Cal gave Manny a warning look. "I'm sure she is a sweetheart, but I can look after myself—and you all know it."

Manny gave him a half smile. "We do. But I'll let you be the one to convince Nina of it. And you might want to wait until after you've met her friend."

"Who—?" Ryan began, but Cal cut him off by shoving his chair back and getting to his feet.

"I have some errands to run, so if we're really done for the day, I'll get to them. I'll see you all at the Boathouse later."

Manny caught up with him as he made his way out to the parking lot. "Will you be there or was that just the standard Callahan; tell them what they need to hear to get them off you back?"

Cal chuckled. "I haven't decided yet."

"I figured. If you don't come, do you want to join me for a run in the morning? I'll be going around seven."

"Sure."

"Okay." They'd reached Cal's car. "But don't use that as a built-in excuse not to come tonight?"

"I won't. I think I'll be there. I need to get a haircut, get some groceries and …" He shrugged. "That's about the extent of what I have to do so …"

Manny smiled. "So, I'll see you later. You'll only be climbing the walls otherwise."

Cal got into his car. "Seven-thirty, then."

~ ~ ~

"We'll see you in six weeks." Teresa handed the appointment card to Elaine Summers with a smile.

"Thanks, Terry." Elaine shot a glance over at Elle. "Do you think she'll still be here by then?"

Teresa shrugged. "I hope so."

"Me, too. You should get her more involved. Let her step up and run the place. You take it a bit easier."

Teresa gave her a rueful smile. "I'm just playing it by ear."

Elle looked over, as if she somehow knew they were talking about her even though there was no way she could hear them over the hairdryer in her hand.

Teresa met her gaze. She was hoping with all her heart that Elle would decide to stay, but she knew better than to think she'd get a say in her daughter's decisions—or her granddaughter's future.

"I'll see you next time, if not before," Elaine said as she left.

Teresa checked the clock on the wall. Mel Thomas should be here any minute, and she was just a blow dry ready for the weekend.

She reached for the phone when it rang. "Mane Street Salon. This is Teresa—"

"Teresa! I'm so sorry. It's Mel. I'm supposed to be there and I'm not going to make it."

"Is everything okay?"

"Yes. Don't worry. Everything's fine. It's not an emergency or anything. It's just me. I swear my short-term memory's starting to fail. I completely forgot. I'm at the mall down Route Twenty. It was only when Barb called to check that I'm still going tonight that I remembered that for one thing, I'm going out tonight and for another, I'm supposed to be getting my hair done for it."

Teresa laughed. "Don't worry about it, it's not a problem. You were my last appointment, so I'll make the most of it and go home early."

"You do that, but be sure and charge me the cancellation fee, won't you? I don't want to mess you around."

"Thanks."

"Of course. We're friends but this is business. I wouldn't take advantage."

"Thanks."

"I'll give you a call on Monday morning and rebook for next week, if you can fit me in."

"Sure, but don't leave it too long, my schedule's mostly full."

"I'll tell you what, do you have this same time next week?"

Teresa checked the screen. "No. Sorry. Elle can take you if you like?"

Elle glanced over at her. Teresa was trying to help her build her clientele up now that she was back, even though neither of them knew if she wanted it.

"I'll take it. Thanks. I'll see you then."

"Bye." Teresa hung up and tapped in the appointment before she got to her feet. She went to stand beside her daughter, who was brushing out the gorgeous cut and balayage she'd spent the afternoon on. "Wow, you look gorgeous," she told the girl sitting in the chair.

"Isn't it perfect?" The girl looked up at Elle. "You're amazing! Thank you so much! Please say you're going to stay?"

Elle smiled at her, then met Teresa's gaze in the mirror. "I'm not sure yet."

Teresa nodded. At least it wasn't a flat-out no. "My last appointment just canceled. So, how would you feel about closing up tonight?"

"Sure. It'd do you good to go home and put your feet up. Are you going to go out with Nina later? You know she wants you to."

"Well … actually … I was thinking I could go and get Skye for you. You know, take her home and—"

Elle was already shaking her head. "I'm not being mean, Mom. I'm really not. But I'm trying to get her into some sort of routine. Jackie's not expecting me to pick her up until six-thirty. I don't want to mess her around."

Teresa nodded sadly. "You're right. I'm sorry. I just …"

Elle touched her arm. "We'll hang out on Sunday, huh? The three of us?"

Teresa had to blink and hope that her eyes weren't too shiny. "I'd love that, sweetheart. I'll see you later. Oh." She rolled her eyes at the sound of the bell when the door opened. "Looks like I might not be leaving after all."

She turned to see what kind of client she'd be facing. Tourist season had quieted down now, but they still got walk-ins. Wow! She pressed her lips together, hoping that she hadn't just said that out loud. The sound of Elle's giggle beside her let her know that she might have. It was hardly her fault; the man standing just inside the door was breathtaking—even if he did look thoroughly uncomfortable as he took in his surroundings. He couldn't be a starker contrast to the soft pastel and undeniably feminine décor of the salon—he was solid, masculine …

"Go get him, Mom!"

Teresa bit back a giggle of her own and hurried toward the door before he could turn around and leave. He looked like he could've walked off the set of an action movie—one of those where all the actors used to be the hot, young things in Hollywood, but these days they were the older generation—but still hot. She'd guess he was around her age. Maybe a little older. She kept herself in good shape, but he looked like he must live in the gym; he was solid muscle. He must be military by the way he carried himself; he even had the whole square jaw thing going on. She made herself focus.

"Good afternoon, what can we do for you?" No way was she going to let her mind wander to all the things she'd like to do *to* him!

He met her gaze. Phew! His eyes were a piercing blue.

She smiled, waiting for him to speak.

He continued to stare for a few moments before shaking his head. "No."

She raised an eyebrow.

His expression softened, though he didn't quite smile. "Can you tell me where I can get a haircut in this town?"

She gave him a puzzled look before casting a curious eye around the salon.

She looked back when he made a noise. It wasn't a laugh, but by the way the corners of his mouth turned up ever so slightly, she'd guess that it was at least an expression of amusement.

"I mean, where can *a man* get a haircut."

She couldn't help it. She looked him up and down.

This time he cracked—and his smile was so worth the wait. She wanted to laugh at the thought of the sun coming out from behind the clouds and birds breaking into song all because of that smile.

"Yes, I'm a man."

Was he ever!

"And yes, I can see that this is an establishment where hair gets cut." He pursed his lips and she'd guess that it was to stop himself from letting any more smiles out. "But it doesn't strike me that this is where men get their hair cut."

She finally let out a chuckle. "I'm sorry. I was only playing with you. It's a small town. There's no barber's shop. The men around here either do it themselves, get their wives to do it, or they come to me." She held out her hand to shake with him. "I'm Teresa."

Whoa! He had big hands. She had to bite back a laugh at the obvious question that raised about other parts of his anatomy.

He held onto her hand for just a moment too long. "Well, I don't like to do it myself and I don't have a wife to do it for me …" He held her gaze and his eyes told her that he wasn't thinking about a haircut any more than she was. "So, I guess I'm coming to you."

Her throat went dry and she had to swallow before she could speak. She was probably just imagining the whole thing. "Well, alrighty then." She gave him her best customer-facing smile. "Do you want to do it right now?"

She realized her unfortunate wording at the same time as he laughed. It was the sexiest sound she'd heard in years.

She smiled at him through pursed lips.

"Now works for me, but I can make an appointment if you'd rather?"

"No need to wait. You're in luck. I just had a cancellation." She motioned for him to follow her to her chair.

"His loss is my gain."

He probably only meant his gain in getting an appointment straight away, but the way he was looking at her when she turned to him made her wonder. "Not a he," she said. "I do women, too."

His laugh was rich and deep.

She covered her mouth with her hand and shook her head. "Oh, my God! Not like that! What do you think, should we start again from the top?"

He smiled. "Sure thing. Good afternoon, ma'am. Is there any chance you can give me a haircut?"

"Why yes, yes I can. Please, take a seat. I'm Teresa, nice to meet you."

He held her gaze. Those eyes were something else. "It's a pleasure to meet you, too."

She'd hoped that he'd tell her his name. When she told Nina about this later—heck, when she replayed it in her mind—she wanted to be able to say his name. He wasn't offering, so she asked. "And your name is?"

"Blake."

"Oh." He didn't look like a Blake, but what did it matter? If he found his way back into her thoughts—or dreams—later, and she already knew he would, she could call him by whatever name she liked. "And what can I do for you, Blake?" She gave him a wry smile in the mirror. "What kind of haircut are you looking for?"

Chapter Two

Cal tensed as she slipped a gown over him and had to close his eyes at the feel of her fingers brushing the back of his neck as she fastened it. She'd knocked him off kilter the moment he'd laid eyes on her. He didn't even know why he was sitting here. As soon as he'd stepped inside the salon, he'd known the place wasn't for him. But when she'd turned and smiled at him …

"Can I get you a drink or anything before we get started?"

He looked up at her. She was beautiful. Her eyes were a light brown color and they seemed to dance when she smiled. She was smiling at him now, waiting for him to answer. He cleared his throat. He wanted to ask if he could get her a drink instead—take her out for one. He shook his head. "I'm fine, thanks."

The phone rang, and she held up a finger. "Sorry. I'll be right back."

He didn't mind. He was glad to be given a minute to pull himself together. He prided himself on being able to handle any situation he was thrown into. He was quick to see and implement the necessary course of action and he always came out on top. He clenched his jaw when he saw Teresa bend over the desk to write something down. He shouldn't start thinking about coming out on top. What had gotten into him, anyway?

She caught his gaze in the mirror as she came back to him. "Sorry about that. And you're sure I can't get you a drink?"

He held her gaze, considering again whether he should ask if he could get her one once they were finished here. No. He wasn't one to be moved by a pretty face—or an attractive figure. He forced himself not to let his gaze travel over her again—he already knew how attractive hers was. But women tended to irritate him. If he still found her as appealing by the time they were finished here, he'd allow himself to reconsider asking her out. "No."

She stood behind him and ran her fingers through his hair. He had to grip the arms of the chair—glad for the cover that the gown provided, so that she couldn't see him grasping the metal frame.

"So, just a trim?"

He nodded at her in the mirror and didn't let out his breath until she stepped away to get her scissors.

She worked in silence for a few minutes, which surprised him. In his experience, women tended to chatter away mercilessly. He frowned as he realized that he'd expected her to be that way just because she worked in a hair salon. That wasn't good. Not only was he buying into a stereotype, but it left no room or curiosity to find out who she might actually be.

He watched her work for another few moments. She was quick and efficient, obviously talented at what she did.

She glanced up and met his gaze in the mirror, and he was surprised to see himself smile. He couldn't help it. He tightened his grip on the arms of the chair again when she smiled back.

"Don't look so worried. I'm not going to talk your ear off. I've been doing this long enough that I have a good sense of what you need."

"Need?" He raised an eyebrow at her. He doubted her sense was so good that she could tell what he needed right now.

"Yeah. You need quiet. Sometimes, people need a listening ear. Sometimes, they need a chat and to catch up on all the gossip in town. Sometimes, they want me to ramble on about nothing in particular." She shrugged and brushed her fingers over the back of his neck, sending electric currents shooting down his spine. "You need quiet." She smiled. "And you need to get out of here as quickly as possible, right?"

He smiled through pursed lips. "You're good. But you're not completely right."

She raised an eyebrow as she continued working. "What did I miss?"

"You didn't miss a thing. When I first walked in here, I would have said that you were spot on. I don't do chit-chat and I wanted to be in and out as quickly as possible."

"But?"

"But now I'm in less of a hurry to leave—and I'm enjoying talking to you."

She straightened up and came to stand behind him. He wondered if he'd blown it. It wasn't like him to talk to a woman like that. He was relieved when she smiled.

"Well, in that case. Do you want to talk some more? Tell me where you're from, what you're doing here? I'm curious, but I thought I knew better than to ask."

He smiled back at her. He should ask her out. Not only was she beautiful, she was smart, too. "I'm from Minnesota …" What the hell, why not? "Would you have any interest in going for a drink with me later?" The phone started to ring again, but she ignored it, so Cal tried to as well and continued, "I'm curious about you, too …"

"Sorry, Mom, can you get that?"

He'd hoped that the blonde girl who'd just finished with another customer and gone into the back would answer it. Teresa gave him a rueful smile. "Hold that thought. I won't be a minute."

As he watched her go back to the desk, he was ninety percent certain that when she returned, she'd say yes. His phone buzzed in his pocket, and he glanced over at Teresa. He'd have time to check his messages before she returned.

He smiled when he saw Darla's name pop up.

Darla: How are you liking California, big brother?

He checked on Teresa again, she'd sat down at the desk and was looking at the computer. He'd have time to answer.

Cal: So far, so good. How are you and the kids?

Darla: We're all good. We miss you though. They keep asking when you'll be coming back.

Teresa was hanging up and coming back to him.

Cal: I'm busy right now. Tell the kids I'll be home when I can.

Darla: Will do. Call when you get a chance. Love you. Miss you.

Cal rolled his eyes. He knew she'd want him to say it back.

Cal: Love you and miss you, too, Darl.

He finished typing and hit send as he braced himself for the feel of Teresa's fingers on his neck again as she stood behind him. He looked up in surprise when the comb raked none too gently through his hair. Her whole demeanor had changed. He tried to catch her gaze in the mirror, but she avoided him. Perhaps the phone call was bad news? It hadn't looked that way. He'd have guessed she was simply taking an appointment.

"Is everything okay?" He had to ask.

She nodded curtly. "Yep. We'll have you done and out of here in just a few more minutes."

Hmm. He didn't think he'd been wrong about her interest in him. It'd been a while since he'd played the dating game, but he'd have sworn she was attracted to him.

She worked on silently and true to her word, just a few minutes later, she stood back. "How's that? Do you want me to run the clippers?"

He gave her a puzzled look, but she didn't meet his gaze. He'd thought it was standard procedure to run the clippers over his neck before the cut was considered finished. She was giving off weird antagonistic vibes, though. "That's fine, thanks." He got to his feet, unsure what had changed, but very sure about the fact that it was time for him to make a quick exit. "What do I owe you?"

She stalked away to the desk, and he removed the gown himself before following her. The girl who'd called her Mom came out from the back and shot him a smile. He didn't smile back. He didn't know what was going on, only that he'd be better off getting out of here.

"That'll be twenty-five." Teresa didn't even look up at him as she said it.

Cal couldn't for the life of him figure out what was going on. He took two twenties from his wallet and set them down on the counter. "That's fine," he said when she started to make change.

"Thank you."

He stood there for a moment longer. Every instinct told him he should turn around and walk out and never look back. This was the kind of thing that women did—and he never understood. It didn't usually bother him. He'd accepted a long time ago that he was so far out of sync with the female psyche that it wasn't worth him even trying to understand. But … he looked her over again … she made him want to try.

"I take it you're not interested in that drink with me?"

"Pft!"

He stepped back at the contempt loaded into that little sound. It made her answer quite clear, even if it left him befuddled as to her reasons for it.

"Okay, then." He turned on his heel and left.

Teresa's shoulders sagged as she watched him go. Even his rear view was gorgeous—that might be the best ass she'd ever seen on a man.

"Mom!" Elle came hurrying to her. "What the heck? What happened? I thought I was witnessing the beginning of a beautiful friendship there. I heard him ask you out. He's hot—for an older guy. What changed?"

Teresa let out a little laugh as she shook her head. "He is hot, but I'd guess his wife thinks so, too."

"His wife?" Elle looked shocked.

"Yeah. He was texting her while I took that call. I could see his phone when I went back to him."

"Are you sure it was his wife? How could you tell?"

"Well, even if she's not his wife, she's someone he calls darling. He told her to tell the kids he'd be home when he could, and he said, love you and miss you, too. Wife or not, I doubt she'd be happy to know that he'd just asked me out for a drink."

"Ugh! Men." Elle made a face. "They're all the same, aren't they? No matter what age."

Teresa felt bad. Elle's boyfriend had cheated on her and dumped her and little Skye. That was why they were back here at the lake. "No, sweetheart, they're not all like that, but ..." She blew out a sigh. "Don't give up on them. Just be careful."

"No. I've given up. They're more trouble than they're worth."

"Not all of them. Just look at Nina's daughter, Abbie. She had a rough go down in the city, just like you did. Then she came home and met Ivan; he's wonderful."

"He is, but ... you know I don't really want to stay, Mom. And even if I did, I doubt I'd get as lucky as Abbie did. It's different. I have Skye. I should give up on men until she's grown up. I don't want her to—" She stopped short and Teresa's stomach sank, wondering if Elle had been about to say that she didn't want her daughter to follow in their footsteps.

Elle touched her hand. "I felt bad asking you to get the phone when he was asking you out like that. Now, I'm glad I couldn't get it, or you would have gone out with him, wouldn't you?"

Teresa nodded sadly. "Yeah. He was a good-looking guy and he seemed nice."

"You should go out with Nina and Manny tonight. You might meet another good-looking guy—a single, decent one."

Teresa laughed. "I'm not looking for a guy, Elle. You know that."

"Yeah, but you should go anyway. You haven't been out once since we came home. It'd do you good."

"You might be right. First though, I need to run to the grocery store, and then I might stop in and see Austin on the way home."

Elle gave her a stern look. "I've told you. I don't want you kicking any of your tenants out to give me a place. I'll find something myself … if I stay."

"I know. I wouldn't kick them out. In fact, that's not what I want to talk to him about anyway. I heard that the Marshalls want to sell their place and I wouldn't mind buying it."

"I love that you've turned into this property tycoon. It's awesome. I'm so proud of you, Mom."

Teresa's heart filled up and overflowed. To hear her daughter say she was proud of her was the best feeling in the world.

~ ~ ~

Cal stopped at the house before he went to the grocery store. He'd told Teresa that he didn't like to do his own hair, and that was true. But he did have clippers, and he wouldn't feel finished until he used them. He let out a short, humorless laugh as he ran up the stairs. He'd need to get used to using them, anyway. He didn't plan on going back to the salon any time soon.

When he was finished, he went back down to the kitchen and took inventory of the contents of the fridge and the cabinets. He wanted to stock up so that he wouldn't be tempted to stop at the restaurant in the resort for takeout every night. This wasn't just an assignment; he planned to be here long-term, so he should make it feel like a home.

Ten minutes later, he was pulling up in the parking lot of the grocery store. He started to get out of his SUV but stopped and pulled the door closed when he saw Teresa walking toward him. He held his breath wondering if he should call to her and ask her what the problem had been earlier. No. Ducking back into the car had been his first instinct, he should roll with it. First instincts were the ones that kept you alive. He smiled to himself. That might be a bit over-the-top, she was hardly likely to kill him. But he didn't want to risk tangling with her again. She was a beautiful woman, a very attractive woman, the tightness in the front of his pants verified that. But as much as he liked beautiful, he didn't need it. He needed a quiet, drama-free life. So, he waited for her to pass. He wondered if he should wait here until she returned to her vehicle, that way he'd be assured of not running into her inside the store. No. He watched her enter the building. He was a covert ops specialist. He might not have been in the field for years, but he had faith in his ability to negotiate the aisles of the grocery store without running into her.

He was in and out and back to the house within twenty minutes. Once he'd put the groceries away, he checked his watch. He still had plenty of time to kill before he met up with the guys. He looked around the house. There was nothing much that needed to be done. He didn't like the place and he didn't think he'd be staying, so there was no point in attempting to make it feel lived in. It would be just one more temporary post. He smiled. But this time, he'd be using it as a base while he looked for the place that would become home. And that thought gave him an idea: Austin, the realtor who'd found him this place had said he'd be happy to help him search when he was ready to buy. He wasn't sure he was ready yet, but it'd do no harm to check the listings, see what was available. He could do that online of course. But just for the sake of not sitting here, watching the time tick by, he could pay Austin a visit and get some intel on the market.

He parked on Main Street, a few doors down from the realtor's office. When he reached it, he spent a few minutes looking at the listings in the window. He liked that Austin displayed a little of everything right out front. Sure, there were big waterfront homes, and the modern new-builds over on the other side of the lake, but there were also pictures of smaller, modest homes right here in town, too.

He pushed his hands into his pockets as he read the details beneath a photo of a super-modern looking place which stood right by the water. The address was Four Mile Creek; that was the development over on the other side of the lake where Manny was buying a place with Nina. Cal wondered what it'd be like to have them as neighbors. He smiled at the thought and went to push the door open.

He stopped dead when he saw Teresa inside, glaring at him.

Austin shot her a puzzled look before greeting him. "Hi, Cal. I'll be with you in a few minutes."

Teresa scowled. "That's okay Austin. I'm leaving." She came to the door, fixing Cal with an angry look the whole way.

He stepped aside and held it open for her.

"Stop following me!" She spoke in a low voice as she passed him.

Once she'd gone, Austin raised an eyebrow at him. "Do you two know each other?"

Cal shook his head. He was still trying to get a lid on his reaction to her. While his mind reacted angrily and wanted to set her straight that he wasn't following her—that he'd gladly stay the hell out of her way—his body felt as though it had come to life again in her presence and wanted nothing more than to do exactly what she'd just told him not to.

"No." He ran his hand over the back of his neck. "She cut my hair this afternoon. She ... I ... I ran into her at the grocery store a little while ago." He shrugged. "I guess seeing me here, too, made her think ... it must seem ... three times in one afternoon?" He shrugged again. "I guess I can see it."

Austin nodded. "I guess. But it's a small town. Teresa knows what it's like, we all run into each other all the time. Anyway, that's not what you're here for. What can I do?"

Cal forced himself to focus on what he was here for. "I'm ready to start looking. I wanted to pick your brain about what the market's like."

Austin nodded, but Cal could tell he wasn't thrilled. He shot a glance at the clock on the wall. It was almost five-thirty. Damn. He should have thought. Just because time didn't hold much meaning for him when he was working didn't mean that Austin would feel the same way. "What time do you close?"

"It's okay."

Cal fixed him with a stern look. "What time do you close?"

Austin laughed. "Five."

Cal laughed with him. "So, you're already late. Forget it. I can look at your website."

"I don't mind. I just need to call Amber and let her know …"

"No."

Austin laughed. "Wow. I bet no one ever argues with you when you talk like that, do they?"

Cal shrugged. He didn't like to spell out that no, not many people did. He was used to giving orders and used to them being followed—and it was a habit he was trying to get out of now that he was retired. It came in handy sometimes, though. "Do you have the details on the place at Four Mile Creek? I'll take those for now and you can call me on Monday to set something up."

"Sure. Which one …"

"The one on the water."

Austin smiled and pulled out a brochure.

Cal nodded when he saw the photo on the front. "That's the one. Is it open for showings?"

"It is. I'm out of the office next week, but I can …"

"I can wait. I'm not in a hurry."

"I was going to say I can ask Dallas, my brother, to set it up for you."

Cal frowned. His sister-in-law was a realtor, and it was his understanding that they clung to every potential sale—they didn't hand buyers over to other agents, there was too much commission at stake. "It's okay. I can wait for you."

Austin held his gaze long enough that Cal wanted to tell him to spit it out. Eventually, he did.

"Can I be frank with you?"

"I expect you to be."

Austin smiled. "Of course. It's just that Dallas just got his license. He's good, and I'll be his backup, I'll watch all the details. But I'd like him to get his first sale, and if you're looking at Lakeside … it'd be a good first deal for him."

It would. Even three percent of the sale price would be a handsome commission and a great start to a career. "What about you?"

"I want him to find his feet. I want him to stick around."

Cal grasped his shoulder, liking him even more. "Okay, then. You have him call me and set something up. Do you want me to take it easy on him or …?"

Austin chuckled. "I'll let you be the judge of that. That's why I asked you. I get the feeling he could probably pick up some life lessons as well as real estate experience from working with you."

"Have him call me." Cal let himself out. He'd be happy to help. His smile faded when he remembered the look on Teresa's face when she left. Ah, well. She was beautiful, but he didn't need to deal with that kind of crazy. He'd be happy to stay out of her way.

Chapter Three

"Are you sure you don't want to go out? I can stay home and watch Skye for you. I don't mind, sweetheart."

"Thanks, Mom, but really, I'm pooped. It's been a long time since I've done a full week like this at work. We're going to play for a while." She dropped a kiss on top of Skye's head. "Then, once she's gone to bed, I'm going to do my nails and watch a movie."

Teresa wished that Elle would show some interest in life here. She'd love for her to pick up with some of her old friends and settle back in. But so far all she'd wanted to do was work and hang out at home with Skye. Of course, she was a wonderful mom, and that was the life she'd been used to from what Teresa could gather. While her boyfriend had thought it was just fine to go gallivanting with his friends—and other girls—it sounded as though he'd been domineering with Elle and Skye. He'd wanted them at home.

Elle waved a hand in front of her face. "Hello? What are you thinking? Don't tell me that you're changing your mind about going out? You deserve it, Mom. I feel bad that you almost had a date, but he turned out to be a pig. You should see what this friend of Manny's is like. She waggled her eyebrows. Nina's

done well for herself there. I never did like Abbie's dad ..."
She stopped. "That's a horrible thing to say now that he's
dead, isn't it?"

Teresa shrugged. "No. It's just how you feel." She wanted to
move on from that subject. Elle's instincts about the man Nina
had been married to for thirty years were spot on. But she
couldn't tell her that. Abbie still thought the sun had shone out
of him.

"Anyway. You should go."

"I think I will." She went to little Skye, who looked up at her
with a smile.

"See you tomorrow, Grandma."

Teresa wrapped her up in a hug and then set her back down
again. "See you tomorrow, sweet pea." She looked at Elle. "I'll
give Nina a call and then take a shower and get ready."

Elle smiled. "Don't be on the phone with her too long. You
know what you two are like; you'll chat all night. Keep it short
and talk to her when you see her."

"I'll try." Teresa took her phone through to the kitchen and
dialed Nina's number.

She answered on the second ring. "Hi. I was about to call
you. You are coming, aren't you?"

"I am."

"Good. I had a feeling you were going to drop out. I know
you love having Elle and Skye home, but I haven't seen you in
ages. And I need you to even up the numbers tonight."

"Even up the numbers?"

"Yeah. Leanne's out of town, she had to go back to San
Francisco, so Ryan will be by himself, and Manny's friend, Cal,
is going to come out. I don't want to be the only woman with
three men."

Teresa laughed. "I think a lot of women would envy you. Three good-looking men all to yourself. Well, two and what's Manny's friend like?"

"I don't know. I haven't met him yet. But I'm hopeful."

"I hope you don't mean on my behalf?"

"Of course, I do! Can you imagine? Don't you think it'd be great if you ended up getting together with Manny's friend?"

Teresa laughed. "We're not in high school anymore, Nina. It's been more than thirty years since our days of double-dating."

Nina laughed with her. "I know. I'm getting carried away. But it is a nice thought."

"Yeah. Nice, but hardly realistic. And besides, I'm off men."

"What? Why?"

"Nothing."

"No, come on, tell me. Last time I saw you, you were talking about going on another one of those adventure vacations—in part to meet an adventurous man. What's changed? Oh … is it because of Elle? Because she's home?"

"No! It's not that at all. It's just … there was a guy in the salon today."

"Ooh. Tell me more?"

"There's nothing to tell. He was a good-looking guy, sexy. Just my type. We hit it off, there was something there. He even asked if I wanted to go for a drink afterward."

"And you didn't go?"

"No. Because I went to take a call and when I came back, he was texting. I peeked; I know I shouldn't, but I'm glad I did. He was texting his wife saying to tell the kids he'd be home when he could get there and love you, miss you." She shuddered, mostly at the fact that she'd had a narrow escape—

but partly in disappointment, too. He might be a horrible human being, but they'd definitely had chemistry.

"Oh, Terry, that's awful. Did you throw him out?"

"No, he was almost done anyway. But perhaps I should have told him what I'd seen. I'm hoping it was just coincidence, but I ran into him two more times after that. I'd swear that he followed me to the grocery store, and then he came into Austin's place when I was there, too."

"No?"

"Yeah, but like I say, hopefully it was just a coincidence."

"I'm going to tell Manny."

Teresa laughed. "There's no need. Just because you had your own stalker doesn't mean that I have one now, too. And even if I did, it wouldn't be Manny's problem."

"I won't tell him you said that. He'd be mad at you. He takes care of all his people and you're one of his people because you're one of my people. He'll take care of it."

"There's nothing to take care of, Nina, really. You're just getting carried away. And besides, I'm not sure I want to hear any more about how you have this big, strong wonderful man who's so in love with you that he'll look out for me, too, just because I'm your friend, while all I have is a creepy married dude following me around—even if he was a very good-looking creepy dude."

"Sorry."

"Don't be. Listen. I'm going to go and get ready, otherwise I'll be late. And we don't need to be talking on the phone. We can talk properly later."

"Okay. Do you want us to come get you?"

"No! I'll see you there."

"I just thought …"

"I know, and you're the sweetest. But honestly, I'm fine. I'll see you there."

~ ~ ~

Cal walked into the Boathouse at seven-fifteen. He liked to get the lay of the land before others showed up. He wasn't surprised to see that Ryan was already there, sitting alone at one of the picnic tables out on the deck.

"Hey, boss."

Cal smiled. "How long's it going to take you to stop calling me that?"

"I'm not sure I ever will."

"You know that, technically speaking, you're my boss now, don't you?"

Ryan shrugged. "Sure, I do, but that doesn't make any difference. Do you mind? Do you want me to quit saying it?"

"No. It's fine by me. Do you need a drink?"

"Yeah, I'll come to the bar with you. I had dinner here; Leanne won't be back till tomorrow."

"How are things with you two?"

Ryan didn't need to say a word, Cal could see the answer in his eyes and his smile. "They're amazing. Better than they ever were."

"I'm glad. And she doesn't have a problem with me being here?"

Ryan's smile dimmed momentarily. "She'll be fine. She says she doesn't, but I think part of her still believes that you might have been behind those messages."

"I figured as much." He blew out a sigh.

"Before you say anything else, I don't want to go there. It's the past. It's behind us."

Cal met his gaze. "*You* don't think …"

"Hell, no. And I never did, not even for a minute."

"Okay. Good."

When they had their drinks, they took them back to the picnic table. Cal liked this place. He liked the whole town, and from what he'd seen so far, the Boathouse seemed to be the heart of it.

He smiled at Ryan as they sat down. "Will Manny be late?"

Ryan chuckled. "No, but he won't be early."

Manny used to show up fifteen minutes early just like Cal and Ryan, but now he had a woman to take into account. Cal was curious to meet her.

Ryan smirked at him over his drink.

"What?"

"I'm wondering about you. I don't know if Nina's friend's coming or not, but would you be interested? I never thought I'd see Manny settle down but now that he has, it's making me wonder if you're next."

Cal shook his head rapidly. "Hell, no! And if I say any different, you remind me?"

Ryan laughed. "If you want. Is there a story behind the look on your face?"

Cal blew out a sigh. "Let's just say that this afternoon I almost forgot that women and I don't mix. I was interested in … but I got a timely reminder. The female of the species might as well be an entirely different species, as far as I'm concerned. I don't understand them."

"Maybe you just need some practice?" Ryan grinned at him. "You know, use it before you lose it?"

Cal laughed. "I don't have a problem in that department. It's the talking to them, the figuring them out, that I'm no good at."

"From what I've seen, you've just never cared to learn. You're good at everything you put your mind to."

"Maybe." Cal pondered Ryan's assessment; could he figure a woman out if he chose to try? And what did it matter anyway? Well, he knew the answer to that last part. It might matter if he couldn't get the hairdresser Teresa out of his head, and so far he hadn't been able to—no matter how strange her behavior had been.

"I take it I should drop it?" asked Ryan.

"Yep."

"Okay, and look, there's Manny anyway."

Cal turned to follow Ryan's gaze. Manny looked more relaxed and happier than Cal had ever seen him. He had his arm around a woman's shoulders. It made Cal smile. They looked right together.

He got to his feet when they reached the table. Manny grasped his shoulder. "I'm glad you came." He turned to the woman. "Nina, this is Cal."

She stepped forward and ignoring the hand he extended to shake with her, she reached up to hug him and landed a kiss on his cheek. "It's so good to meet you. Welcome."

He smiled back at her. Now he understood what Ryan had been saying. She really was a sweetheart. "It's a pleasure to meet you, too, Nina."

He glanced at Manny and gave a slight nod of approval.

Manny grinned back at him, and Cal had to wonder what it must feel like. Manny had been divorced right around the same time he had. He'd been a single guy, focused on work for …

more years than Cal cared to count. Yet here he was, engaged to Nina and from what Cal could tell, in his late fifties his life was better than ever.

~ ~ ~

Teresa looked around when she entered the restaurant. It was busy, but that was nothing unusual. She couldn't see Nina straight away, so she headed to the bar first.

Kenzie greeted her with a smile. "Hey, lady. What can I get you?"

"Vodka, lime, and soda, please. A double."

Kenzie raised her eyebrows. "You okay?"

"I'm fine. It's just been a day, you know?"

"Oh, I know how that goes." Kenzie turned away to fix her drink and then set it down in front of her. "Here you go. The day's over now and if I know you, you've earned that."

Teresa took a drink and smiled. "I have."

"Well, now you get to kick back. Are you meeting Nina?"

"Yes." She looked around. "Have you seen her?"

"I sure have. She's like the queen bee, tonight. She's over there."

Teresa looked but couldn't see her friend through the crowd.

"She's out on the deck holding court with three men all to herself." Kenzie waggled her eyebrows. "Manny's with her of course, and Ryan because Leanne's out of town. But Manny's friend?" She fanned herself with her hand. "Damn! You need to see him to believe it. If I were you, I'd get over there and stake my claim. You've got the in because of Nina and Manny, but if you're not quick about it he'll get snapped up in no time."

Teresa made a face. "I'm sure he'll make some lucky lady happy. But I'm not interested."

"Tell me that again later, after you've seen him." Kenzie smiled. "Go on, get over there and see for yourself." She moved along the bar. "I can't stop anyway."

Teresa took another sip of her drink and watched Kenzie serve a couple who'd just come in. She was looking forward to seeing Nina and Manny, and Ryan was fun—he was fun to look at, too, but she was too old to be looking and he was well and truly spoken for anyway. She wasn't thrilled at the prospect of meeting Manny's friend. He was probably a nice guy but even if he were as good-looking as Kenzie made him out to be, she doubted he'd catch her attention the way Blake had this afternoon. Wasn't it just typical that he'd turned out to be … a pig, as Elle had put it?

She took another sip of her drink and set out toward the deck. She was relieved when she reached the table to see that there was no friend with them. Nina came to greet her with a hug and Manny got to his feet and did the same. He was an amazing guy. Teresa was so happy for Nina that she'd met him—and they were getting married.

Ryan greeted her with a smile as she took a seat.

"How's everyone doing?" she asked.

Nina nodded happily. "We're doing great. Cal should be back in a minute." The way she held Teresa's gaze said that she was keen for her to meet him.

Manny raised an eyebrow at her. "Nina's quite taken with him."

Teresa had to laugh. "We all know you've got no worries. She only has eyes for you."

Manny laughed with her. "That wasn't what I meant. I think she might have plans for you." He turned and smiled at Nina through pursed lips. "Even though I've warned her that Cal's not really a ladies' man."

"I haven't … I wouldn't …" Nina shrugged. "I wouldn't meddle."

Manny patted her hand. "I'm only teasing you, but I didn't want you," he looked at Teresa, "to think that this was a set up."

"That's okay. I didn't. I don't. And I wouldn't be interested even if it were."

"Oh!" Nina turned to Manny. "I was going to tell you. There was a guy in the salon this afternoon and he might have been following Teresa around afterward."

Manny's eyebrows came down and Ryan leaned forward.

"What happened?" they asked in unison.

Teresa had to laugh. "You two need to get your business up and running. Look at you, both so eager to have someone to protect! Nothing happened. I'm fine. It was just a bit strange that after this guy left the salon, I ran into him two more times in the next hour."

Ryan frowned. "And you came by yourself tonight? I'll walk you home when we leave."

Teresa had to laugh. "That's sweet of you, but there's no need. Leanne would skin me alive!"

Ryan chuckled. "Nope. She trusts me absolutely these days."

"Even so," said Nina. "We could get Cal to see you home."

Teresa rolled her eyes at Manny, and he laughed and said, "We can take you."

"I'm a big girl. Thank you. I'm more than capable of taking care of myself."

"There he is."

She turned to follow Nina's gaze and her heart thudded to a halt when she saw him—Blake. He looked even more handsome in jeans and a black shirt than he had this afternoon. He was coming toward their table. She looked past him, wondering where Cal might be and hoping this didn't turn ugly. She didn't like Blake's chances if he said anything to her in front of these guys.

He smiled at Manny as he got closer but stopped dead when he saw her. She glanced around at the others, wondering if they'd even noticed him.

It seemed they were all looking at him—did they know somehow that he was the guy from the salon? Apparently, not. Manny grinned and waved him over. "Cal! Come and meet Teresa."

Her heart was thundering in her chest. Cal? Manny had called him Cal? She'd thought Austin had called him Carl this afternoon, but that had only made her think that he'd given her a fake name in the salon. She'd known he didn't look like a Blake.

She watched him approach the table cautiously. She couldn't figure it out. Was he Cal? It didn't make sense.

Nina smiled at her. "Teresa, this is … Cal." She turned her smile on him. "I never thought to ask the rest of your name."

He smiled back at Nina, and it had the same effect on Teresa as it had this afternoon—that was one hell of a smile. "Callahan."

He turned to her. His blue eyes were unreadable. If she was shocked, how must he feel? "*Blake* Callahan."

"Oh." She knew she should say something more than that, but she had no idea what it might be. She could hardly tell the others that he was the creepy dude from this afternoon. It just didn't make any sense.

Nina nudged her arm, as if she were being rude. Teresa ignored her and took a sip of her drink. There was no way she was going to say she was pleased to meet him.

Manny shot her a puzzled look. What could she say?

Blake, Cal—whoever the hell he was sat down across from her and studiously avoided her gaze. Silence descended around the table—this was going to be awkward.

She caught Manny giving Cal a questioning look. Should she put them all out of their misery and explain? She shot a glance at Cal. No. She wasn't going to tell them that he'd been hitting on her. She frowned as she thought about it. She didn't want to tell them that their friend was asking other women out while he was away from his wife. But she was almost certain that their friend, Cal, wasn't married. It didn't make any sense.

She looked up to find those piercing blue eyes watching her warily. Why would he be cautious of her—unless he thought she was going to land him in it?

Manny got to his feet and held his hand out to Nina. "Abbie's over there; we should go and say hi."

Teresa swallowed as Nina got up and followed him. It wasn't like Nina to abandon her. Next, Ryan looked at Cal and then at Teresa.

"I have no idea what's going on, but I'm out, too." He gave Teresa a half smile and followed the others.

Teresa had half a mind to go after him. She was disappointed that they'd all abandoned her to her fate with the creepy dude—but they didn't know he was the creepy dude; to them he was Cal, a great guy.

She sucked in a deep breath and looked at him, deciding to let him speak first and maybe help her figure out just what was going on.

There were no signs of the attraction or interest he'd shown in her this afternoon as he met her gaze. He looked wary—almost as if *she* might be the creepy one.

She bit down on her bottom lip to stop herself from asking questions.

When he finally spoke, it only reminded her how sexy his voice was. "Whatever I did this afternoon, I'm sorry."

"Pft!" She couldn't help it! But then she realized that he didn't know that she'd seen what he was texting to his *Darl.* "There's no need to apologize to me. I just feel sorry for your wife."

He leaned back, and the lines around his eyes deepened. He looked at her as though she might be crazy. "I don't understand."

She blew out a sigh. "Then let me explain. When I answered the phone this afternoon, you were texting. When I came back, I saw what you'd written. And I'll hold my hands up; it was wrong of me to read it over your shoulder."

His eyebrows knit together, and his lips puckered—she really wished that she were the kind of woman who could be so turned off by his behavior that she didn't notice his looks anymore—but he was a handsome brute.

He reached in his back pocket and pulled his phone out. Without a word, he scrolled though it, and she saw the moment understanding dawned on his face.

"You get it now?" she asked. "You can see why I didn't want to go for a drink with you? Why … you disgust me?"

His head jerked back at that. "I disgust you?"

She nodded. She should clarify that she meant his behavior, but what was the point?

He nodded slowly. "Are you interested in the truth?"

She raised an eyebrow. "Sometimes."

"Now? About this?" He held his phone up.

"I'm not sure there's any need for you to explain."

"I think there is." He got to his feet and came around to sit beside her. She sucked in a deep breath and tried to ignore the effect his closeness had on her—was she just a terrible person? Another woman's husband shouldn't be able to affect her like that.

She started to move away from him, but he put his hand on her arm and she froze. His *big* hand sent warmth coursing through her veins.

"Look." He held his phone up in front of her and scrolled through his contacts. He stopped at Darla.

Oh. Not darling then. She pursed her lips and watched as he opened the conversation. She saw the same words at the end:

love you and miss you, too, Darl.

Hmm, capital D there. He scrolled up a little further to the beginning of the conversation:

How are you liking California, big brother?

She swallowed. Brother? Uh-oh. She continued to stare at the screen. Oops! She waited, but he didn't speak. Eventually, she turned to look at him.

"But you can see why?"

He nodded curtly. "I can."

She held his gaze for a long moment, trying to figure out what this meant. He wasn't married then. But ... she cringed at how she'd behaved since she'd read—make that misread—his text. "I wasn't very nice to you, was I?"

He shook his head.

"You must have thought I was a crazy lady—changing so fast on you and you had no clue why."

He nodded, looking as though he might still think she was crazy.

Crap! Wasn't this just her luck? A guy like him landed in her lap and she went and blew it, big time.

"I'm sorry." She peeked at him.

His expression didn't soften. "So am I."

Chapter Four

Ryan caught up with Manny and Nina just as they reached the bar. "What's going on?"

"That's what I want to know," said Nina. "Abbie's not over here. She's outside with her friends." She gave Manny a puzzled look. "I know you must have a reason, and I trust you. But I don't like leaving Teresa like that. She didn't look happy."

Ryan nodded his agreement. "She didn't, and neither did Cal. What's going on?"

Manny folded his arms across his chest and watched Cal and Teresa for a moment. Cal had already moved to sit beside her, and he was showing her something on his phone. "I might be wrong, but I just have a hunch …"

Ryan laughed. "I knew you must have." He turned to Nina. "And believe me. When he has a hunch, just roll with it."

He didn't understand the smile they exchanged as Nina said, "That's okay, I already know. That's why I came, but I still want to know what your hunch is."

Manny chuckled. "I hope I'm not wrong. I don't want to blow your faith in me. But you both saw the reaction they just had to each other?"

"Err, yeah," said Ryan.

Nina frowned. "I did but I don't understand it. I was convinced that Teresa would like him. I know you said Cal wasn't a ladies' man, but I'd hoped …"

"What did you see that we didn't?" Ryan asked.

"It's not so much what I saw as what I pieced together. When he left the office this afternoon, Cal said he was going to get a haircut."

"You think he went to Teresa?" asked Nina.

Manny nodded.

"You don't think he followed her around afterward?" Ryan didn't believe that for a minute.

"No. But he said he had some errands to run. And we all know how small this town is and how easy it is to run into people constantly."

"I guess that could be it," said Ryan.

"No." Nina shook her head. "Cal's not married."

Ryan and Manny both turned to her.

"Teresa said that the guy in the salon this afternoon asked her out, but it turned out that he was married."

"How did she find that out? Married guys who ask other women out aren't usually upfront about their circumstances," said Ryan.

Nina made a face. "She said he was texting his wife—she saw what he was saying, talking about the kids."

Manny chuckled. "I'll bet he was texting Darla, his sister. Her kids love him."

Ryan had to laugh with him. "And for all the years I've known him, it's always irritated the hell out of him that before she lets him get off the phone, he has to say he loves her." Now, it all made sense. He glanced over at them again. It might make sense, but it didn't look like Cal or Teresa was happy.

He looked at Manny. "Should we go back and help them out?"

Manny's eyes twinkled as he smiled. "No. Didn't you hear what Nina said?"

"Which part?"

"That the guy this afternoon asked Teresa out."

"Shit!" Ryan grinned, then gave Nina an apologetic look. "Sorry."

She laughed. "No need to apologize but you can explain. I'm guessing your reaction means that he doesn't often ask women out?"

"No." Ryan and Manny spoke at the same time.

"And that's why," said Manny, "I think we should leave them to it. If we don't go back over there, they'll have to sort this out for themselves."

Nina smiled up at him. "I thought I had to behave myself and not try to set them up, and now you're doing exactly what you warned me not to."

Manny wrapped his arm around her shoulders. "I am, but only because he already asked her out." He grinned at Ryan. "He wouldn't be happy with us meddling—so we're going to do the exact opposite and stay the hell out of the way."

Cal slowly put his phone back in his pocket. He didn't know what else to do, what else to say. He looked around to see where the others had gone. He couldn't understand them all leaving like that—especially leaving him to fend for himself with the crazy hairdresser. He slid a sideways glance at her. She looked embarrassed, not crazy.

Then it hit him. She wasn't crazy. Her explanation made sense. In fact … it made him like her more. No, not like … appreciate? He appreciated that she was the kind of woman who thought married men shouldn't ask other women out. He risked another look at her. And like wasn't completely the wrong word. She was beautiful. His opinion about that hadn't changed even when he thought she was crazy.

She set her drink down and turned to him. "I should probably go. I don't know where the rest of them went and this is just too … embarrassing. I apologize again."

She started to get to her feet, but he put his hand on her arm and she sank back into her seat, her eyes wide. He got the impression that she felt it too. Every time they touched, heat and electricity coursed through him. He didn't know what he wanted to say yet, but he did know he didn't want her to leave.

He held her gaze while he searched for words. Her eyes were fascinating. Light brown, green flecks … dammit. He was supposed to be figuring out what to say.

"I'm sorry." He'd already said that once. This time sounded a little more like he meant it.

She nodded but didn't give him anything to go on. She was embarrassed. He could understand it. She wasn't the crazy he'd thought her to be—he was adapting to that revelation as quickly as he could. Where did it leave him? It left him back where he'd been before her total one-eighty in attitude in the salon this afternoon. It left him liking her, curious about her, and wanting to ask her out—although now, they were out.

He smiled when he saw a way to maybe rescue the situation. He echoed her words from this afternoon back to her. "What do you think? Should we start again, from the top?"

Her face relaxed and she smiled back. "Sure thing. Hi, it's nice to meet you, I'm Teresa."

He took hold of her hand. Just like earlier, he liked the way it felt, so small and soft inside of his. "It's a pleasure to meet you, Teresa. I'm Blake." He gave her a wry smile. "Blake Callahan. My friends call me Cal."

She chuckled. "I didn't think you looked like a Blake."

"I've been Cal for most of my adult life."

She nodded. "You know that begs the question why you introduced yourself as Blake earlier."

"It's a fair question. I'm not sure I know the answer. Except perhaps …" He really didn't know. No one called him Blake anymore. Andrea was about the only person who had since high school. But he wasn't going to question that too deeply. "I can assure you that it wasn't about trying to deceive you, though."

"Good." She looked around. "Why do you think they all ran off like that?"

He ran his hand over the back of his neck. He didn't know, but he'd guess that the look Manny had given him when he left the table had something to do with it. "I think perhaps Manny sensed something was amiss. He's perceptive."

She laughed and the sound seemed to reverberate in his chest. "It wouldn't have taken much to see that there was something very amiss when they introduced us. I should warn you; I told Nina all about the creepy dude in the salon this afternoon who proceeded to follow me around town."

He sat back. "I wasn't following you."

She laughed again. "I understand that now."

He frowned as he processed the rest of what she'd said. "Creepy?"

She brought her hand up to cover her smile. "Sorry. But think about it. As far as I knew, you were asking me out one minute and the next you were texting your wife."

"I—"

She put her hand on his arm when he started to explain. "I know. I understand now. But I'm telling you how it was, how I saw it at the time. I was so disappointed that—"

She stopped abruptly, and he guessed that she'd perhaps realized she'd given away too much. She was disappointed? That was good. It made him believe that she would have said yes to that drink with him. He didn't push her though. He just stored the information away for now.

"So, Nina thinks you have a stalker?"

She nodded. "And Manny and Ryan do, too." She laughed again. She did it a lot, and he liked it. "They're all planning to escort me home later to make sure that I get there safely."

Cal wanted to offer to be the one to escort her home, but he didn't. He wasn't one to move quickly when it came to women. He wanted to proceed with caution, but he was starting to wonder why.

Teresa watched his face, wondering what he was thinking. She was still playing catch up herself. He wasn't married. He hadn't been following her. And now that she knew that, she could see why he'd been wary of her—why he might think *she* was the creepy one. It made her laugh again. And that probably didn't help. She'd been laughing a lot, partly out of embarrassment, partly out of relief. When she'd first figured out that Cal and Blake were the same person, she'd thought it was going to make life difficult since he was such good friends with her best friend's man.

He raised an eyebrow at her.

"I'm sorry. I promise you I'm not crazy. I just keep seeing the funny side of this whole situation."

That smile! It seemed to get better each time he used it. He was gorgeous. And she'd almost put her foot in it and told him how disappointed she'd been when she'd thought he was married.

"I'm glad we got things straightened out."

"Me, too. Do you think we should find the others and let them know it's safe to come back now?" She'd love to keep him all to herself. But that was hardly realistic.

"Ah." His smile disappeared. Perhaps he wouldn't have minded being left alone with her after all? "We should."

He got to his feet and waited for her to join him. Her breath caught in her chest when his fingertips brushed the small of her back as he guided her through the bar. Whoa! Every time he touched her it sent her heart rate soaring. Shaking hands with him made her swoony—his hands were so damned big— she had to wonder about the rest of him. And when he'd put his hand on her arm earlier? There was no way she could leave—the heat from his touch had made her knees go weak.

She frowned when they reached the spot where Nina and the guys had been standing. There was no sign of them. Cal stopped beside her, and she pressed her lips together at the feel of his palm against her back. Fingertips had been tantalizing. His whole palm resting there made her want to forget about finding the others and take him home.

He moved closer when someone squeezed by on his other side. She looked up into his eyes. At five-eight, she wasn't short, but it was still a long way up.

He smiled. "Don't worry. We'll find them."

She laughed. Man, she needed to stop doing that! "I'm not worried." Oops. She needed to get herself under control.

The corners of his lips quirked up. "You're not?"

She shook her head.

"Can I ask you a question?"

"Sure." She was amazed that she sounded so calm.

"If you hadn't gotten the wrong idea this afternoon …"

Crap. She was hoping that they could move on from that. Now she was less eager to hear what his question was.

"Would you have gone for a drink with me?"

His face was completely still as he waited for her answer. He should look intimidating, standing there all tall and straight and stern-looking, but for some reason he didn't. Not to her, and then it struck her. He wasn't interrogating her about her actions and motives. She smiled and wasn't surprised when he did, too. "I would have. And …" She might be wrong, but she didn't think so, and what the hell, it was worth the risk. "And now that we've sorted that out, I'm hoping that you might ask me again, sometime."

His fingers splayed across her back, and he leaned in closer. For one crazy moment, she thought he was going to kiss her. But instead of bringing his lips to hers, he brought them closer to her ear and murmured, "I'm asking."

She swallowed as she nodded. The man was dangerous! With shivers chasing each other down her spine and her whole body on high alert, he could be asking anything, and she'd say yes, eagerly.

The stern face didn't match the whispered words, but she knew she hadn't imagined them. "Yes." She wanted to say something more, something funny or … anything. But at this point all she could do was agree.

He didn't smile. She'd been hoping for another one of his killer smiles.

"Can I ask another question?"

She nodded, wondering what was coming this time.

"Do you want to go for that drink now?"

She didn't understand.

This time he did smile and, even better, it turned into a laugh. She joined him; she couldn't help it. Her mind was terrible, and it was thinking that if his smile could make the sun come out, his laugh could make panties drop.

"I know we're here, in a bar, and it could be said that we're already out for a drink. But I meant …" He hesitated. "I was going to suggest that we could go somewhere else; somewhere less crowded. Escape from having to explain everything to our friends and …" He shook his head. "But that wouldn't be right."

"Why?" She'd been loving where he was going.

"Because until a little while ago you thought I was a *creepy dude*." She had to laugh at the way his lip curled when he said it.

"That's not entirely true. I didn't think you were the creepy dude. I thought the married guy at the salon was—and you're not him."

He chuckled. "I want to question your logic, but since it goes in my favor I won't."

She nodded happily.

"But perhaps we should wait? We could go for a drink tomorrow, or next weekend?"

"You don't want to go now?" They probably shouldn't. Nina and Manny would wonder what was going on.

Her breath caught in her chest again as his index finger traced a circle on her back. "I want to. But you should take your time. Be sure that you do. Be sure that you're comfortable."

She looked up at him. He was deadly serious. So serious, it was cute! "So, what? You think maybe I should check your references between now and tomorrow, or next weekend?"

He frowned and started to speak.

"Oh, my God! I'm teasing you! Don't worry about it. I'd like to go now. I'm not worried." She smirked at him. "And I trust you to behave yourself—and to see me home safely afterward. You know—in case there's a creepy dude out there somewhere."

He smiled through pursed lips and gestured for her to go ahead of him. His other hand never left the small of her back.

Chapter Five

Cal reluctantly let his hand fall to his side as he followed Teresa out through the main door of the restaurant. Part of his mind was questioning what he was doing. Manny and Ryan would no doubt give him grief for leaving with her. He still felt traces of wariness whether it was a wise idea. She was beautiful, and he liked the way she laughed so much, her seemingly lighthearted approach to life. But he'd liked those things about her this afternoon, too, and that had gone sour quickly.

Still … he lengthened his stride to catch back up to her after letting a girl go out before him … he couldn't deny that he was eager to get back to her side, or that he was already looking for an excuse to put his hand on her back again. He might not have been with a woman for a long time, but that didn't explain the intense connection he'd felt as he guided her through the bar.

She smiled when he reached her. "I should let Nina know that we're leaving."

"Of course." He wasn't looking forward to hearing what Manny and Ryan would have to say about this turn of events, but he was going to let them know, too.

He watched her pull out her phone and then did the same. Teresa smiled and tapped away at hers while he just stood there wondering what he should say. He didn't get the chance to wonder long. His screen lit up with an incoming text.

Manny: Fast work. Where are you going?

He looked around without lifting his head, hoping to spot Manny without making it obvious.

Manny: On the corner of the deck outside.

Cal smiled through pursed lips and looked over to see Manny and Ryan standing there grinning at him. Nina was tapping away at her phone.

He made a face at them and typed a reply.

Cal: Since all our friends disappeared, we thought we'd go get a drink somewhere quieter – where we can hear each other talk.

He watched them both read Manny's phone. Ryan smirked at him while Manny replied.

Manny: And where exactly do you plan to take her?

Cal: Don't look at me like that! Like I said. Someplace quieter – to talk.

It occurred to him that even though he wasn't thinking what Manny was implying, he didn't know where he could take her. He knew there was another restaurant in town, some Italian place, but he didn't know if there was a bar where they could sit and talk. The only other place he could think of was the Lodge at Four Mile Creek, and that was away on the other side of the lake. He didn't think that driving her all the way out there would be appropriate.

Manny: I wasn't giving you a hard time. I'm trying to help.

I know you wouldn't suggest your place – and she wouldn't suggest hers.

So … Giuseppe's has a terrace out back where you can sit and have a drink.

Cal had to smile. He looked over at them again and instead of the kind of teasing he'd expected, both Manny and Ryan were giving him encouraging smiles.

He glanced at Teresa. She was still engrossed in her phone.

Cal: Thanks, guys.

He put his phone away and she looked up at him. "Did they ask you what's going on?"

He shook his head with a smile.

She laughed. "Lucky you. Nina's giving me twenty questions here."

He frowned. "She doesn't like the idea?"

"She loves it! She's excited and wants to know everything." She stopped abruptly and gave him an embarrassed smile.

He didn't mind. He liked that she had a friend who would look out for her. And even more, he liked the way she spoke before she stopped to think and censor herself. It was … refreshing. Refreshing wasn't the first word that came to mind. No, the first word he'd thought had been sexy. But he should probably stay away from that—for a while, at least.

He smiled back at her, wanting her to know it was okay— that she had no need to feel embarrassed. Plus, her eyes seemed to dance whenever he smiled at her.

"You should give her a wave and let her know that you're okay."

She frowned, and he pointed to where Nina was standing with Manny and Ryan on the edge of the back deck of the restaurant.

She rolled her eyes when she spotted them. Manny touched Nina's arm and said something, and she looked up and waved. Judging by the smile on Nina's face, Teresa hadn't been exaggerating when she'd said that she was excited.

Cal jumped when his phone buzzed in his back pocket. He pulled it out and laughed when he read Manny's message.

Teresa raised an eyebrow at him. "Dare I ask?"

"Yeah. Nina says we both have to text to let them know when we're home safe."

It felt strange to walk across the square beside him. Strange but good. It made Teresa wonder when the last time she'd walked beside a man had been. It'd been a while that was for sure. In fact, it must've been the last time she went on vacation. She liked to go away a couple of times a year on adventure trips. She'd been white-water rafting, rappelling, and horseback riding on a pack trip in the wilderness. She'd even done a three-day trip in a hot air balloon one year. Most of the time she lived a hum-drum little life, but she did love her adventures—and she'd had some fun with some adventurous guys on those trips, too.

She looked up at Cal. None of them were in the same league as him though. He was so big, not just tall, but solid, too. He made her feel small beside him. It wasn't just his broad shoulders—or big muscly arms—it was all of him. He was probably twice as wide across as she was—and there wasn't a scrap of fat on him.

"Are you sure about this?"

She looked up at him. "I am, are you? You can change your mind if you like. You don't have to be stuck with me." Why had she said that? Maybe it was the serious look on his face.

"I'd like to have a drink with you, but you're quiet now. I wondered if you're perhaps regretting your decision?"

She smiled. "Not one bit. To be honest, I was thinking …" She wasn't going to tell him what she'd been thinking, was she? No, she wasn't. "That this is an unexpected turn to the evening—a pleasant one."

He stopped beside a black Suburban. "As long as you're sure. I don't want you to feel uncomfortable." He opened the passenger door and gestured for her to get in.

When he came around and climbed into the driver's seat, she smiled at him. "Would I be right if I guessed that it's you that's uncomfortable?"

His lips pressed together before he replied, and she'd guess that the honest answer was yes, he was.

He turned to look at her, and her heart raced when he smiled. "I'll admit that this is outside of my comfort zone, but that doesn't mean I don't want to go." He started the engine and pulled out of the square.

She wanted to talk to him while he drove, wanted to ask him what he thought of Summer Lake so far, what had brought him here, all kinds of things she was curious to know, but just like she had this afternoon, she got the sense that he needed quiet. So, she waited.

He didn't speak again until he pulled up in the little lot outside Giuseppe's. He cut the engine and turned to face her. "Are you sure you're okay?"

She had to laugh. "I'm fine. But you're not, are you? We don't have to do this, you know. We can go home. It doesn't have to be awkward. We'll no doubt run into each other around town, but it's all good."

His eyebrows drew together. He looked intimidating, but she already knew better. He was just serious. Very serious indeed.

She loved the thought of lightening him up. She reached across and rested her hand on his arm. "It's okay."

Her heart leaped into her mouth when he covered her hand with his. "No. It's not okay. I'm making a complete mess of this." He sought her gaze and held it as he continued. "I'm … I guess you could say, I'm out of practice with this … with taking a woman out. I'm rusty, I guess." His expression relaxed into a smile. "But if you can bear with me …"

"I'll be happy to. There's no pressure. We can just have a drink, have a chat, make a new friend." His hand tightened around hers at that. She shrugged. "You're Manny's friend. I'm Nina's. It makes sense for us to be friends, too." She hadn't been thinking of him that way when they left the Boathouse, but the poor guy seemed so uncomfortable, she wanted to put him at ease again—and she hated to think that the thought of her expecting something more than friendship from him was the cause of his discomfort.

He held her gaze for a long few moments. She thought he was going to say something, but in the end, he just nodded and said, "Thank you." Then he got out and came around to meet her at the passenger side.

It looked like he was relieved to be off the hook. Oh well. She hadn't really expected that she could get that lucky, had she? It wasn't in the cards for her to have a guy like him land in her lap. She should have known better. And she hadn't been lying when she'd said it would be good for them to become friends. That would have to do.

With that thought, she slipped her arm through his as they walked through the restaurant. He looked surprised, but not horrified. He might as well get used to the way she treated her friends.

"Hey, Tino!" she called as they reached the bar. "Is the patio open? Is it okay if we sit out there?"

"Teresa!" Tino came out and greeted her with a hug. "It's good to see you. Of course, you can go out there. Turn the heaters on if you want them. Do you want to eat?"

"No, we're just here for drinks." She smiled. "Cal, this is Tino, a good friend of mine. Tino, this is Cal—a new friend."

She loved the way Tino sized Cal up before he shook with him. He didn't even come up to Cal's shoulder, but his expression made clear that he'd be keeping an eye on him.

"You like prosecco?" asked Tino.

Cal nodded.

"Okay. I'll be out in a few minutes."

The courtyard out back was empty. Teresa went to turn one of the big patio heaters on and took a seat at the table beside it. "Have you been here before?" she asked as Cal sat down.

"No. I like it."

"It's a great place. Obviously, the Boathouse is the main attraction in town, but Giuseppe's has great food. We should pick you up a delivery menu when we leave. Of course, there's pizza, but they'll deliver anything on the menu, too. Wait, where are you …?" She'd been about to ask him where he was staying, but she probably shouldn't. "Scratch that. I don't mean to be nosey. As long as you're not too far out of town, they'll deliver wherever you are." She stopped when she realized she was talking too much.

Cal looked as though he was about to ask her a question, but Tino came out with a bottle of prosecco and two glasses. He set them down on the table. "Enjoy. I won't keep coming out. We're busy in there tonight. Text me if you need anything else, Terry. Otherwise, I'll see you on Thursday." He smiled first at her then at Cal. "The prosecco's on me. Welcome, new friend."

Cal had a puzzled look on his face as he watched Tino go back inside. Teresa poured them each a glass and made herself wait for him to speak first.

"I take it he's a good friend of yours?"

"He is. We go way back—all the way to grade school."

"You've lived here all your life?"

"I have." She had to wonder how that must sound to him. From what she knew he'd lived and worked all around the world doing top-secret, dangerous work. "What about you? You said you were from Minnesota—"

She stopped mid-sentence when he leaned forward and put his finger to her lips. She couldn't quite believe it. There probably wasn't another man on earth who'd get away with doing that. But he smiled, and she swallowed and waited for him to explain.

He slowly lowered his hand but left her just as speechless when he rested it on her knee. "I'm sorry. I just ... Tell me if I'm wrong?"

"About what?"

"You're just talking to cover the awkwardness I created earlier, aren't you? I didn't explain myself properly, and now you think that I'm not interested in you, not as ... as a woman." His hand tightened on her knee as he spoke the last few words, making her stomach tighten.

She nodded, not trusting herself to speak.

"Can I clear that up then, before we go any further?"

"What ...?"

He was leaning toward her, coming closer. She didn't know how it had happened, what had changed but ... his lips brushed over hers. It was soft, fleeting, but it was one of the best kisses she'd ever had—and definitely the most unexpected.

He sat back with a smile, though his hand remained on her knee. "I told you. I'm rusty. But that doesn't mean I'm not interested."

Her fingers came up to touch her lips. She was dazed.

His smile faded. "Was that—?"

She held her hand up to stop him before he could say anything that might detract from the magic of that brief kiss. "That was amazing!" She grinned at him. "I would never have guessed …"

He chuckled. "Then I'm glad I made myself clear."

~ ~ ~

Her eyes sparkled as she smiled at him. It made Cal want to kiss her again. But he should wait. The whole time she'd been chattering away he'd known that he'd messed up earlier—that when he'd told her he was outside his comfort zone she'd somehow taken it to mean that he wasn't interested in her. He was. Very much so. Even if he was more than rusty on how the whole dating thing worked.

He looked down when he realized that his hand was still resting on her knee. He should probably remove it, but he didn't want to. And she didn't seem to mind.

She still traced her finger over her lips, making him wish that he'd lingered there a little longer himself. He was tempted to lean in again, but he no longer had the element of surprise in his favor—and it seemed he no longer had the nerve either. He'd made the most of his moment of spontaneity, but now he'd have to fall back on conversation and the more conventional means of getting to know each other.

"So …" He didn't know what he wanted to say, but the silence was lengthening, and it didn't seem like Teresa was going to fill it.

She smiled. "So?"

He got the impression she was teasing him. She wasn't going to let him off the hook easily.

"Are you going to put me to the test here—see just how rusty I am?"

She lifted a shoulder. "Honestly? I don't know what to say next, so I'm waiting to see where you go."

"That's fair." He chuckled.

"But I'm impatient, too." She laughed with him. "So, where are you going to go? What direction are we taking this conversation?"

He rubbed his hand over his chin as he thought about it. "How about I lay out the options I see and then you choose which you want to pursue?"

"Okay."

"We could talk about the weather."

She laughed.

"Or you could tell me all about this little town of yours."

She shrugged at that.

"You could tell me all about yourself and your life."

"There's not much to tell. You already know I've lived here all my life. It's a great little town, but not much happens here."

"I could try to impress you with stories about my life."

"I thought you weren't allowed to talk about your life—about your work?"

"I'm not."

He was relieved when she smiled. "Then how about you tell me about you—who you are." She gave him a rueful smile. "About your sister, Darla, and her kids?"

And that was all it took for Cal to relax. He didn't date much because while he was still working for the agency, he didn't like the only options available to him. Those were the options he'd laid out for Teresa. The nature of his work had always meant keeping things superficial with a woman, keeping the focus on her, and never really knowing if her interest in him went any deeper than in the perceived mystery and danger.

Teresa wanted to know about him, about who he was, who his family was. And perhaps telling her about it might help him figure out who he wanted to be now.

Chapter Six

Teresa looked up when the patio lights flashed on and off three times. She looked at her watch and couldn't believe that it was just after midnight.

"Is that your friend, Tino, giving us a hint?" asked Cal.

She laughed. "Yep. I can't believe it's gotten so late. We've been here for hours."

He checked his watch and shook his head in disbelief. "I had no idea."

"That's a relief. I'd hate to think that you'd been watching the minutes drag by while I kept you here and talked your ear off."

"You know that's not the case. I've done as much talking as you—perhaps more."

It was true, too. At first, she'd caught herself chattering, but that had been nerves. After a while, she'd relaxed and when she'd asked Cal about himself, he'd opened up.

He got to his feet and held his hand out to her. She got up, wishing that the night didn't have to end. They'd talked and laughed for hours already but she still felt like they were just getting started.

When they reached the back door of the restaurant, it was locked. "I guess Tino wanted to get home," she told Cal. "We can go around the outside." She turned to go back, but Cal didn't move out of her path.

Instead, he put his hands—damn they were big hands!—on her shoulders and looked down into her eyes. "I had a great time tonight."

She nodded. She didn't have breath to spare for words, it was all caught in her chest somewhere.

She couldn't stop her hands from reaching out to touch him. Her palms flattened themselves against his chest, and all her breath finally came out in a big, involuntary sigh.

He leaned in closer, and her eyelids drooped. She wanted to look at his handsome face, but her eyes closed, and her lips parted when his arms came around her and he kissed the corner of her mouth.

She pecked him back tentatively. She wanted nothing more than to claim his mouth in a full-on kiss, but he'd been so hesitant, she didn't want to—Whoa! His arms tightened around her waist and she found herself crushed against his broad chest. It seemed he'd used up all his hesitation over the course of the evening and now he was making up for it. He kissed her like he meant it, and certainly not like a guy who was as rusty as he claimed to be with the ladies. She clung to him to keep herself upright, even though the way he held her told her loud and clear that he wouldn't let her fall.

Eventually, he lifted his head, but he didn't loosen his arms around her. His eyes were a beautiful blue as they looked down into hers.

"From everything you've told me, between the salon and Elle and Skye being home, you have a full and busy life."

She nodded, wondering where he was going.

"Do you have room in your life for more?"

She cocked her head to the side.

"Do you date?"

"Yeah. Sometimes."

He brought his hand up and rubbed the back of his neck and chuckled. "I'm making a mess of this again, what I'm trying to do here is ask if you'd like to date me. You know, go out sometimes?"

She nodded. "I'd love to." She wasn't sure what he meant. Did go out sometimes mean that they'd have dinner once a month? That they could pair up for convenience on occasion since their friends were together? Whatever he meant, she was up for it.

He closed his arms around her again and pressed a kiss to her forehead. "How about more than sometimes?" She looked up at him, and he smiled. "Is there any chance you're free tomorrow night?"

She couldn't hold her smile in as relief and excitement coursed through her. "Yes."

When he brought his SUV to a stop in front of her house, Cal cut the engine. She wasn't going to invite him in. He knew that. Her daughter and granddaughter were there. Even if they weren't, he'd be bidding her goodnight out here. He felt as though he'd made up a lot of lost ground tonight—recovered quickly from his lack of practice with the fairer sex. But he wasn't in a hurry.

Teresa turned and put her hand on his arm with a smile. The heat that surged in his veins at her touch made a liar out of him. She made him want to hurry her straight to bed. Desire and arousal may have become unfamiliar feelings over the last few years, but she'd brought them back with a vengeance over the course of just an evening.

"Thanks, Cal."

He frowned. Thanks sounded like a dismissal. "You're welcome." He wasn't even sure what she was thanking him for. "Thank you, too. I haven't enjoyed an evening this much in …" He didn't know how long. The answer that came to mind scared him, and would no doubt scare her too. He'd sound like the creepy dude if he told her he couldn't remember ever enjoying an evening this much. "… a long time," he finished lamely.

She laughed, and he relaxed. She had such a light-hearted approach to everything; he'd do well to try and lighten up a little himself. "What did I say wrong this time?" he asked with a rueful smile.

"Nothing! You didn't say anything wrong. I was laughing that if this is the best evening you've had in a long time, you should stick with me. I'll remind you how to have fun."

She was only teasing, he knew it. But it felt like she was speaking a deeper truth that she wasn't even aware of. And part of his mind was also shouting that he could take her words on another level, too, if he wanted to—a more physical level. And that part desperately wanted to.

He caught her hand and brought it to his lips. "I like the sound of that."

"Me, too."

"So, tomorrow? Do you want to remind me tomorrow?"

Her eyes widened. So, he wasn't the only one who was thinking along those lines. He wanted to ask her what kind of fun she had in mind. But that wouldn't be fair. He needed to get his act together and be the one to lead, not play the coward like this and put her on the spot.

"You said you're free tomorrow," he clarified. "Would you still like to see each other?"

She nodded.

"Can I pick you up? I could take you over to the Lodge at Four Mile. I heard the restaurant there is great; we could have dinner."

"That sounds lovely."

"Great. What time?"

"Seven-thirty?"

"I'll be here."

He leaned toward her and she came to meet him. Her lips were soft and sweet. She kissed him eagerly. It'd be easy to get lost in her kisses. But not here, not sitting in his car outside her house. He closed his fingers around the back of her neck and took one last taste before he leaned back and smiled.

"You have the most amazing smile I've ever seen!"

He had to laugh. She was a breath of fresh air. "Why, thank you. That may be the best compliment I've ever had."

She chuckled. "I have a feeling you'll be getting more of them in the not too distant future."

He raised an eyebrow, not sure he understood. But she just laughed. "I guess we'll see." She turned and started to open the door. He didn't want her to go but it was time.

He got out and couldn't help placing his hand in the small of her back as he walked her to her front door. She looked up at him and reached up to plant a peck on his lips.

"I'll see you tomorrow, then?"

He nodded. "Seven-thirty." He wanted to kiss her again but knowing that her daughter and granddaughter were inside stopped him. Instead, he closed his fingers around the back of her neck and pressed a kiss to her forehead. "I'll look forward to it."

~ ~ ~

Teresa closed the front door behind her and let out a big breath that was half sigh, half chuckle.

She jumped when Elle popped her head out of the living room. "Are you okay?"

"I'm fine, sweetheart. Better than fine."

Elle raised an eyebrow. "Yeah? Want to tell me about it?"

"If you like? I thought you'd be in bed."

"I couldn't sleep. After Skye went down …" She shrugged. "I'm awake, and I'd love to hear about your night, if you want to tell me. Did you and Nina have a good time?"

"Oh, thanks for reminding me. I need to text her. Let her know I got home okay."

"That wasn't her who dropped you off?"

"Nope." Teresa didn't do a very good job of hiding her smile.

"Who, then?"

"Just let me send her a message and I'll tell you all about it."

Elle grinned. "Does this call for a glass of wine?"

"It sure does." Teresa didn't need another, but she wasn't going to pass up the chance to hang out with Elle like this. She didn't know if it was deliberate, but they were falling back into their old after-a-night-out routine. When Elle had still lived at home, before Tristan had come along, they used to sit in the kitchen when *she* came home from a night out. They used to share a glass of wine and she'd tell Teresa about her friends and her boyfriends. Teresa missed those times and had often wished for them back—but she hadn't seen things turning around like this; that she'd be the one coming home after midnight to find her daughter still up.

She sent Nina a quick message to let her know she was home—and that they'd talk tomorrow. She wanted to tell her friend about the night's events, but it was more important to spend this time with Elle.

She was relieved when Nina's reply came back short and sweet.

Nina: Thanks. I know it's late now. But call me tomorrow.

She found Elle in the kitchen and took a seat at the island beside her.

"So?" Elle took a sip of wine and slid the glass toward her.

Teresa grinned.

"Who brought you home?"

"The guy who was in the salon this afternoon."

"Mom!" Elle looked horrified.

"It's okay. He's not married. It wasn't what it looked like."

Elle frowned. "Are you sure? How do you know he's not just talked his way out of it?"

Teresa laughed. "Because I don't need to take his word for it. He's Manny's friend."

"He is? You're serious? The guy Nina wanted you to meet is the same guy who asked you out this afternoon?"

"Yep."

"That's some coincidence." Elle didn't look convinced.

"I know. I couldn't believe it. You would have laughed. Nina and Manny were telling me about this great guy, and of course,

Nina told him about my creepy dude from this afternoon. Then he came back from the bathroom and they were saying here's Cal but all I could see was Blake."

"Oh, my God!"

"Yeah. The poor guy was texting his sister—he even showed me the conversation. Her name's Darla. I saw darl' and …"

"So, you gave him a hard time over nothing?"

"Yes, but in my defense, I think any woman would have read that the same way I did. The way he talked about the kids and said love you and miss you, too."

"I guess. And he got over it?"

Teresa chuckled. "He did. He wasn't very happy about it at first though."

"I can imagine! Poor guy. I bet he thought you were crazy. I mean, he didn't even know that you'd seen what he texted, did he?"

"No. But we got it all straightened out."

"And he's a nice guy?"

"He's lovely."

"Are you going to see him again?"

"Tomorrow night."

"Wow. You don't waste any time, do you?"

"It was him. He asked. At first, I thought he was just trying to be nice, you know, trying to get things on a good footing with me since we're kind of friends of friends. Then he made it sound like he wanted to maybe have dinner occasionally, and then …" Teresa traced her finger over her lips and smiled at the way he'd stunned her with that first kiss.

Elle laughed. "Then he made a move? Made it clear that he wants more than the occasional dinner?"

"That he wants to go out again tomorrow."

Elle chuckled. "Hey, I'm not judging."

"I know." Elle had always been supportive of her dating life. She hadn't been one to date around a lot, but she'd had the occasional boyfriend over the years.

"Anyway, what about you? Did you do anything with your evening?"

"I did. I did my nails." She held them out for Teresa to inspect. They were long and pointy and sparkly—pretty, but Teresa had no idea how she managed to work with them. "And Abbie called, too. We had a good catch up. She wants ... Oh, you know what, never mind. She sounds so happy ..."

"She wants what?" asked Teresa. She had a feeling she knew what her daughter had been about to say.

"Nothing. It doesn't matter."

Teresa frowned. "Yes, it does. Did she ask you to go out with everyone tomorrow night?"

Elle dropped her gaze. "I can go another time."

"No." Teresa shook her head adamantly. "You should go. I'll watch Skye. You were going to ask me to, weren't you?"

Elle shrugged. "I'm not that worried. And you have a hot date." She waggled her eyebrows. "He is hot, you're not going to deny that. And no way am I going to let you miss out on that because of me."

"Then don't. Let me miss out on it because of Skye. I've been pestering you to go out so I can get her to myself ever since you came home."

Elle rolled her eyes. "Watch my lips, Mom. No! No freaking way. You wouldn't get Skye for long anyway. You'd put her to bed and sit here all evening by yourself. You do that enough. Go have some fun with—what's his name?"

"Cal. But I wouldn't have fun now anyway."

"Well, you'll just have to try."

"No, Elle. This is important. This is the first time you've wanted to go out since you've been back. Please go."

"No. It's sweet of you, Mom, but no. You deserve a date more than I deserve a night out."

Teresa chewed on her bottom lip. Her daughter was just as stubborn as she was. But this was important. Of course, she wanted to see Cal again. But she wanted to see her daughter start enjoying life back at the lake more.

She smiled when a solution hit her. "So, why don't I invite him over here? That way everybody wins."

Elle chuckled. "I don't think I like the idea of you and him *winning* here while Skye's asleep."

Teresa laughed and slapped her arm. "Have a little more respect for you mother, young lady!"

"I do. I'm only teasing."

"I know." Teresa had suggested it before she'd given it any thought. But it could work. She didn't know what Cal would think about the idea, but she could ... She frowned as she realized that no she couldn't call him and see. They hadn't exchanged numbers. He'd said he'd pick her up here at seven-thirty.

Elle watched her face. "See, you know it's not a great idea."

"No. I'm thinking that I'll call him tomorrow and see what he thinks."

"You don't have to—"

"I know, but I'm going to. And if he says yes, you'll probably want to make yourself scarce. You wouldn't want to be here to join in on my date, would you?" She smiled. "So, if I can talk him into coming over, would you mind giving us some space and going out? You could go to the Boathouse or something."

Elle shook her head with a smile. "I love you, Mom. But will you make a deal with me?"

"What?"

"If he doesn't like the idea of coming over here, you go out with him still? I'll admit, I wouldn't mind going out—but only if it doesn't cost you a date."

"Deal."

Elle laughed. "You sound pretty sure of yourself."

Teresa waggled her eyebrows. "I am."

Chapter Seven

Cal put the vacuum away and looked around. The house was clean—spotless. There was nothing else to do. He'd taken care of every mundane detail he could think of. Now what? He blew out a sigh and went to get a glass of water. He'd find his feet soon, establish a new routine. He was only feeling so unsettled because this was his first weekend here. Granted, he usually found his feet quickly in a new place—he was used to having to, but that was for work. This wasn't work. This was retirement.

He took a drink and set the water bottle down on the counter. This was different. He didn't have a predetermined timeframe or a predetermined goal. He was just here. This was to be his life now. It was unsettling. He had to smile at the contradiction—the prospect of settling down was unsettling.

He sat down on one of the stools at the island. He needed a plan. He'd done okay through the week, but that was because he'd been working. He'd gone in early and come home late. That was a familiar routine, but Dan had already made it clear that he shouldn't expect it to be the norm. He was only supposed to be working part time.

He was enthusiastic about the operation Dan had set up. They were going to provide security services—physical and cyber security, though these days the two went hand in hand. Dan had contracts with a couple of agencies and Cal had no doubt that the work would start rolling in soon. He was here to oversee operations. Dan headed up the cyber side, Ryan was field ops, and as Ryan had put it, Cal was to be the overlord, masterminding the whole operation. What that really meant was that he'd be running interference, troubleshooting, and overseeing the big picture. If Dan were the left hand, and Ryan the right hand, they'd brought Cal in as the brain who coordinated their actions.

His phone buzzed, bringing him back from his musings. He smiled when he saw Manny's name. Cal had texted him last night to let him know that he was home—after delivering Teresa safely to her door. He'd declined the invitation to go for a run this morning. He wasn't ready to face Manny's questions about last night. He knew he wouldn't be able to put him off again, though. He picked his phone up to see what he wanted.

Manny: You busy?

Cal: No.

Manny: You want to take a ride over to Four Mile?

Cal: No, thanks.

Manny: Why?

Cal: You guys don't need me tagging along.

Manny: Nina's not coming. She's out.

Hmm. That was a different proposition.

Manny: That a yes, then?

Cal laughed.

Cal: Yes.

Manny: Great. I'll pick you up in 15.

Cal set his phone down with a smile. It wasn't that he didn't like Nina. He liked her a lot. But he didn't want to get into the habit of hanging out with the two of them. And especially not today, not after last night. He didn't want to face the questions from Manny—he sure as hell wouldn't know how to handle any from Nina.

He let himself out the front door ten minutes later and wasn't surprised to see Manny pulling up. He jogged up the path and climbed into the passenger seat.

Manny smiled. "What's the place like?"

Cal glanced back at the house and shrugged. "It's a place. I don't plan to stay here long."

"You mean here at this house, not here at the lake, right?"

"Don't look like that. I'm not changing my mind about staying already. Yes. I mean the house. In fact …" He pulled the brochure Austin had given him out of his back pocket. "When we get over to Four Mile Creek, you can drive me by a couple places I might be interested in."

Manny swiped the paper from his hands and let out a low whistle when he saw the picture. "Nice!" He handed the brochure back and pulled away. "You're thinking about being my neighbor then?"

"Yeah. If you wouldn't mind. From what I can make out it's just down the way from your place. Is it your place yet? Have you closed?"

"No, not yet. But it looks like it should go through in the next couple weeks."

"That's great."

Manny chuckled. "It is. Nina wasn't sure about leaving her place when I first asked her, but now she's so excited she has almost everything packed in boxes waiting to go already."

Cal had to smile as he remembered Teresa last night saying that Nina was excited to hear about the two of them.

"Something funny?" Manny was giving him a puzzled look.

"No. I think it's great. And seriously, you wouldn't mind if I ended up being your neighbor?"

"Mind? I think it'd be great."

They drove on in silence for a little while. Cal watched the lake through the window as they headed up the East Shore toward Four Mile.

"Are you deliberately not saying anything?" asked Manny.

"About?"

Manny laughed. "Never mind. If you don't even know what I'm curious about, then I guess it wasn't that big of a deal."

Cal smiled through pursed lips. "Of course, I know what you're talking about. But I'm waiting for you to ask specific questions, so I don't give away more than I need to."

"Come on, this is me you're talking to. I'll get it all out of you one way or another. You may as well just dive in."

He had a point. "Okay. But at least tell me where to start?"

"I want to know the backstory before you tell me why you both reacted the way you did when you first saw each other. That wasn't the first time, was it?"

"No."

"And I figured that she must have cut your hair after you left the office?"

He nodded.

"Come on. Between Nina and Ryan and me we pieced it together last night, but I want to hear your version of events."

Cal blew out a sigh. "Okay. Yes, she cut my hair." He chuckled. "I actually sat in her salon—have you been in there? It's …"

"Not a place I could imagine you ever setting foot!" Manny laughed.

"Yeah. I realized that as soon as I got through the door, and I was about to leave but …"

Manny waited.

How was he supposed to explain that the moment he'd seen Teresa's smile his feet had rooted themselves to the floor? He'd sound like a complete idiot. He sneaked a glance at Manny. Maybe he'd get it? He was a different guy with Nina. And not just *with* her. He was a different guy since he'd met her.

"But then you met Teresa," Manny finished for him.

"Yeah. And Nina already told you that I asked her out, and that she saw me texting Darla and got the wrong idea. That she ended up thinking I was some creepy dude—some creepy married dude."

"Yep. Ryan and I were ready to hunt you down. At least to hunt down the creepy dude."

"So I heard. And that's all. So, you know everything that happened before what you saw last night."

"I do now. Up until now I only had hearsay and a few assumptions."

"And now?" Cal knew he was getting at something else.

Manny shot a smile at him. "Now I know that you're taken with Teresa and way out of your depth."

"I didn't say that."

Manny laughed. "You didn't need to. It's all in what you don't say."

When they reached the development at Four Mile, Manny took a left down onto the lane that ran along the shore. There were only a few houses here by the water's edge. Cal nodded appreciatively. It was nice.

"This is us," said Manny when he brought the car to a stop.

"Are you going in?" asked Cal. "Is that what we're here for?"

"No. But what do you think of the place?"

Cal looked it over. It was a nice house. It was obviously a fairly new build. It sat behind a row of evergreens that looked as though they still had some growing to do. There was a porch on this side of the property, but he'd guess this was just the entrance.

"It doesn't look like much from here," said Manny. "But out front it opens up to the lake. There's a dock, and a pool out there."

Cal raised an eyebrow. "I like it. It's an upgrade from your apartment in Sacramento. But … a pool?"

Manny chuckled. "Nina's always wanted one and there's a bit of story behind why she never got one."

Cal could swear he saw a hint of pink color Manny's cheeks and ears. "And you're happy to be the guy who makes sure she gets one now?"

"Yeah."

"I like it."

"You do? I thought you might bust my balls."

Cal laughed. "Fair's fair; you haven't busted mine yet."

Manny laughed. "And I don't intend to, but I can't speak for Ryan and like I told you, he brings out the worst in me."

Cal laughed. "I can handle Ryan."

"True. I forget that. Anyway …" He pulled away and carried on to the end of the road. "Let's see what your place looks like."

Cal smiled when he saw the house. It surprised him that it looked better in the flesh than it did in the photos. He'd expected that to be the other way around.

"Is it empty?" asked Manny. "Can we take a look around?"

Cal pulled his phone out. "I'll check." He dialed Austin's office number and waited.

"Summer Lake Realty, this is Crystal, how can I help you?"

"Hi, Crystal. This is Blake Callahan. Austin's supposed to be setting me up an appointment to see the house at Lakeside. No need to find him, you can probably tell me. I took a drive by and want to know if the place is empty, if it'd be okay to take a walk around."

"Oh, okay. Hold on. I know it's empty. Just let me …"

She put him on hold and Cal frowned. That was all he'd needed to know.

She came back after a few moments. "Mr. Callahan?"

"Yes?"

"I checked with Austin. I knew the contractors had been out there this morning. Austin said that even if they're not there now the back door should be unlocked. He said to go on in and take a look since you're there."

"Thanks!" He hadn't expected that.

"Of course. And call me back if you have any questions, won't you?"

"Thanks. I will." Cal hung up and smiled at Manny. "I'm glad I checked. She said it's unlocked, and we can take a look around."

Manny pulled forward into the driveway. "Great!"

Cal smiled when he walked into the living area. The whole place was light and airy. It felt new and modern, all open plan. The front wall was mostly glass, giving onto a view of the lake that made it feel as though he was on a boat instead of in a house.

"Is it love at first sight?" asked Manny beside him.

Cal's throat went dry. Was that what it was? Was that why he hadn't been able to turn around and walk straight out of her salon yesterday? Why he'd made such a fool of himself through the course of the evening while he tried to remember—or perhaps learn for the first time—how to treat a woman?

Manny raised an eyebrow at him. "You like the place so much it's rendered you speechless?"

Oh! The house! He was talking about the house. "Yeah." Cal swallowed. "It is. I have." He frowned. He needed to get his shit together! "I love it."

"I can see it suiting you. It's not to my taste. Too modern for me."

Cal looked around. Manny was right. The place was all straight lines and right angles. Brushed steel and light-colored wood floors. To Cal it was perfect; clean, efficient. He had to wonder what Teresa would think of it.

"Would I be right if I guessed that you're thinking about more than the house?"

Cal raised an eyebrow as if he didn't understand—he wasn't going to come straight out and admit it.

Manny smiled. "I can button it if you like. It's just ... straight up? I'm fascinated, but I'm kind of embarrassed, too."

"Embarrassed?" Cal hadn't seen that coming.

"Yeah." Manny folded his arms across his chest and leaned back against the kitchen island.

Cal mirrored his actions as he waited for him to elaborate. He folded his arms and leaned back against the column that supported the staircase. He looked up and could see the ceiling about thirty feet above them.

"I'm embarrassed because I think I see what's going on with you, but I might just be projecting my own experience."

"We won't know till you explain."

"True. So, I'm guessing that you were wondering what Teresa would think about this place—whether she'd like it."

Cal pressed his lips together. How did Manny always know?

"But at the same time, I don't know that's what you're thinking. So, I question whether it's just me ... because I ... because I think about how Nina would see things, what she'd think. And I did right from the beginning. Maybe it's not like that for you. Maybe Teresa ..."

"It's okay." Cal had to put him out of his misery. He wasn't going to let Manny think that he'd gone soft—or at least, not that he was the only one. He blew out a sigh. Wondering what to say. Wondering what he even thought. "You're not projecting."

Manny smiled. "But you don't want to talk about it?"

Cal shrugged. "I ... wouldn't know how. I don't know ..." He let out a short laugh. "Would you look at us? With all that we've seen over the years, all that we've done? And yet we can't string a sentence together when it comes to talking about this stuff."

"I know." Manny chuckled. "I didn't know what had hit me at first. I thought maybe it was to do with getting old. Then Ryan got Leanne back—and he's just as bad, if not worse." He shrugged. "If I can do anything to help you, I will. How about that?"

"Thanks." Cal pushed away from the column. "And on that note. Let's finish looking around what I have a feeling is going to be my new home."

"Sure thing, neighbor."

Teresa went through to the back and sat down with a sigh in one of the comfy chairs in the break room. It'd been a busy morning, but then it was Saturday; it was always busy. She wondered again about what Elaine had said the other day. Could she get Elle to step up and run the place so that she could step back and start taking life a bit easier? She made a face. She wasn't that old! But then that was kind of the point too. This was a hard job physically, and she didn't want to keep doing it until she was too old and too worn out from it to enjoy doing anything else.

She took her phone out of her purse. Nina had been only too happy to give her Cal's number this morning. She'd wanted to know every last detail about last night. And she was supportive about Teresa's tentative plan for tonight. She got it. It wasn't that Teresa was trying to tempt Cal over to her place. She had to laugh at the thought. She wouldn't mind—and she hoped that at some point they might go in that direction, but she had other priorities.

Elle and Skye were her priorities. If Cal didn't want to come over, she'd see him another time. If he did, well, he'd get to know her better—not just as a woman out on a date, but as a mother and a grandmother. That was who she was.

She looked down at her phone and tapped in the number Nina had written down for her. She hit save before she hit the call button.

"This is Callahan."

His voice brought a smile to her lips. It was so deep and sexy—and very businesslike.

"Hello?"

Oops. She really needed to say something. "Cal? Hi. This is Teresa."

"Teresa?"

"Yeah." She let out a nervous chuckle. "Sorry. Nina gave me your number. I'm not stalking you, I promise."

His laugh tickled her insides. "I believe you."

"It's about tonight."

"Oh." His tone changed completely. He sounded … he was! He was disappointed.

"I'm not canceling on you," she assured him quickly. "At least, I don't want to. I'm calling to see how you might feel about a change of plan."

"Sure. Whatever you like."

She had to smile. So, he had been disappointed. "Well, the thing is … you see …" Damn. She needed to pull herself together. This wasn't like her. "Elle, my daughter, she's going out tonight and …"

"And you have to watch Skye?"

"I don't have to. I want to."

"Okay. Tomorrow, then?"

"No. I'm … I mean …" She laughed. "Now I'm the one making a mess of this. I'm calling to ask if you would like to come to my place for dinner tonight. I can't go out. But you could come over if you want. I can make us dinner. And once Skye's gone down, we can sit out the back with a drink."

"That sounds great. Thank you. Well, except for one thing."

"What's that?" Her smile faded wondering what his problem might be.

"You don't need to be cooking dinner while you're watching the little one. So, how about I pick us something up from the resort on my way over?"

"Wow! You just get better and better, don't you?"

He laughed, and she had to laugh with him.

"It just ... it makes sense."

"It does. Thank you."

"How about I text you around six-thirty and you can tell me what you'd like so I can call the order in."

"Perfect!"

"Okay, then."

"Yeah. Okay." She couldn't stop smiling and she could hear the smile in his voice too. She just wished she could see it. "I'll see you later, then."

"I'll look forward to it."

"Me too."

Chapter Eight

It was busy when Cal got to the Boathouse, even though it was only just after seven. Ben, the guy who ran the place, did a good job. From what Cal had seen the resort was thriving, and the restaurant was the heart of the place.

He looked around when he reached the servers' station. He'd called the order in and they'd told him it'd be ready to pick up at seven-fifteen. He checked his watch. They had another ten minutes yet.

He smiled when the bartender spotted him and waved. "I'll get Kallen to come and take your order," she called.

"That's okay. I've ordered. I'm here to pick up, but I'm early."

She nodded and finished serving the customers in front of her. Once she was done, she came over and leaned on the other side of the bar.

"What are you doing getting takeout on a Saturday night, sugar? You should stay and eat here. Everyone will be out in a while. You should get to know people. I mean, sure you know Manny and Ryan, but we're a friendly bunch around here. You'll know everyone before too long. There's no need for you to take your dinner home and eat by yourself." She laughed. "You won't be by yourself long if you eat here."

Cal smiled through pursed lips. Kenzie was quite a character. He knew that already and he'd only chatted with her a few times so far when he'd come in to pick up takeout.

She raised an eyebrow at him. "Are you considering it? First drink's on me if you stay."

He chuckled. "Thanks, but ..."

"Is my wife bothering you?"

He turned to see one of the guys who sang with the band standing behind him. He didn't want to be the source of any friction between them.

"No. She's just trying to welcome me to the neighborhood. Suggesting I should eat here instead of getting takeout."

To his relief, the guy laughed. "Sorry. I didn't mean it like that. I didn't think she was hitting on you." He held his hand out. "I'm Chase. You're Cal, right? Don't worry. You'll get the hang of how things work around here soon enough." He made a face at Kenzie. "And one of the things you'll learn is that my wife likes to play matchmaker."

Cal shook with him and smiled. "Duly noted." He turned to Kenzie. "Thanks for the thought. But I'm good."

She gave him a puzzled look. "You're good? What does that mean? I can tell you that most of the women in here last night would agree with you." She laughed. "Though they might use the word fine, rather than good. But I don't think that's what you mean."

Chase laughed beside him. "Now you understand why I asked if she was bothering you?"

Cal chuckled. Yes, he did. But he wasn't going to admit that. "It's fine. Like I said. I appreciate the thought but I'm ..." Hmm. What should he say? Would Teresa mind if he told them that he was seeing her? He didn't know.

He was glad when Chase rescued him. "You're under no obligation to say a damned thing. Leave him alone, lover."

Kenzie shrugged. "I'm only trying to help."

"Hey, guys!"

They all turned, and Cal was surprised to see Teresa's daughter, Elle, standing behind them.

"Hey you!" Kenzie greeted her with a smile. "Are you having a wild night in with your mom and takeout again? One of these days I'm going to drag you out."

Elle gave Cal a sly smile before she spoke. "You're too late, Kenzie. Abbie had me under orders to come out tonight or else." She glanced at Cal again. "Someone else is in charge of a wild night and takeout with my mom."

Kenzie frowned and then looked at him. She was so transparent Cal could see the moment she grasped what Elle was saying. "You!"

He stared at her, wondering what he should say. He needn't have worried. He didn't get the chance to say anything.

"Oh, my God! That's awesome! You didn't waste any time, did you?"

He had to laugh, partly at the delighted expression on her face, and partly because it saved him from having to answer what he hoped was merely a rhetorical question.

Elle smiled at him. "If you're just here killing time, I'm sure she won't mind if you arrive early. And if you're here for a shot of Dutch courage before you go, then it's only fair to tell you that she needed one, too."

He hadn't been sure how Elle would feel about him going over like this—about him having a date with her mom or being around her daughter. So, her words came as a relief.

"Thanks. I'm just here to collect dinner."

"Why didn't you say so?" asked Kenzie.

"Probably because you didn't give him the chance to get a word in edgewise." Chase winked at Cal.

"Let me go and see where it is." Kenzie disappeared into the back.

Chase waved at someone across the other side of the bar. "I need to have a word with Michael. I hope you both have a great evening."

Once he'd gone, Cal looked at Elle wondering what he should say. She was Teresa's daughter, not her father, but the situation had him feeling like a nervous teenager asking permission to take a girl on a date.

She put him out of his misery with a friendly smile. "I'm glad you two figured things out."

He smiled back. "She told you what happened?"

"Yeah! After you left the salon yesterday, I thought you were a total pig."

He shook his head. "Good to know that I made such a wonderful first impression. You thought I was a pig, your mom thought I was a creepy dude."

Elle laughed. "You might not have gotten off to the best start but look on the bright side—the only way is up from here."

He laughed with her. He liked her. She reminded him of Teresa; bright and upbeat and judging by her comment about Dutch courage, not afraid to tell the truth. "I hadn't thought of it that way."

"Well, you should." She looked more serious now. "And don't just think of it that way, be that way. I know this is just a first date and everything, but she's an awesome lady. She deserves the best, and you'd better be good to her."

"I will. I give you my word." He nodded solemnly, then turned at the sound of Kenzie squealing behind him.

"Oh, my God! You're awesome!" She looked at Elle. "Isn't he? Did you hear that? See it? He stands there all tough guy, all muscles and blue eyes, looking like he might kick ass and take names and he solemnly gives you his word that he'll be good to your mom?"

Elle nodded happily, though she at least seemed to sense his discomfort at Kenzie's outpouring. She touched his arm. "I did. And I appreciate it."

Cal looked at the bag Kenzie had set on the bar, eager to get out of here now. "What do I owe you?"

The two girls didn't wait for him to be out of earshot, and he smiled through pursed lips as he walked away.

"If I didn't have Chase, I'd be jealous of your mom."

"You mean if you didn't have Chase and you were twenty years older."

He shook his head at Kenzie's dirty laugh. "No, ma'am. I don't."

~ ~ ~

"One more story, Grandma."

Teresa held Skye a little closer. She really should put her down before Cal arrived. Elle had given her a bath and changed her into her PJ's before she left, and the two of them had made the most of their time snuggling on the sofa with one of Skye's favorite books.

She glanced at the clock. She had ten minutes left. They could fit in one of the shorter stories. "Okay, how about the one with the mouse?"

"Benji Mouse!" Skye nodded happily and started flipping through the pages. She stopped abruptly at the sound of the doorbell. "One more story, Grandma. You said."

"I did, and we will, sweet pea. But I have to let my friend in."

Skye's little eyebrows knit together. "Cal."

"That's right. You stay there a minute while I let him in. See if you can find the picture of Benji with his friend, Frankie."

Skye started flipping through the pages again, but as soon as Teresa got up, she slid down from the sofa after her.

Teresa's breath caught somewhere in her chest when she opened the front door and saw Cal standing there. He was something else. Tonight, he was wearing jeans and a light blue shirt that matched his eyes.

"Hi."

"Hey." That smile! "Sorry, I'm a bit early. I …"

"You're Cal! Hurry up. We're going to read Benji Mouse."

When she'd suggested that he should come over this evening, Teresa had thought she could put Skye down before he arrived. But she hadn't been able to resist getting the time with her. Now, she was curious to see how he'd handle it. In her experience, most men didn't know what to do with little kids.

She was thrilled to see Cal squat down in front of Skye so that he could talk to her on her level. She was even more thrilled to see that he was holding flowers behind his back. "Benji Mouse? Who's he?"

"He's a venture mouse."

Teresa had to laugh. "He goes on adventures. Come on in. I'll get you a drink before I read her the story and put her down. I won't be long."

He followed her through to the kitchen and set the takeout bag on the counter. Then he brought his other hand out from behind his back and presented her not with a bunch of flowers, but with a beautiful purple orchid in a pot.

"Oh! That's beautiful! Thank you!"

She loved every version of his smile that she'd seen so far, and the bashful one he gave her as he handed over the orchid might just be her favorite yet. "It's … for you."

"Thank you! It's lovely. That's so thoughtful."

He nodded, then looked down at Skye, who was tugging on his hand. "Benji Mouse. Come on, it's story time."

"Only one more and then you have to go to bed." She gave Cal an apologetic shrug. "I promised her one more story. Do you want to wait in here and I'll—"

"No, Grandma." Skye pouted at her. "He needs Benji Mouse."

"No, Skye. Cal wants to …"

"Cal wants to read Benji Mouse. Don't you?" Skye looked up at Cal with big, pleading brown eyes as she tugged on his hand again. "Cal wants to sit on the sofa and read." She spoke with a finality that indicated she expected to get her way—the little madam.

Teresa sighed. She didn't want Cal to have to witness a battle of wills, but …

He raised an eyebrow at her, seemingly indicating that he didn't mind.

She raised one back and he nodded. Well, okay then.

He squatted down in front of Skye and looked her in the eye. "I would like to hear the story. But Grandma said just one. Is that okay?"

Teresa's heart clenched at the smile that spread across her granddaughter's little face. "Just one. Then I'll go to bed." She looked at Teresa and added, "like a good girl."

Cal chuckled and stood back up. Skye caught hold of his hand and then Teresa's too and led them both into the living room where she pointed at the sofa for Cal to sit. He did as he was told, and to Teresa's amazement, Skye scrambled up into his lap and held her book up in front of him. "See? This is Benji Mouse."

Teresa eyed him warily wondering if this was enough to scare him away permanently. He no doubt wasn't used to little kids, let alone a precocious little madam like Skye. To her surprise, he smiled up at her and patted the space beside him. "Come on, Grandma. I want to hear the story."

Her heart thudded to a halt. Hearing him say that—hearing him call her Grandma, took her back. All the way back to when Steve used to call her that. She hadn't been a grandma then, though. She shuddered and forced herself to smile back at Cal and sit down and take the book.

They had so much fun with the story that she ended up reading two, and by the time the second one was finished, Skye's eyes were drooping.

"Come on, sweet pea. Time for bed." Teresa held her arms out to take her, but Skye wrapped her arms around Cal. "I want him to take me."

Before Teresa could tell her no, Cal raised an eyebrow at her and nodded slightly. Well, If he didn't mind.

"Okay, then."

Skye wrapped her arms around his neck, and Teresa wanted to take a picture when he stood up and seated her on his hip. He looked perfectly at home with her there, and she looked tiny—and so very happy, tucked under his arm that was probably wider around than her waist was.

"Okay, then." Teresa had to pull herself together. "Up the stairs we go."

When they reached Skye's bedroom, Cal's smile faded, and he handed her over to Teresa. "Goodnight, Skye."

She clung to him and planted a sloppy kiss on his cheek before she let go. "Goodnight, Cal. See you in the morning."

Teresa didn't correct her. It was easier to let it go than to get into an explanation of why Cal wouldn't be here in the morning.

Cal reached out and touched her nose with his thumb, making her giggle. "I'll see you soon, okay?"

"Okay." She let out a big yawn and rested her head against Teresa's shoulder.

"I'll be down in a few minutes."

~ ~ ~

Cal went back to the kitchen and looked at the takeout bag sitting on the island. It'd be cold, or at least on the way there, but he didn't feel right to start dishing it or heating it. Instead, he stood there, arms hanging at his sides. He didn't know what to do. He looked at the orchid, wondering whether it had been a dumb idea. He'd guess not, given the way Teresa's eyes had lit up when she saw it.

He would never admit it to a soul, but he'd actually spent some time this afternoon Googling which flowers were appropriate to give on a first date. The first article he'd read had declared that flowers were a complete no-no for a first date, that it was too old-fashioned a gesture. But he hadn't let that deter him. He wasn't a kid trying to impress a girl. In his day flowers had been a good thing—and girls had loved them.

As he'd read on, he'd learned that every flower had some significance attached to it—though he couldn't help but wonder who had assigned the significance; whether it was all just some marketing ploy by a clever florist.

He'd read until his head spun. In the end he'd decided on an orchid because they were supposedly highly prized and reflected the esteem in which you held a woman—while at the same time somehow representing her beauty, luxury, and strength. Plus, he hadn't quite been able to shake the uncertainty over whether giving flowers really was so far outdated as to be laughable—in which case giving her a plant in a pot could almost be passed off as a hostess gift—maybe? He should have asked Darla. But that would have led to a full-on interrogation. And besides, if he was going to do this, he wanted to figure out how to do it himself—not just follow his sister's instructions.

"Sorry about that."

He turned to Teresa when she came back into the kitchen.

"Please, don't apologize. She's a sweetheart. I'm honored that I got to share in story time."

"Aww. Thank you. You did so well with her. You surprised me. I thought she might be enough to scare you away."

"No. I enjoyed it. It took me back."

"You have kids?"

"No!" He was shocked that she might think that. "I would have told you before now if I did."

"I thought so, but ... What did it take you back to?"

He chuckled. "Darla's kids. It seems I'm making a habit of giving you the wrong impression about them. I should probably explain."

"Only if you want to. And what do you think, should we dish this up first? We can eat outside if you like."

"What about Skye?"

Teresa pointed to a baby monitor on the countertop. "We can take that."

Once they were seated at a table outside on the back patio, Teresa cocked her head to the side. "Still want to tell me about your sister's children?"

"I do. Abigail, Anthony and Henry, they're fourteen, thirteen and eleven now."

"And you're close with them?"

"Very. Their dad died six years ago."

"Oh, I'm sorry. That must have been so hard for their mom, your sister."

Cal nodded. "It was. It still is. I took leave from work and stayed with them for the first few months. Henry was a little older than Skye is now." He could see her doing the math in her head. "Darla's twelve years younger than me, but we've always been close. Our dad wasn't around growing up, and I was somewhere between big brother and father to her."

Teresa nodded as if she understood, but he knew she couldn't.

"Anyway. That's why I said reading with Skye like that took me back. I used to read to the three of them."

"They must miss you. Was it hard to move away from them?"

He lifted a shoulder. "Yes and no. I stayed with them for the first few months after Calvin died, but then Darla needed to find her feet again. It wouldn't have been right for me to stay. It was hard on all of us, but I supported them through the early days and then … then I went back to work. When I first retired, I thought I should go back there and be around. They're going into their teenage years now and that's not going to be easy, but Darla met a guy eighteen months ago. He's a good man." Cal could feel the tension in his jaw and rubbed at it absently. "That's why I moved away. Graham's a good man. He's willing … he wants to step in and become their dad, but they all need me out of the picture for that to happen."

He swallowed when she reached out and touched his arm. She understood somehow. Her eyes told him that she did. He loved those kids. Letting Graham step up and become the man in their lives was the right thing for them. But damn, he missed them. He blew out a sigh.

"Anyway, look at me talking your ear off again."

She laughed. "It's okay. I doubt anyone would believe me if I told them."

"That's probably true. I've talked more around you than I can remember talking to anyone."

"Well, thank you. I like it."

They both turned when the baby monitor crackled. Skye muttered something and then it went quiet again.

"She's fine," said Teresa. "Do you want another drink?"

"Please." He got up with her and helped clear the plates and take them to the kitchen. She stacked them on the counter next to the sink, and he raised an eyebrow.

"What?"

"Do you want me to take care of these while you check on her?"

Teresa laughed. "That's fine, they'll keep. But how did you know I was going to check on her?"

"Because it's what I'd do, just to make sure after hearing her like that."

"I'll only be a minute."

"Take your time."

Once she'd gone upstairs Cal poured them fresh drinks and looked around. The kitchen was bright and airy and spacious. The cabinets were all white, the countertops marble, but it still felt welcoming, not sterile. There were lots of little feminine touches around, a bunch of bright pink feathers displayed in a vase like flowers. A splash of rainbow colors in a frame on the wall. It suited her.

He stared at the pile of dishes. She'd said they could wait, but they didn't need to. It wouldn't take him long. He rinsed them and wiped down the countertops

He was just closing the dishwasher when she came back. She stopped dead and looked around wide-eyed.

"I just ..." His heart hammered as he wondered if his actions might appear creepy somehow.

"You cleaned my kitchen?"

He cringed as he nodded, waiting for her to pass judgment that he was some kind of weirdo and demand that he leave.

Instead, she shook her head in wonder. "Are you for real?"

He gave her an apologetic smile. "I'm sorry. I … I'm not good at doing nothing. And I like order."

She laughed and looked around again. He might have straightened a few things while he was wiping the counters.

"So, I can see. I'm with you on not liking to do nothing, but if you like order …" Her smiled faded. "You might not like me."

"No." He crossed the distance between them in two strides before he even stopped to consider his actions. He closed his arms around her and pressed a kiss to her forehead. "I do like you."

Her eyes were even wider as she looked up at him, but they were dancing and the gold flecks in them sparkled.

"I like you, too, Cal."

He smiled. "I was hoping."

She reached up and traced her finger over his lips. "With that smile, you don't need to hope, you can know. I like you a lot."

He lowered his lips to hers and was soon lost in one of her sweet kisses. Her arms came up around his shoulders and she pressed herself against him as her tongue met his eagerly. He held her closer to his chest and had to hope that she wouldn't mind knowing—feeling—just how much he liked her, and how eager he was to get to know her better.

Chapter Nine

Teresa looked up when Nina came into the salon. "Hi, I'll be with you in a few. We're almost done here." She smiled down at Mrs. Etheridge who was sitting in her chair. The old lady barely had enough hair left to style, but she'd been keeping this Wednesday afternoon appointment for a blow-dry since before Teresa had bought the place.

Mrs. Etheridge smiled back up at her. "I think we are done." She patted her hair and peered at the mirror. "I know you've done a good job, even if I can barely see myself. I just don't ever want to become that scary old bat with a shock of white hair standing on end who all the kids are afraid of."

"You could never be that Mrs. E," called Elle from where she was sweeping around her chair. "All the kids love you and always have. You've been the favorite Halloween house and the favorite Christmas decorations house ever since I was little."

Mrs. Etheridge laughed. "And I know you think that's a long time, Elle. But believe me, when you get to my age the last thirty years seem like the blink of an eye. You have to remember that when you were born, I was older than your mom is now."

She winked at Teresa, and they both laughed at the stunned look on Elle's face.

"It's true. And you might want to remember that. Whenever things look bad or feel like they're going wrong, more than likely it's only a blip in the grand scheme of things. When you're having a tough time, it might feel like you're in a bad chapter of your life. When you get to my age and look back, you'll see it wasn't even a chapter, it was barely a couple of pages."

Teresa rested her hand on the old lady's shoulder. She wanted to thank her for trying to help Elle see her troubles in a new way, but she didn't know what to say. She didn't need to. Mrs. Etheridge reached up and squeezed her hand. "And you, Teresa. You'd do well to think about it. Elle was born thirty years ago."

Teresa laughed. "That just makes me feel old."

"That's my point. You're not. You're only at the beginning of the next thirty years. You're not old, you're at the beginning of a new chapter." She winked again. "If I were you, I'd make the most of it." The twinkle in her eye gave her away.

"Are you trying to tell me something?"

"I am, but I'll spell it out for you if you like. You're the talk of the town girl, you and that handsome young fella, Callahan. You're the talk of the town and the envy of half its women. You've been by yourself a long time. Like I said, it's time for a new chapter."

Teresa rolled her eyes. "I've been out with the man twice."

Elle laughed. "No, you've only been out with him once. The second time he came over."

Mrs. Etheridge waggled her eyebrows. "I heard that, too, but I wasn't sure if I should believe it."

"It's true that he came over. But you shouldn't believe the rest. There's no truth to what I can only imagine people are saying."

"And you," she made a face at Elle, "can vouch for that, young lady."

"Yeah. Okay. I'm only teasing."

Teresa helped Mrs. Etheridge up from the chair and led her over to the front desk to write out her appointment card for next week. She didn't need it, but it was part of the ritual they went through every week. After she'd handed it over, she came around the front desk to give her a hug.

"Is Kevin out there?"

Teresa peered out through the window and saw the cab sitting outside as it always was. "He is."

Elle came hurrying over and looped her arm through the old lady's. I'll walk you out, Mrs. E."

When the door closed behind them, Nina grinned at her. "So, there's no truth to the rumors then?"

"No!" Teresa blew out a sigh. "But I'm not going to lie to you and tell you that I hope to have to admit they're right at some point soon."

"You like him then?"

"Like is such a little word."

"Especially for such a big man."

Teresa laughed. "I didn't like to mention that."

"Ooh! So, you'd know?"

She rolled her eyes. "I mean, I didn't want to start rattling on about how tall he is and his big arms and all his muscles and ..." She couldn't help laughing. "His huge hands!"

"But you don't know if they're an indication of …?"

"If I had to guess, I'd say that absolutely they are."

"But you don't have to guess … you know?"

"No, not … directly. Like I said. The rumors aren't true, yet. But we did kiss, and he held me to him and … well … Let's say he was so pleased about that, that I got the impression that he's …" she tried to find the right words but couldn't. She laughed when it came to her. "That he's a big boy."

Nina laughed with her. "And when are you seeing him again?"

"Not until the weekend. He's all in on his new job. By the sounds of it he's going in early and staying till late."

"Yeah, Manny said that Dan's already worried about him working full-time when he's only supposed to be part-time."

"He said it's only until he sets everything up the way he wants it, that he has to get all his systems in place so that when they open for business everything will run as he wants it to."

Nina smiled. "You sound defensive on his behalf."

"No! I … I do, don't I? It's just that he told me about it. He said they all think that he's a workaholic and he used to be. But that he doesn't plan to be that way here. That he's looking for balance. His job used to be his life but now he wants to have a life and a job."

"And does he want you to be part of his life?"

"I don't know. It's too soon to even think about that. We've only been out … once."

"Yeah, and stayed in once. You wouldn't have shared your Skye time with him if you didn't like him a lot."

"I know. I just … I don't know where it's going, and it doesn't have to go anywhere, does it?"

"I guess not. Anyway, are we going or are we going to stand around here talking all night?"

"We're going. Come on through to the back while I get my purse."

Nina sat down while Teresa straightened the back room a little. She didn't normally bother but the way Cal had cleaned her kitchen on Saturday night had left her wondering if she was perhaps a little too disorganized.

"What are you doing with him at the weekend?" asked Nina.

"Well, he's going to come over again on Friday night. We're going to watch Skye so Elle can go out." She glanced at the door that led back to the salon. "I'm so thrilled, Nina. She said she had a good time, and they'd asked if she wanted to go again. I'm hoping that she's finding her feet and will want to end up staying."

"I'm hoping right along with you. Abbie said it was great to have her back and that she got along with everyone—all the new kids."

"Yeah. I'm keeping my fingers crossed. Though there is one downside to it."

"What?"

"Apparently, Steve's talking about coming up to see her and Skye."

"Ugh." Nina's face summed up the way she felt about Teresa's ex-husband more eloquently than she could have put into words.

"Yeah. My sentiments exactly."

"We could go out of town when he comes—whenever it is."

"Thanks, Nina. But I'm not going to run and hide. You know what he's like. He makes out that I'm the one with the problem. I don't care. He doesn't bother me. I just don't like how he tried to turn Elle against me. And I don't like the way—" She stopped abruptly when Elle stuck her head around the door.

"What are you still doing here? I thought you were going for dinner with all the girls?"

"We are. We did it again, though. We got to talking."

"Well, take your talking over to the Boathouse so you can have a good chinwag with all your cronies!"

"Elle! You make us sound like old witches!"

"I said no such thing," Elle grinned at them, "but if the shoe fits!"

Teresa grabbed for one of the brooms. "More like if the broom's handy, I'll chase you with it."

She chased Elle back into the salon, and Nina followed, the three of them laughing, until the door opened, and they all stopped at the sight of Cal standing there.

Teresa sucked in a deep breath. He was like that. He made you stop and stare. He stole her breath.

He folded his arms across his chest and raised an eyebrow. "Am I interrupting something?"

"No!" cried Elle and ran to him, ducking behind him and peeking out around his side. "You're just in time to rescue me."

He chuckled and gave Teresa a puzzled look. "You were about to beat your daughter with a broom?"

She laughed and set it down. "I guess you'll never know."

Elle came out from behind him. "Thanks, Cal. You saved me." She went to Nina and slipped her arm through hers. "Come with me while I get you those things for Abbie."

Teresa was aware of them going into the back and closing the door behind them only because Cal watched them and visibly relaxed when the door clicked shut.

"I hope it's okay to just drop by like this?"

"It's more than okay. It's wonderful." She'd been disappointed when he'd asked if she wanted to see him again on Friday. She'd said yes, of course she did. But she wasn't thrilled at having to wait a whole week before she could.

He still had his arms folded across his chest. She loved the way he did that, it showed off his forearms—complete with tattoo that she had yet to ask him about. He looked serious again. If she didn't know better, she'd think he had a problem. But she did know better. At least, she hoped she did. The intimidating stance and seemingly shuttered face had so far proved to be merely cover for uncertainty. He wasn't mad at her; he was unsure about something.

She knew how to put him at ease. And if she was wrong? Well, even if she were wrong it'd be worth it.

She went to him and slipped her arms around his waist and reached up to press a little kiss to the corner of his mouth.

For a moment, she thought she'd misjudged him. He tensed, frozen for a second like a statue, but then he relaxed, and his arms closed around her and he pecked her lips.

"I wasn't expecting that," he murmured.

She looked up at him. "Does that mean you don't want ..." She started to take a step back, but his arms tightened around her waist.

"No. I said I wasn't expecting it, not that I don't like it, or didn't want it. I expected to have to earn it"

It was her turn to relax. "You already have."

He looked down into her eyes. "How?"

"Just by being you." She pressed another kiss to his lips. She couldn't help it. "But I'll probably have to let you go in a minute." She glanced back at the door to the breakroom. "That was sweet of them, but I doubt they'll stay in there long."

Cal pressed a kiss to her forehead. "I can't stay long anyway. I'm going back to work. I'm almost done with everything I wanted to get set up. Which means …"

"What?"

He looked doubtful now, as if he'd come here with something on his mind but was about to change it.

"Tell me what it means, Cal. Don't back out on me now."

He laughed. "Okay. I wondered if you wanted to go out tomorrow night … as well as Friday. I'm looking forward to Friday. I'm not saying tomorrow instead. I'm asking for tomorrow as well … if you'd like?"

She grinned. "I'd like. I'd like very much. What do you want to do?"

"I thought we could go over to Four Mile."

"I'd love to."

"Great. I'll call you tomorrow then about coming to get you. Does around seven work?"

"That'll be great."

"Okay. He glanced at the breakroom door over her shoulder. "I should go."

She laughed. "You probably should. I'll see you tomorrow."

When Cal got back to the office, he sat down and waited for his computer to fire up. He'd been wondering all day if he should ask Teresa out tomorrow night. Now that he had—and she'd said yes—he wondered why he'd waited so long.

He smiled as he entered his password. He only had a couple more hours to put in and then he'd be happy that his systems were as good as they could be for now. Of course, he'd have to adjust on the fly once they were tested in the real world. But he knew he'd set the organization up with a solid foundation.

"You're back?"

He looked up to see Ryan standing in the doorway.

"I am."

"I thought you left for the night. You know Dan's starting to wonder about you."

"What about me?" Cal frowned. He liked Dan. He'd thought they were establishing a good working relationship.

"Don't look like that. He's wondering if we're going to be able to afford you. This was only supposed to be a part time gig, remember? You've put in more hours in the first couple weeks than we budgeted for the entire month."

"That's not a problem. I know what my official hours are and I'm not expecting to be paid for going over them. It's just …" He shrugged. "You know how it is; we've never worked in an environment where you keep track of your hours. We do what it takes to get the job done. At the beginning of an op, it takes a bit more to get set up, that's all."

Ryan smiled and came into the office. "I know. I get it and I've tried to explain it to Dan, but he's concerned. He doesn't want to take advantage."

Cal raised an eyebrow, and Ryan laughed.

"I know, I did try to tell him that no one takes advantage of Blake Callahan. But you know what he's like. He's from a different world than we are."

"Yeah. Thanks for the heads up. I should be able to set his mind at ease now anyway. I'm only back tonight to run through everything one last time. Barring any unexpected glitches, I'll be able to stick to my scheduled hours from now on."

Ryan smiled. "There's no need to sound so formal. This isn't me delivering a directive from above. I'm just letting you know that you're appreciated—and that no one wants you overdoing it."

Call narrowed his eyes. "That's not some veiled dig, is it? Am I supposed to hear the unspoken *at my age?*"

Ryan laughed. "Hell, no! My self-preservation instincts are still strong. There's no way I'd give you the kind of shit I give Manny."

Cal held his gaze as he considered that. "Why, though?"

Ryan's smile faded. "What do you mean?"

"Why's it okay for you to give Manny shit, but not me?" He frowned. "Am I no fun?"

Ryan gave him a puzzled look and came to sit down across the desk from him. "What brought that on? Of course you're fun. You think we would have survived on the inside for as long as we did without all the laughs?"

"No." Cal regretted asking now. "Forget it."

"Nah, come on. Tell me what's eating you?"

He shrugged. "Nothing. I'm probably just … I don't know … feeling old maybe."

"I call bullshit."

Cal met his gaze. "I hate to break it to you kid, but all joking aside, I am getting older."

"Brush it off if you want. But I'm going to tell you what I think."

Cal waited. He doubted Ryan would have any clue what he was really thinking.

"I think it's Teresa who's got you questioning yourself."

"No! She ... she's not ..."

Ryan held his hand up. "I don't mean in a bad way. I mean being around her. She's all upbeat and out for the laughs, right? You like her. She likes you, but you haven't found your feet yet, so you're questioning if you might be a bit too ... formal for her?" He raised an eyebrow.

Cal stared at him for a few moments before blowing out a sigh. "Pretty much."

Ryan grinned. "Well, don't."

"Don't what?"

"Don't sweat it. Don't second guess yourself. Get over any doubts you're having."

Cal chuckled. "What, just like that, because you say so?"

"Yeah. And if that's not enough. Then because according to Leanne—who got her hair done yesterday—Teresa is besotted with you."

"She told Leanne that?"

"Not in so many words, no. But while Lee was in there, her daughter kept teasing her about you and she didn't deny a thing. She even looked embarrassed, which according to Lee is something that Teresa doesn't do very often."

Cal mulled that over, not sure what to think.

"Relax, boss. I'm trying to reassure you here. She's into you. So, what are you going to do about it? Want me to help you come up with a plan of attack?"

Cal smiled. "Thanks, but I don't need one. I just stopped into the salon to see her—and asked her to have dinner with me tomorrow."

Ryan grinned. "And she said yes?"

"She did."

"Good for you. See, I told you; you don't need to worry about whether you're fun enough."

"I guess not."

Ryan got to his feet. "I need to get going. I'll see you in the morning."

"Yep. Say hi to Leanne for me."

"Will do. And she's been talking about inviting you over for dinner soon."

"Okay."

Ryan laughed. "Don't look like that. I told you. She doesn't think you were behind those messages. The sooner I get the two of you together, the sooner we can all put the past behind us."

"Sounds good. I'll see you tomorrow." Cal turned back to his computer. He wouldn't mind having dinner with Ryan and Leanne and putting the past where it belonged, but he was more interested in having dinner with Teresa and focusing on the future. He frowned as he entered his next password and waited for the database to load. He was thinking about her in the same breath as thinking about his future? Apparently, he was.

Chapter Ten

Teresa checked herself over in the mirror and smiled. She looked good. The dress flattered her figure. She knew she was lucky to have good genes. She'd been tall and willowy as a girl. Now, in her mid-fifties, she was still slender. She had to work harder for it than she ever had before, but it was a price she was willing to pay. She went to the gym a couple of times a week and did circuits with Russ. He was a good guy, and they had a laugh. She'd piled on a few too many pounds when she hit her forties and … and she didn't need to be thinking about that tonight.

She dabbed a little perfume on her neck and wrists and headed down the stairs. Cal had said he'd be here at seven, and she suspected he'd be early. He was that kind of guy.

"Ooh!" Elle grinned at her when she reached the kitchen. "The poor guy's not going to know what hit him. Should I expect you home later … or not?"

Teresa made a face. "Of course, I'll be home."

"Sorry. I'm only teasing, but by the same token, just text me if you change your mind."

She held her daughter's gaze for a moment. "Thanks."

"You look pretty, Grandma!" Skye came toddling toward her holding her arms up.

Teresa scooped her up and planted a kiss in her hair. "Thank you, sweet pea."

"Come and read Benji Mouse?"

"Grandma can't tonight, Skye," said Elle. "Grandma's going out. Once she's gone, we'll read."

Skye's bottom lip slid out. "I want to go."

"No," said Elle. "Grandma's going out with Cal and—"

Skye's face lit up. "Cal? I like Cal! He likes Benji Mouse. He can read, too."

Elle raised an eyebrow at Teresa. "He likes Benji Mouse?"

Teresa chuckled. "He does. He was very good with Madam here last week." She looked down at Skye. "And if you're good, he might read with us tomorrow when he comes. But for tonight, Cal's taking Grandma out."

Skye made a face and wriggled to get down. She was on her way back to the living room when the doorbell rang, and she diverted to get it. Teresa hurried after her, and when she opened the door, Skye flung herself at Cal's legs, wrapping her arms around them.

"Cal! Come and read Benji Mouse!"

Teresa marveled at the way he scooped her up and sat her on his hip. "Hello, Skye."

It seemed her granddaughter was just as taken with him as she was. A big, goofy smile spread across her face as she looked up at him. "Hello, Cal."

He pressed her nose with his thumb, making her giggle. "Are you being a good girl?"

She glanced at Teresa and nodded.

"She is, come on in a minute."

Elle came out of the kitchen and her eyes widened when she saw Skye snuggling against Cal, her arms as far around him as she could reach and her little head resting on his shoulder.

"Hi." She greeted him with a smile. "Come on, Skye." She held her arms out, but Skye turned her head away and clung tighter to Cal.

"I want Cal to read Benji Mouse."

He smiled through pursed lips.

"Skye!" Elle's tone held a warning this time.

Cal raised an eyebrow at her, and Elle nodded. He reached up and tapped Skye's shoulder. Teresa's heart melted a little bit as she watched her granddaughter lift her head and look at him. "I can't read with you tonight, Skye. But maybe tomorrow."

Her little eyebrows knit together.

"I'm going to give you back to your mom now." She clung tighter to him again. "Because I'm going out with Grandma. But will you do me a favor?"

She nodded.

"Will you draw me a picture of Benji Mouse for when I come tomorrow? I'll be here again at the same time before you go to bed and I'd love to see your picture."

A smile spread across her face and she wriggled to get down. When her feet hit the floor, she ran to Elle and took hold of her hand. "Come on, Mommy. Want my crayons."

Elle looked back over her shoulder at them as she let Skye lead her away. She grinned at Teresa and spoke in a low voice. "Damn! He's good. He has my approval. You guys have a great night."

With that she let Skye drag her to the dining room in search of crayons.

Teresa smiled up at Cal. He was wonderful.

He gave her a bashful shrug, making her laugh. "Are you ready?"

"Yep. Let's get out of here while we can."

Once they were in his SUV, she looked over at him and he turned toward her. "Are you okay? I didn't do wrong back there with Skye, did I?"

She shook her head.

"So …" He raised an eyebrow. "Am I allowed to ask why you're looking at me like that? What are you thinking?"

She chuckled. She might as well tell him. "I'm thinking that you are amazing, and I'm looking at you like this because … I like what I see."

His smile transformed his face. He was handsome even when he looked serious, but there was something about that smile that just melted her insides.

Her breath caught in her chest when he leaned toward her and his hand closed around the back of her neck. He claimed her mouth in a kiss that stole her senses. When he finally lifted his head, he smiled again.

"Wow!" she breathed.

He chuckled. "I was going to ask if that was okay, but I think you just answered that question."

She nodded rapidly. "Okay doesn't do it justice, but if you meant was it okay to do, that'd be a yes—any time you like."

He chuckled. "Good to know."

He started the engine and pulled away. When he reached the main road, he surprised her again by reaching over and taking hold of her hand.

It was a surprise, but she didn't want to question it. Instead, she linked her fingers through his and gave him a smile. "Do you know the way? Have you been out to Four Mile yet?"

"I have. I was over there on Saturday with Manny. He showed me his house and …"

Teresa frowned when her phone started to ring. "Sorry." She fished it out of her purse, she didn't want to answer, but she needed to make sure it wasn't Elle needing her for something. It wasn't. She scowled when she saw who it was. She let it ring and didn't answer.

"Is everything okay?" asked Cal. "Take it if you need to."

"I don't want to." She waited for the beep that would indicate she had a voicemail. But it didn't come. Instead, it started to ring again. She blew out a sigh. Damn him. She didn't hear from him for months at a time, but when he wanted to talk, he'd blow up her phone until she answered. She considered turning it off. She didn't want him spoiling this evening.

Cal glanced over at her. "Get it if you need to. I don't mind. Or …" The look on his face made her wonder what he was going to say. "Or I can pull over and get out while you take it, if it's personal."

"Pft!" The sound was out before she could stop it. "That's so sweet of you, but it's nothing like that. It's Elle's father and I'll be honest. He pisses me off!"

"Do you want me to pull over?"

"No. This won't take long." She scowled as she swiped to answer it. "What do you want, Steve?"

"Is that any way to greet me, Grandma?"

Teresa didn't bother to answer. She wasn't going to get into it with him, she wanted to keep this as short and to the point as possible.

"What's up, are you busy?"

"As a matter of fact, I am. So, is this something urgent or can I call you back?"

"Hey, there's no need to be like that. Maddie and I are trying to figure out when's the best time to come up to see Elle and Skye. You know you make Maddie uncomfortable, so I wanted to check if you have any trips planned. We can come while you're not around."

Teresa rolled her eyes. She'd only told Nina the other day that she wouldn't run and hide if Steve came to town but since he was asking her to ... "When are you thinking?"

"Next weekend or if not, it'll have to wait until the end of the month."

"The end of the month would be better."

"Are you really going to make this so easy?"

"For Elle and Skye's sakes, yes, I am."

"Okay. Thanks. How are you doing?"

She pursed her lips. He only ever pretended to show an interest in how she was. He was just nosey—and jealous of how well she'd done for herself since they'd split. "I'm okay thanks. I hope you are, too." She really did. Whenever things were going well in his life, he tended to leave her alone. "I'm busy right now though. Call me and let me know when you make arrangements?"

"Will, do. Thanks, Terry."

"You're welcome. Bye." She ended the call and looked over at Cal. He was keeping his gaze fixed on the road ahead.

"Sorry about that."

"No need. Have you eaten at the restaurant in the lodge before?"

Bless him. He was trying to move on from what might be an awkward moment. She didn't want him to, though. She didn't want him to feel like he was the stranger on the outside. She wasn't going to let Steve put him there. It was probably too early in their friendship to give him the whole story of her divorce, but …

"I have. It's great. But can I be honest for a minute?"

He glanced over at her. "I hope so."

"That was Steve. Elle's father. My ex-husband …"

"You don't owe me any explanations. I'd guess that you need to talk to him sometimes, especially with Elle and Skye back at home with you."

She rested her hand on his arm. "You're far too sweet and far too understanding. You're right. I don't owe you an explanation, but I want to give you one so that you understand. Okay?"

He nodded.

"The man is an asshole!"

The corner of his mouth quirked up in what she guessed— hoped—might be an attempt to hide a smile.

"And I don't say that lightly," she continued. "I'm not being the bitter ex-wife either. We were good for a few years. We had Elle. We were decent parents to her when she was small. But once she was older it became obvious that she'd been the only thing holding us together. It was obvious that we weren't going to make it. But Steve, well I guess he wanted to try out his options before he threw in the towel with me. He got himself quite a reputation around town before I found out about it. Apparently, none of them were worth the upheaval of divorcing me for. But then he met a tourist at the resort, Maddie. She was worth walking out the door without so much as a goodbye for. She's ten years younger."

"I'm sorry."

"I'm not. I'm not telling you this for sympathy. I'm well rid of him. My life's been so much better since we divorced. But like I said, he pisses me off. He knows how to make me angry and I don't want you to see that and think that I'm still affected by him. Well, I am, but not in that way. He makes me angry because he tries to turn Elle against me. Even little Skye."

Cal frowned and took hold of her hand. "I'm sorry."

"No. I'm sorry. I don't want to let it affect our evening." She smiled brightly. I just wanted to explain, and now that I have, can we forget about it?"

"About what?"

That smile of his could make her forget most things. "Thanks."

They ate dinner out on the terrace. Cal liked this place even better than the Boathouse. He liked the atmosphere over on the other side of the lake, the small quaint town, the down-home feeling, and everybody-knows-everybody vibe at the Boathouse. But he wasn't sure how much small-town *closeness* he'd be able to handle. The lodge here and the restaurant were more his speed.

Teresa set down her fork and smiled at him. "That was wonderful. I'd forgotten how good the food is over here."

"Do you come over here much?"

"Not too often, no. I come sometimes because I ..." She hesitated, as if weighing a decision, before she continued. "I have a place in phase one of the development."

He raised an eyebrow.

"It's a rental property. I was all in on this place from the moment I heard about it. I knew it'd be a goldmine. Do you know Pete and Jack?"

"No. They're the guys who own the Phoenix Corporation, aren't they? The developers?"

"They are. They're good kids, too."

"Kids?" That surprised Cal.

She chuckled. "Well, they're not kids, but they are to me. Elle went to school with one of them. Pete Hemming grew up here, he was always a smart kid. Always going to make something of himself, you could just tell. And his partner Jack, he's not from here, but he married one of Pete's best friends, Emma. And Ben—you've met Ben who owns the resort?"

Cal nodded.

"He owns this place too, the lodge. I think he's in partnership with them on the whole development, but I don't really know. The land belonged to his family."

"Wow. I didn't know any of that."

Teresa chuckled. "And you probably didn't want or need to. I was just trying to explain why I bought one of the first houses off the plan when they started up here. I knew it'd be a good investment."

"Sounds like you're a savvy businesswoman."

He didn't understand the scowl that flickered across her face. There was no sign of it when she answered. "I like to think so."

He wanted to move on from the subject. Something about it made her uncomfortable and he'd been enjoying the laughter up until now. "Do you want dessert? Anything else?"

She laughed. "I couldn't even if I did. I'm stuffed!"

He had to laugh with her. She was definitely a lady, no question about it, a beautiful, elegant one at that. But he loved the way she talked. She wasn't trying to put up a front, wasn't trying to impress him. She felt more like a friend than any woman he'd known apart from Darla. But there was nothing brotherly about his feelings toward her.

He called for the check and then reached for her hand. "Well, I don't want this evening to end yet, so how would you feel about showing me around the plaza? We could walk some of that dinner off."

She smiled and squeezed his hand. "I'd love to. I just need to pay a visit first."

He nodded expecting her to get up, but she pulled out her purse first and set a card down on the table. "In case he comes before I get back."

Cal scowled. He could feel it on his face before he could stop it.

"What? You brought dinner to my place last week."

"And I asked if I could take you out to dinner tonight."

She made a face. "You have a problem with me paying?"

He looked down at her card and then back up into her eyes. It seemed like it was important to her, but it was important to him too. "Honestly, I do. I'm sorry. It probably makes me look like some old school jerk. I don't mean it that way. But I can't just …"

She held his gaze for a long moment, and he wondered if he'd blown it. She surprised him when she laughed and picked her card back up. "Then for now, all I'll say is thank you. If it's important to you, I can respect that."

"Thanks."

He took hold of her hand as they left the hotel and crossed over to the plaza. "Do you like it over here?"

She looked up at him. "The plaza you mean? Or Four Mile?"

"Both, either?" The question had slipped out before he'd thought about it too much. What he was really interested in knowing was whether she preferred that side of the lake to this. He didn't want to get ahead of himself, but he already knew that he wanted to keep seeing her—to see a lot more of her, so if she was set on staying in town, perhaps he should start his search for a house over there.

She surprised him when she reached up and took his face between her hands and landed a kiss on his lips.

"What was that for?" he asked with a smile.

She laughed. "It was for *that*." She traced her finger over his lips, sending a shiver down his spine. "I wanted to see you smile again. You have such a killer smile, but sometimes you look so serious it's scary."

"Scary?"

She nodded but her eyes danced with laughter. "I don't think you understand how scary you come across. You're a big guy." She ran her hand up his arm and he had to bite down on his bottom lip. His only consolation was that her action seemed to have the same effect on her. Her pupils dilated and her tongue ran across her bottom lip.

He slid his arm around her shoulders. He had to feel her close, feel her soft body against his. "Well, I wouldn't ever want to scare you away."

She looked up into his eyes. "I don't think you could, even if you tried."

His heart beat a little faster at that. She was being more open with him than he'd dared to hope. "Still, I take it I should try to be less intimidating? Maybe smile sometimes."

She laughed. "More than sometimes. That smile?" She put her hand over her heart and blew out a sigh, making him laugh. She was fun. And she wasn't making fun of him. She meant it.

He chuckled. "Keep talking like that and you won't be able to wipe the smile off my face."

She stopped walking and looped her arms up around his neck. His hands closed around her waist of their own accord, pulling her against him. Then he was lost in her sweet kiss. One part of his mind stood sentry, acutely aware that after a lifetime of moving in the shadows he was now engaged in a very public display of affection. But even that part of his brain didn't want him to disengage from her kiss.

When they finally came up for air, she smiled at him. "Wow, Blake Callahan. You are something else. Has anyone ever told you that?"

He chuckled. "I can honestly say that no, no one ever has."

She gave him a sassy smile. "How about that? I get to be your first at something."

He tightened his arms around her. They were both a few decades past the point of firsts in the sense he was thinking about, but just the fact that she mentioned it heightened his desire for her.

Her eyes widened as she looked up into his. She felt the change in him, and her expression told him that she understood what it was about.

She pressed herself against him, making his eyes close and the blood surge in his veins.

Chapter Eleven

"What are you up to today?" Elle looked up from her laptop when Teresa came into the kitchen.

"I'm meeting Nina for lunch. What about you?"

Elle shrugged. "I think I'm going to take Skye to the park."

"By yourself? I can come if you—"

"That's okay. Not by myself, no. I got to talking to Emma on Friday night and she wanted to get Skye and little Isabel together."

"Aww. That's a lovely idea. I've always liked Emma."

"Yeah. She's a sweetheart. I'm glad she's with Jack now. He's awesome. I met up with her in the city a couple of times when she was married to that Rob. He was ..." Elle shuddered and the look on her face spoke volumes.

Teresa couldn't resist. "See, she just needed to come home to the lake and she found her perfect guy."

Elle made a face. "It's okay. You don't need to keep pushing all the merits of this place on me. I get it. And I'm thinking that maybe ..."

Teresa held her breath, hoping she knew what Elle was about to say.

"Maybe it is for the best if we stay here. Skye definitely has a better life here. And I can make it work."

"Oh, Elle." Teresa wrapped her up in a hug. "You know I'll do everything I can to help. To make life good here for you. If you want one of the houses, just say so. Tell me which one. You know I won't throw anyone out, but all the three of the leases are coming up soon. And I have a feeling that the Sullivans are ready to move out of the place at Four Mile."

Elle raised an eyebrow. "Really?"

"Yes. I heard that he's been offered a job in San Francisco. They love it here, but her mom's getting older and they want to move back to be closer to her. They haven't told me that themselves yet, but you know what the grapevine's like."

Elle laughed. "I sure do. If that place does come vacant, I'd love to rent it from you."

Teresa frowned. "You don't need—"

"I do, Mom. I need to stand on my own two feet. I'm not coming home to sponge off Mommy. And besides, that place is part of your income."

"It's not income. It's savings. And the only thing I'm saving for is you and Skye."

"I don't want to argue with you. If the place is available, I'd like to rent it from you. That's all."

Teresa nodded and managed to stop herself from saying anything else. She needed to just be grateful that Elle was thinking about staying. That was enough for now.

"And you wouldn't mind me staying on at the salon with you?"

"I'd love it. And … I know it's probably too soon to talk about it, but I'm just going to plant the seed. I'd like you to think about taking over if you want to. I'd like to start cutting back. I'm getting too old to be in there full-time."

"You are not!"

Teresa laughed. "Well, I feel it, put it that way. I'm ready to do more with my life than spend all my days in there. So, you have a think about it and when you're ready we can talk about what it might look like. Okay?"

Elle nodded. "Okay."

"Awesome!" Teresa was thrilled.

"Can I ask you something?"

"Anything."

"Does this have anything to do with you and Cal?"

"What do you mean?"

"I mean … I know it's none of my business, so tell me to butt out if you like, but are you two getting serious?"

Teresa laughed. "What makes you think that?"

"Err, I don't know. Maybe the fact that out of the last four nights you've been out with him twice and he's been over here twice."

Teresa's heart sank. "Do you mind? That's not why you—?"

Elle laughed. "I don't mind at all. He's awesome! Not only is he good to you, he's good to Skye and me, too. And this probably sounds weird but he's good *for* you and for us, too."

"What do you mean?"

"I mean none of us is used to having a decent man in our lives, are we? And Cal? He's the most decent person I've ever met." She waggled her eyebrows "And there's no denying that he's all man—or that he's totally besotted with you."

"You think so?"

Elle laughed. "Come on, Mom. The guy's crazy about you. Do you think he'd come over and hangout with your daughter and your granddaughter if he wasn't? We both know he'd rather have you all to himself, but he'll take whatever time you'll give him. How many guys would come over on a Sunday afternoon to grill for his new girlfriend's family?"

Teresa couldn't hide her smile. "Wasn't it a good time?"

"It was. I'm glad you argued with me and made me stay. I would have taken Skye out to give the two of you time together. But it was such a good time. It felt like …"

"Like what?"

"Like we were a real family. Skye's never known that, and I never really did either. Dad wasn't exactly …"

"I'm sorry, sweetheart."

"Don't be! I didn't mean it in a bad way. After Dad left, I loved what we had, you and me. I had the best girl mom around—just ask any of my friends. Hair, nails, makeup, clothes, I was the go-to girl because of you. You did everything you could and more. But I did kind of envy my friends who were close with their dads. You know, the ones who got to go out on the boat or go four-wheeling." She shrugged. "I guess having Cal here yesterday reminded me of that. And it made me want it for Skye, too. You know?"

Teresa nodded. She knew exactly what Elle was talking about.

"So, back to the original question. Do you want things to get serious between you and him?"

"It's way too soon to think about that. We've only known each other a couple of weeks. And he's …"

Elle laughed. "He's nuts about you. I only asked if *you* want things to get serious; I can already tell that he does."

"Do you think so?"

"I'd put money on it." She made a face. "I'll come clean, too. I've asked around about him. I got Abbie to dig the dirt through her mom and Manny. And the info I got back is that he doesn't normally date at all. And he isn't the kind of man who does anything in half-measures."

Butterflies took flight in Teresa's stomach at those last few words. Cal had spoken them himself on Saturday night before he brought her home. When they'd left the Boathouse, he'd suggested she come back for a drink at his place, but even though she'd agreed—eagerly—he'd brought her home instead. She hadn't understood what was going on until he'd turned onto her street, parked his SUV outside her house and cut the engine.

The way he'd kissed her had left her in no doubt that he wanted her. But he'd explained that he didn't do anything in half-measures and that if he'd taken her back to his place there was no way he would have brought her home before morning.

Elle was watching her closely. "You want it, don't you?"

Teresa felt the heat in her cheeks, and Elle laughed.

"I meant you want things to get serious between you. But the look on your face says you want *it*, too. And I don't blame you. I think half the women in town wouldn't mind getting it either."

Teresa recovered and laughed. "I'm not going to deny it. Any of it. But I still think it's too soon to be thinking about it."

"I think you're wrong. But it's your call. I just wanted you to know that not only do I not mind. I like the idea—a lot. For you, of course. But selfishly, too."

Teresa nodded. She loved the idea of Cal becoming a part of their lives. He was such a good man, and he was so good with Skye, and with Elle for that matter. Her smile faded.

"Have you heard from your dad?"

Elle rolled her eyes. "Yeah. He wants to come up and bring Maddie."

"I know. He called me about it the other night."

"Would you mind?"

"Of course not. He's your father."

Elle shrugged. "I'll keep him out of your way."

"You don't need to. He asked if I had any trips planned—or if I could plan one. I told him the end of the month."

"He shouldn't be able to run you out of town."

"He's not. I volunteered. I can go …"

Elle grinned. "You can go away for a dirty weekend with Cal!"

Teresa laughed. "Oh, my God! You're so bad."

"I am my mother's daughter."

Teresa slapped her arm but had to laugh with her.

They both stopped when Teresa's phone rang.

"That's probably Nina wondering where you are."

"No. It's the salon. Even after all these years I can't train people that we're closed on Mondays. They still call for appointments."

"Well, let it go to voicemail and I'll deal with it. And in the future, we can start forwarding the calls to my phone."

"Thanks, sweetheart. That'd be great."

Cal looked up at the sound of a knock on his office door and smiled when he saw Ryan and Manny standing there grinning at him.

"What's up?"

"We're finishing up for the day and we've come to take you to the Boathouse for a drink."

Cal frowned at his screen. He wanted to—

"Don't even think about making excuses or claiming you have more work to do," said Ryan as he came into the office. "You've been doing better this week. But I was serious when I said that you need to lighten up. You're supposed to be taking life easier here."

Cal blew out a sigh. "Okay."

"Okay?" Ryan laughed. "Just like that?"

Cal chuckled. "Yeah. Just like that. We're halfway through the week already and I need to save something to do to keep me going until the weekend."

"Awesome! Let's go then."

Manny grinned at him as he got to his feet. "I wish you hadn't made it so easy on him."

"Why's that?"

"He was bragging that he was going to drag you out of here if you said no."

Cal raised an eyebrow at Ryan and rolled his sleeves up a little higher.

Ryan just laughed. "Okay! I admit I'm full of shit. There's no need to go baring your tree trunks at me to remind me I'd have no chance whatsoever of dragging you anywhere."

Cal winked at Manny. "You just have to remind him who's really the boss every now and then."

When they got to the Boathouse, Cal looked around as they made their way to the bar. It was early, so it was still quiet. He frowned when he saw Dallas, Austin's brother, the kid who was supposed to be showing him the house over at Four Mile. He was sitting in a booth by himself.

"I'll catch up with you guys."

"You want a beer?"

"No, just a water. I'll be right there."

"Hi, Mr. Callahan."

Cal smiled and sat down opposite him. "Dallas. How's it going?"

The kid ran a hand through his hair, the gesture belying his words. "Great, thanks. How about you? Have you figured out when you'll have time to go and see the Lakeside house? I can make time whenever suits you, just say the word."

Cal thought about it. "How about this time tomorrow?"

"Perfect. Let's do it. Do you want me to drive you over there?"

"No. There's no need. I'll meet you there. Five-thirty?"

"You got it."

Cal met his gaze. "Don't be late."

Dallas's eyes widened. "I won't."

Cal wanted to help Austin out, and Dallas seemed like a good kid, too. "Is everything okay?"

"Yeah. Fine. Great."

Cal sat back and folded his arms across his chest. He raised an eyebrow and waited.

A flurry of emotions flitted across the kid's face before he spoke. "Do you mind if I ask you something?"

"That's what I'm here for."

"You're used to having people working for you, right?"

"I am."

"And sometimes people screw up."

"Everyone does, sometimes."

"So, if someone who worked for you screwed up. Would you want them to fix it before they told you about it? Or would you want to know first?"

"That'd depend."

"On what?"

"On how sure they were that they could fix it by themselves. If it were something small and they were one hundred percent sure that they weren't going to make things worse then I'd be okay with them doing so. But ..." He paused for effect, and Dallas eyed him warily. "If there was any chance that they didn't know enough to fix it, or that they might screw things up further, I'd expect them to come to me."

The expression on Dallas's face told him which scenario they were talking about.

Cal got to his feet. "That answer your question?"

"Yes, sir."

Cal turned as if to walk away, but he took pity on the kid and looked back over his shoulder. "If that person came to me and told me that they'd screwed up, I'd help them fix it and teach them what they needed to know so that it didn't happen again. And I'd have a little more faith in them going forward. It takes balls to admit when you've screwed up, Dallas."

"Thanks. I appreciate it."

"You're welcome. I'll see you tomorrow."

When he reached the bar, Manny gave him a puzzled look. "What was that about?"

"I was just helping Austin out."

"I thought that was Dallas?" asked Ryan.

"Yeah, it is," Cal said with a smile. "Anyway, what are the two of you doing coming for a drink after work in the middle of the week? I thought you'd be eager to get home."

Manny smiled. "Nina took a shift in the gift shop and I'm not allowed to pick her up until seven."

"And Leanne's working with Donovan on some legal files." Ryan lifted a shoulder. "I may have gone in and checked on them a few too many times already this afternoon."

Manny laughed. "Yeah. She kicked his ass out of there."

Cal gave Ryan a puzzled look. "You have a problem with Donovan? I like him. He's good."

Manny laughed again. "You don't know the story about when Leanne first came up here?"

Ryan groaned. "I didn't believe she was with him for a minute."

Manny winked at Cal. "That's what he says. But you'll notice that whenever Leanne and Donovan lock themselves in an office, Ryan here worries that they're working on something other than legal files."

Ryan punched his arm. "Quit it, old man."

Manny clipped the back of his head. "You know it's true."

"Children, please!" Cal folded his arms across his chest and gave them a stern look.

Ryan laughed. "Uh-oh, he's displaying the tree trunks again."

Cal rolled his eyes but didn't get the chance to speak before Kenzie called his name.

"Cal! They managed to get you out, then? How are you doing?"

"Fine thanks, Kenzie. And you?"

She nodded. "All's well in my world. Are the ladies joining you?"

"No."

Kenzie made a face. "Where is she?"

Cal frowned and looked at Manny, but he was no help, he just grinned.

Kenzie laughed. "Oh, come on! It's not as though the whole town doesn't know that you and Teresa are seeing each other. I thought she might be coming to join you. And Leanne and Nina, too." She looked at the others.

"They're both working," said Ryan.

"Shame. You should bring them all out together."

Manny nodded his agreement. "Nina's mentioned that a few times now." He looked at Cal. "What do you think, Saturday?"

Cal nodded. What else could he do? "I'll ask her."

"We should ask Ted and Diego, too." Ryan looked at Cal. "Have you met Audrey and Izzy yet?"

"No." Of course, he knew that Ted and Diego were living here now and that they'd both met women and settled down. But he hadn't made the time to catch up with them yet.

"It'll be like old times," said Manny. "How many years has it been since the five of us were in the same room?"

Ryan laughed. "I'm not sure we've ever all been in the same room at the same time, have we?"

Cal shook his head as he thought about it. They probably hadn't, despite all the work they'd done together. Ted and Diego had had business in Colombia back in the day. That was how their paths had crossed with his. It'd be good to see them again and it'd be interesting to see the dynamic between everyone now that they were not only in civilian life, but also had partners.

Teresa wasn't exactly his partner. Not in the same way as the others, but … he knew that he'd like her to be.

He looked up to find Manny watching him curiously. "Are you up for it?"

He nodded.

"Do you think Teresa will be?"

"I'll ask her."

"Hey. I didn't think," said Ryan. "I only ever think of you working or going home to do whatever it is you do when you're not sleeping or working. You're not seeing her tonight, are you? We didn't mess up your plans?"

He smiled. "I'm seeing her later. She's working and then she had another appointment."

Ryan gave him a puzzled look, but he didn't elaborate on what the other appointment might be. He couldn't since he didn't know himself. She'd just said that she couldn't do dinner tonight because of it, but yes, she'd love to meet him for a drink afterward.

Chapter Twelve

"Three more. And two. And last one. Good job!"

Teresa flopped back down and then curled up one more time before the blood rushed to her head. She slid her legs out from the ab bench and climbed down and grinned at Russ. "I'm glad that's over with. I feel like a bat hanging down like that."

Russ laughed. "That's why you don't stay down long." He poked her in the ribs. "And your abs appreciate the effort."

She laughed with him and flicked him with her towel. "I know." She checked her watch, wanting to make sure that she was going to have enough time to go home and shower before Cal came to get her. She'd said she could meet him at the Boathouse, but it seemed that he liked coming to pick her up. She liked it, too. It felt very chivalrous. She hadn't ever cared about that kind of thing in the past, but with Cal it was different—he was different. He was a real gentleman. She pressed her lips together to keep in a smile; she was hoping to discover his less gentlemanly side soon.

Russ smirked at her. "I was going to offer a penny for your thoughts, but I'd pay up to five bucks to know what caused that dirty smile!"

She laughed and pushed at his arm. "Oh, stop it. You don't know that it was a dirty thought."

"Yeah, I do, Terry. I've known you for—"

"A long time," she interrupted. "More years than either of us cares to count."

"True. Do you want to do fifteen on the treadmill before you go?"

"You mean the torture's over?"

"Yep. You worked hard tonight."

"I might just sneak out then and go home."

"Hot date?"

She smiled through pursed lips. "Maybe."

"He seems like a good guy."

She had to laugh. "Who does?"

"Frosty the freaking snowman! Who do you think?"

"Ugh, so the grapevine even reached in here? I thought you were above gossip."

"I am! But I can't help overhearing and when I heard your name come up ..." He shrugged. "I look out for you."

"Aww," she leaned in and pecked his cheek. "If I weren't such a sweaty mess, I'd hug you."

"Evening."

They both turned at the sound of a deep voice, a very familiar voice that sent a shiver down Teresa's spine. Wow! She swallowed at the sight of him in workout gear. That was an awful lot of muscle with very little tank top to cover it.

"Cal!" She couldn't keep the smile off her face.

He didn't smile back. His eyebrows were drawn together, his arms—those arms!—were folded across his chest. He looked … and then she realized … she'd just been kissing on Russ. He didn't think …?

"Hey, Cal," said Russ. "I hope you don't think I was making a move on your lady?"

Cal's face—and the rest of him—was almost completely still. Only a tiny muscle twitching in his jaw gave away the fact that he wasn't a statue.

Russ laughed. "I can imagine how that must have looked. But," he turned and smiled at Teresa, "Terry's like another sister to me."

Teresa watched Cal's face as she tried to process her own reaction. Part of her wanted to be mad at him that he could assume she was up to something with Russ, but she could see how it might look that way. Another part of her liked—make that loved—the fact that it bothered him. It felt like minutes but was probably only a few seconds before his face relaxed and he treated them to one of his smiles.

"I'm sorry. I …"

"No, need." Russ went and grasped his shoulder and shook his hand. "I get it," he said before walking away and heading back to the office.

Cal slowly lifted his gaze to meet Teresa's. "I'm sorry."

She went to him and put her hand on his arm—how could she not? "It's okay. I'm sorry. I know how it might have looked. But I can't say you won't see it again in the future. It's just how we are. I've known Russ since we were tiny tots."

The corners of his lips twitched up.

"Funny?" she asked.

"The thought of Russ as a *tiny tot* is amusing. The thought of you is … I'll bet you were a little cutie."

She laughed. "According to my mom, I was a little terror."

This time the smile broke the surface and made her want to sigh. "So, this was your appointment?"

"Yeah. I come in twice a week. Three when I can make it, and Russ works me out."

His face tightened again at that. She'd have to make sure that he understood that Russ was just a friend. He might be another big, muscular, good-looking guy, but like he'd said himself, he was more like a brother to her than anything else.

"Do you come in here a lot?" She laughed and tightened her grip on his arm. "I know you must work out a lot, but I haven't seen you here before."

"I've been coming in the mornings. I wanted to come tonight to kill some time."

She looked at her watch. "I can't imagine having time to kill. I'm always running somewhere. And right now, I need to run home for a shower." She waggled her eyebrows at him. "Before you arrived, I was telling Russ that I have a hot date tonight."

"You were?" That might be the biggest smile she'd seen on his face yet.

"I was, and I need to go and get cleaned up and try to make myself look beautiful."

"You *are* beautiful." His voice was so low she wondered if she'd imagined it. But looking up into his eyes, she saw the truth of his words reflected there. He really meant it.

She reached up and pressed a kiss to his lips. "Thank you."

Cal brought the SUV to a stop outside her house at eight-twenty-five. He'd done his best to not arrive too early. She'd said it was going to be a rush for her when she left the gym.

He pursed his lips. Seeing her there had been a surprise. Seeing her in workout gear had sent his heart rate soaring but then seeing her lean in to kiss Russ had sent a rush of adrenaline through his system. He closed his eyes. He hadn't been prepared for that. It didn't bother him now; it had only been a momentary urge to throw Russ across the room. What he hadn't been prepared for was what it made him realize. It made him understand that he wanted Teresa to be his. The thought of her with someone else?

He rubbed his hand over the back of his neck. He couldn't even entertain the thought. He'd never understood how some guys went all caveman over a woman. He'd had a few relationships over the years since his divorce—with some nice women—but he'd never, even when he was married, felt the way he did now. Now he got it. He supposed it kind of made sense. He didn't do anything in half measures, so why would he be any different when it came to falling in love?

He raised an eyebrow at himself in the rearview mirror. Love? His reflection smiled back and gave him a slight nod. Apparently, yeah.

He blew out a sigh and opened the door. Just because he'd figured it out, didn't mean that he should go scaring Teresa with it. What he needed to do was let her get to know who he was, give her time, and hope that she might discover that she felt the same way about him.

Elle opened the door and greeted him with a smile but didn't get the chance to speak before Skye came barreling past her and wrapped her little arms around his knees then held them up to him.

"Cal!"

He chuckled and raised an eyebrow at Elle. To him, it felt like the most natural thing in the world to pick the kid up, but he didn't have a good feel yet for how comfortable Elle was having him around her daughter.

He needn't have worried. She grinned at him. "You don't have to, but if you want to."

He reached down and swung the little girl up in the air. "Skye!"

She giggled and looked down at him as he held her up.

"I missed you, Cal!"

His breath caught in his chest. It reminded him of when he used to go home after an assignment. Little Henry, and Abigail and Anthony, too, but mostly Henry because he was that bit younger, used to greet him this same way. "I missed you, too, sunshine." He said it before he thought about it.

Skye giggled. "I'm Skye, not sunshine!"

He brought her down and sat her on his hip. "Well, doesn't sunshine come from the sky?"

She was cute as a button as she wrinkled her nose to consider that one.

"Come on in," said Elle. "Mom will be down in a minute. She was running late after the gym."

Cal followed her through to the kitchen. Skye rested her head on his shoulder as they went, but then decided to start pawing at his face. He pretended to bite at her hands making her giggle.

Elle grinned at him. "She adores you."

He caught Skye's finger between his lips and shook his head like a dog with a toy, making her giggle even more. "The feeling is mutual."

"Will you be my grandpa?"

Cal's heart thudded to a halt. He'd love to be.

Elle reached out to take her. "Skye!" She rolled her eyes. "Sorry. Don't let her scare you off."

Skye turned away from Elle and buried her face in his neck. "I want you to be my grandpa. I don't have a grandpa."

Elle blew out a sigh. "Sorry, Cal."

"It's fine. It's no problem. I thought she ... your dad ..." He stopped. He shouldn't ask and he knew it, but he was curious.

Elle made a face. "My dad makes her call him Papa Steve."

Cal tried to keep his expression neutral, but he didn't get it.

"Skye. Will you run upstairs and tell Grandma that Cal's here?"

Cal was relieved when she let him set her down and she trotted off upstairs.

Elle glanced after her before turning back to him and lowering her voice. "I don't know how much Mom's told you about my dad. He's not a bad guy, not really, but he can be a bit of a jerk. He used to call my mom Grandma, long before I ever had Skye. It was just a kind of dig at her, saying she was like an old lady. She wasn't! It's just that she's always been more responsible about … well, everything. She had the business, and me to take care of, and she's always been sensible with money. He used to call her that meaning that she was no fun. But she is. You've seen that."

Cal nodded. He had. She was a lot of fun, she had such a light-hearted approach to life, she was always laughing. Her ex must be an asshole was the only conclusion he could reach.

"Anyway. Sorry. I didn't mean to dump all that on you. My point was that he makes Skye call him Papa Steve, as if he thinks people won't realize he's her granddad. And his wife, Maddie, she says she's not old enough to be a grandma, either. So, they had Skye call her Nana. I think Dad did that on purpose so that Mom would only be left with Grandma." She smiled. "I think it's kind of backfiring on him now though because all Skye's friends here have a Grandma and Grandpa and she wants that, too." She smiled. "Not that I'm trying to rope you into anything."

He smiled back at her. He liked her, and he loved how much she loved and looked out for her mom.

"Unless you want roping in?" She gave him an inquiring look.

What the hell? She'd shared more with him than she needed to. If this was ever going to work out the way he hoped it would, Elle and Skye would become part of his life. It wouldn't do any harm to get onside with her from the beginning.

He glanced at the hallway before he spoke. "I wouldn't mind."

Her eyes widened and she brought her hand up to cover her mouth, just like Teresa did. "Oh, my God! Are you saying what I think you are? That you wouldn't mind being her grandpa—for real? Not just letting her call you that?"

Cal couldn't keep the smile off his face as he nodded. "I'm not going to rush anything though."

Elle nodded rapidly. "Yeah! I mean, no! I mean. Oh, Cal, that's awesome. I'm in your corner, okay?"

"Thanks."

~ ~ ~

"Is something going on?" Teresa asked when they got into Cal's SUV.

"What kind of something?"

She'd guess that there was. There was a twinkle in his eye that she hadn't seen before, and Elle had been giving off weird vibes when Teresa had come back downstairs with Skye.

She pushed at his arm. "Don't play the innocent with me."

When he turned to her, his smile looked anything but innocent. "I would never do that. I am many things, but innocent isn't one of them."

All the muscles in her stomach and lower tightened in the heat of that look. It was a new one, and she liked it—a lot.

"So, tell me what you and Elle were scheming? You were, weren't you?"

He chuckled. "Perhaps. But even if we were, I might have to ask you if it would be okay if she and I shared a secret—for a while, at least. A secret that I hope you'll like when you discover it."

Teresa put her hand over her heart and was about to make some smart remark about him being sweet, but she was taken by surprise when her eyes filled with tears.

Cal's smile evaporated. "Hey. I'm sorry. I don't …"

She held her hand up to stop him. "It's okay. It's great. I'm just." She shrugged. "Sorry. It's lovely. I love the idea of you and her sharing something. I love that …" She shook her head. "But I don't want to freak you out or scare you off. So, are we going for that drink?"

His expression turned serious, as though he was about to say something, but instead he nodded. "Okay." He started the engine and reached across to take hold of her hand as he drove.

She could tell he needed silence. She was already used to that with him. What surprised her was that she didn't mind it. She enjoyed it, too. Usually with people in the salon who didn't talk much—mostly the men—she spent the quiet moments wondering what they were thinking or trying to get ahead on what they might say when they spoke again. With Cal she was comfortable to just be. She enjoyed sharing space with him, being beside him. It didn't need to be anything more than that for her to feel relaxed—and happy.

She only realized that they'd passed the Boathouse when he reached the other end of Main. She squeezed his hand and raised an eyebrow when he looked over.

"I should have asked first. I didn't feel like getting the third degree from Kenzie again, so … I thought we could go to my place. You haven't seen it yet."

Her heart started to hammer in her chest. Now, that, she hadn't been expecting.

"Do you want to?"

Her eyes darted to his face, it sounded like he was asking another question entirely. But she couldn't tell, he had his gaze fixed on the road ahead.

"I'd love to." Whichever question he was asking, that was her honest answer.

When they got there, he opened the door and let her go in ahead of him. "Come on in, I'll get us a drink and we can sit outside if you like. There's a deck out the back."

"Okay, thanks."

She wandered around while he fixed the drinks. The place looked bare. Sure, it was only a rental, she knew that, but there were very few signs that there was anyone living here. There was a photo sitting on the mantel, and she went to it. It must be his sister and her kids. She smiled. They were gorgeous. The little girl, Abigail, looked like her mom. Anthony, the middle one had an air of Cal about him. He didn't look that much like him, but there was a seriousness in his expression that she'd bet he'd learned from his uncle. She hoped that Darla's new man would bring some fun into their lives. The little one, Henry, was laughing at the camera. She imagined Cal must miss them. It was telling that this photo was the only personal item she could see in the whole place.

She jumped when he appeared in the doorway from the kitchen. "Wine?"

She nodded. "Whatever works."

He shrugged. "Wine, beer, whisky, vodka. I guessed you'd like wine best."

She grinned. "Do you have soda water?"

"Yup."

She grinned. "Any chance you'd have such a thing as a lime?"

He smiled. "As a matter of fact, I do. And I should have known. You were drinking vodka, lime, and soda that first night."

"Do you pick up on all the little details?"

He smiled back at her. "I do and usually I store them. My only excuse is that I was mildly traumatized by the first part of that evening."

She had to laugh. "You weren't the only one."

He crossed the room in two strides and closed his arms around her. "I'm glad we figured it out and got past that."

She looked up into his eyes and slid her arms up around his shoulders. "Me too."

Chapter Thirteen

They took their drinks out onto the back deck. It was nice enough out here, but Cal couldn't help wishing that he already had the house over at Lakeside. He could happily picture sitting out on the deck there with her, watching the sun go down over the lake.

"Do you have a lease on this place?"

Cal set his glass down on the table. It didn't surprise him that she seemed to be thinking along the same lines he was. He didn't have huge experience talking with women, but he generally found that they chattered away, chasing their own train of thought with no awareness of his. Teresa wasn't like that. She was in tune with him somehow.

"Only month to month. Austin, the realtor, he owns it and he said he usually rents this one on a monthly basis to newcomers."

Teresa nodded. "I like Austin. He's done well for himself."

"It sounded that way. He said he set up the brokerage himself, and it seems he does well on the property management side, too."

"He does. He manages my properties for me. I've known him since he was a little kid. He's a year older than Elle, but his brother, Dallas was in her class in school."

"What do you think of him?"

She smiled. "He's a good kid. He's a different story from Austin. Austin's the steady, reliable one. Dallas was always a bit wilder. Well, maybe wild is too strong a word, he was always getting into scrapes, but he's a charmer and could always talk his way back out of them. Why do you ask?"

"He's going to show me a place over at Four Mile tomorrow. Austin said he's just got his realtor's license and I might be his first sale."

She sipped her drink and looked out across the yard. He'd hoped that she might ask about the house, but she didn't. He watched her without turning his head, wondering what she was thinking. If he had to guess, he'd say that she was curious but didn't want to ask.

"Do you want to come with me?"

She turned to him and cocked her head to the side.

"To see the house tomorrow. I like it. I've already been inside. Manny and I were over there on the weekend. I'd like to know what you think."

Her eyes danced as she smiled. "I'd love to see it. Where is it? Oh, wait, what time are you going?"

"I said I'd meet Dallas there at five-thirty, but I can ask him to make it later. What time do you finish work?"

She took her phone out of her purse and checked it. "That's perfect! I should be done by four-thirty tomorrow."

"Great. Should I pick you up from the salon?"

She smiled. "I can drive you know."

He chuckled. "I know. I'm sorry. I just … I like to …" He shrugged. "Am I too old school?"

She winked at him. "Maybe a little, sometimes."

He pursed his lips. "Does that mean a lot and more than sometimes, but you're too nice to say so?"

She laughed. "Let's just stick with sometimes. And I don't mind too much, not when it's about coming to pick me up. But there will be times when I want to drive." Her smile faded. "And times when I want to pay, too. I let it go the other night because you said it was important to you, but … I'm not a helpless little lady, okay? I can pay my way and hold my own."

"I know. I don't mean it that way. I don't think you can't." He smiled. "I see you as totally competent, not helpless in any way. I'm not trying to be the big man. I … I guess, you just bring so much to the table, I need to do whatever I can to let you know that I have something to offer, too."

She put her hand on his arm with a mischievous smile. "Oh, you have plenty to offer."

His throat went dry when she ran her hand up his forearm and back down again. He linked his fingers through hers and tugged her toward him.

"You think so?"

She only hesitated for a moment before getting up from her seat. When she stood before him, he pulled her down into his lap and closed his arms around her. His heart was hammering hard, and he shifted trying not to let her feel how badly he wanted her. He should have known better. She wasn't going to let him gloss over the way his hard-on was pressing into her ass.

She dropped a peck on his lips and wriggled against him. "You're pleased I'm here, then?"

He had to laugh. She wasn't shy about it, so why should he be? He tightened his arms around her and held her closer. "Very."

"Me, too." She traced her fingers down the side of his cheek, sending shivers chasing each other down his spine and making him press more eagerly against her. She'd have to be careful about how much encouragement she gave him. He wasn't sure he'd be able to resist too much—but he wasn't sure if it was too soon to go there.

He reached up and sank his fingers into her hair, pulling her down into a kiss that left him breathing hard. He couldn't tear his eyes away from the way her chest rose and fell when he let her lift her head.

"Wow!" She laughed. "I think that might have been the best kiss I've ever had."

He smiled. "You didn't like the other times I've kissed you?"

She nodded rapidly. "Every single one is better than the last."

He chuckled. "Are you by any chance trying to sweet-talk me?"

She nodded again, and a slight flush spread across her cheeks and neck. "Yep. All the way into bed."

His breath caught in his chest. Here he'd been trying to figure out if it was too soon, if he should wait, how he might even bring it up and she just …?

She wriggled in his lap again, making him close his eyes and suck in a deep breath as her ass tormented his aching cock. "We're going to be honest with each other you and me, aren't we?"

He nodded, wondering what she was going to say next.

She chuckled and the sound reverberated in his chest. "Okay, so if you're being honest, can you tell me that you don't like the way that feels, that you don't want to …?"

He stared at her for a moment, not quite able to believe that she was making this so easy for him. It seemed he hesitated a moment too long. Her smile faded and she started to pull away. "Of course, if I've just embarrassed us both—"

"No!" He pulled her back to him before she could get up. "You haven't. I wasn't hesitating over my answer. I do want you. I want to … I told you in the beginning, I'm rusty at this, but that's no excuse. I shouldn't have made you go out on a limb. You shouldn't have to …" He tightened his arms around her and held her close to his chest. "But I'm glad you did. Thank you. And just so we're clear. I love the feel of you against me." He shifted his hips so she could feel how much he was enjoying it. "And I want nothing more than to feel your body naked underneath mine."

Her cheeks flushed again, but this time it was with desire, not embarrassment. Her eyes danced as she looked into his. "Wow!"

That made him laugh. He ran his hand up and down her back and the way she quivered under his touch left him with no choice but to slide her off his lap as he got up, took her hand, and took her upstairs.

Teresa tried hard to catch her breath as he led her into his bedroom and closed the door behind them. She'd never been backward about coming forward, but she was a little surprised at herself.

When Cal turned back to face her, she was glad that she'd forced his hand. He was such a gentleman; she didn't know how long it would've taken him. Now she didn't have to wait—and the way he was looking at her she didn't think she could wait, not another minute.

He came to her and put his hands on her shoulders. She couldn't allow herself to think about how big his hands were. She'd get her answers about the rest of him soon enough. One hand slid up to cup the side of her neck and his mouth came down on hers.

She sagged against him as he kissed her deeply. Her hands roved over his broad chest. He was solid muscle under his shirt. She slipped her fingers under the hem and moaned into his mouth when those muscles trembled under her touch.

He broke away and pulled his shirt up and off, letting it fall to the floor. She stepped closer and pressed a kiss to his warm skin. He smelled wonderful. She pressed herself against him and looked up into his eyes; they were a brighter blue than she'd seen them before, and they burned with an intensity that took her breath away.

His arms closed around her and his hands slid down to hold her ass. A moan escaped from her lips when he pulled her against him and rocked his hips. Heat pooled between her legs and she rocked in time with him.

His mouth came down on her neck, and she clung to his shoulders as he nipped and sucked, driving her crazy with the need to be naked with him. As if he sensed that need, he got rid of her clothes. To say he was so rusty with women, he made short work of it and in moments, she stood before him in just her panties.

He ran his hands up her sides and cupped her breasts. "You're beautiful."

She tugged at his belt. "Thank you."

He chuckled as she fumbled to free him from his jeans, then helped her out and got rid of them and his underwear.

She heard herself gasp when he stood naked before her but could do nothing to stop it. His hands hadn't lied about the rest of him!

He led her to the bed and sat down, tugging her hand so that she sat beside him, and then in one smooth move, he was somehow on his back and she was on top of him.

She lifted her head with a laugh. "How did you …?"

He smiled and closed his hands around her ass and moved her against his cock. "I couldn't wait anymore."

He mouthed her nipple and moaned as she braced her hands above her head. "I don't think I can either," she breathed.

He felt so good pushing into the heat between her legs, but her panties weren't going to allow what she really wanted.

The next thing she knew, he'd flipped them, and she was on her back. His legs were between hers, but he rested his weight off her. She reached for him; he felt like silk over steel as she stroked him.

He lowered his head and nipped her lips as his hand slid inside her panties. His fingers teased her until she moaned and writhed, desperate for more. Just when she thought she'd need to get rid of her panties herself, he slid them down over her hips and she kicked out of them. She reached her arms up around his shoulders and pulled him down into another kiss, wriggling her way underneath him as she did. This was no time for him to be a gentleman, she wanted him, and she wanted him now.

Her next moan was one of frustration when he lifted his head and broke away. He couldn't stop now!

He smiled and trailed his fingers over her breasts, circling first one nipple then the next.

"Cal," she breathed. "Please …?"

He met her gaze and nodded. "Remember I told you I don't do things in half measures?"

She nodded.

"I want you so badly."

"I want you."

He nodded again. "I don't do this lightly."

"Neither do I."

"It means something to me. It means a lot to me."

"It does to me, too, Cal. I'm not … this isn't just …" She didn't want him to think that she was one to sleep around. But she didn't want to say that in so many words.

"I like you, Teresa. I like you a lot."

"I like you, too, Cal. More than a lot."

He smiled. "Do you want, will you … if we do this …"

"If?" The word squeaked out before she could stop it.

He chuckled and his fingers found their way back between her legs, making it hard to focus on whatever he was about to say.

"Will you be my lady?" His gaze locked with hers. "That's probably too old school to say. But it's what I want. I don't just want to sleep with you, I don't just want to date you. I want you to be my lady."

She nodded. "I would love to be your lady." She reached up and kissed him and then asked, "Will you be my man?"

He pressed her down into the bed as his body covered hers. "I'll be your man."

One of his hands slid underneath her ass and he wrapped her leg around his waist. She clung to his shoulders, holding her breath as his hot, hard head pushed at her wetness.

He thrust his hips and she gasped and clung tighter as he entered her. "Oh God, Cal!"

He looked down into her eyes. "Are you good?"

She nodded.

"Ready for more?"

She nodded again, and he pressed deeper, filling her until she felt like he was becoming a part of her.

"Do you want all of me?"

She looked up into his eyes and understood all the ways he meant it. "I do, Cal."

She closed her eyes, ready for the next thrust.

"Look at me." It sounded almost like a command, but his expression was gentle when she opened her eyes.

"I want to do this together." He held her gaze as he gave one last push until he was seated deep inside her. One little bead of sweat rolled down his brow. She could feel him pulsating, hot and hard. His eyes were filled with a look that made her heart beat even faster. It was full of honesty, and something that looked like—it couldn't be—but it looked a lot like love.

She dug her fingers into his ass, urging him to move, to give her what she needed. She was sure that the connection between their bodies would lead them somewhere good, it would bring them both pleasure; she knew that. She needed to break the connection between their eyes, she was less sure that wouldn't lead to heartbreak.

He drove all conscious thoughts from her mind as he drove deep and hard inside her. He set up a punishing rhythm and all she could do was let him carry her away. His big body proved to be capable of giving her more pleasure than she'd known she was still capable of. He pushed her to the point of no return and didn't relent as she soared away, carried on the tide of the best orgasm she'd had in years—maybe ever. Her hands grasped desperately at his back and when she dug in her nails, it sent him over the edge. His release carried her higher and she clung to his straining muscles as he gave himself to her.

When they finally stilled, he rolled to the side and pulled her with him, wrapping his big arm around her and holding her close to his chest.

She looked up at him and he planted a kiss on her lips and asked, "Good?"

She shook her head slowly, but his pained expression made her stop. "I'm only teasing! But honestly, it wasn't good, it was great, amazing, fantastic." She ran her hand down his arm. "You're wonderful, Cal."

He didn't look thrilled, but she knew what was bothering him.

"I don't just mean in bed. I mean everything about you. You're a wonderful human being. A wonderful man."

He was smiling again now. "I'm glad you think so."

She raised an eyebrow, glad to get back to something more playful. "Oh, yeah? And why's that? Are you thinking you'd like to keep doing this sometimes?"

He chuckled. "More than sometimes. I'm glad you think I'm a wonderful man, because that's how every man wants his lady to think of him."

She raised an eyebrow. "Your lady?"

He nodded his smile cockier than she'd ever seen it. It suited him. "Yes, ma'am. I asked you, and you agreed." He ran his hand down her back, making her shiver before he closed it around her ass. "And then we sealed the deal. I take it you're a woman of your word."

She looked back into his eyes.

"You don't want to back out on me, do you?"

She shook her head. "I don't. We said we're going to be honest, right?"

"We did. I give you my word I will be, and I hope you will, too."

"I will. I'm trying to be. It scares me."

"What does?"

"You saying that I'm your lady—that you're my man. I love the idea, of course I do. But reality has a way of not living up to great ideas."

"I can see that. But … and this may scare you more. I wouldn't have asked you if I didn't believe that we could make the reality even better than the idea. I wouldn't have asked if I didn't know that you're worth it. I don't want to screw up here, it's probably not great pillow talk, but I've weighed this up very carefully. I already know who you are. I know that I want you in my life and I want to be in yours. On paper we may not be the ideal match. But in reality, I've never met anyone more perfect for me." His smile made her heart melt. "And you know I'm not one to brag, but you have to admit that I'm kind of perfect for you, too."

She had to laugh. Everything he'd said made her heart happy, but that last part? That was the best thing a man had ever said to her.

"Funny?"

She laughed again. "Perfect! I'm laughing because if any other man told me that he was perfect for me, I'd tell him he was full of shit! With you, it works; not just because I believe it, but because I know you'd never say it unless you did, too."

He claimed her mouth in a slow, sweet kiss and when he finally lifted his head, he nodded. "I don't just believe it. I know it. You just have to let me prove it to you."

They lay there in his bed for hours talking, touching, kissing. Sometime after midnight, he made love to her again. She felt right, she felt like coming home, and Cal's mind was already moving ahead, wanting to get to the place where she might share his home.

Her eyes had drifted shut a few minutes ago. He liked the thought that he'd worn her out. He brushed a strand of hair off her forehead. He'd love to wrap her up in his arms and go to sleep, but he didn't know how she'd feel about that. She hadn't even known that he was going to bring her back to his place. How would she feel about spending the night? She'd at least want to let Elle know, he was sure. Tempting as it was to let her sleep on, much as he'd love to wake up with her in the morning. He couldn't do it. He had to let it be her decision.

He planted a kiss on her forehead. She smiled but didn't wake.

"Teresa?"

"Mm?"

"Terry?"

Her eyes flew open. "Yes? Sorry. Did I fall asleep?" She smiled. "Did you just call me Terry?"

He smiled back at her. "You did, and I did. Is that okay?"

She reached up and pressed a kiss to his lips. "It's more than okay. I love it. Only my people call me Terry. And I guess if you're my man then you must be my people, too."

He chuckled. "I guess so."

"Crap! What time is it?"

"It's a quarter till two. I wanted to let you sleep, but I didn't know ... do you need to go home?"

She pursed her lips. "I should. I have to go to work in the morning. You do, too. And I didn't say anything to Elle, and ..." She gave him a rueful smile. "I didn't bring my toothbrush."

"I can get you up for whatever time you need to go. I can go into work whenever I'm ready. You could text Elle to let her know where you are and ... I buy my toothbrushes in four packs, so I have a spare one."

She held his gaze for a long moment. "Are you asking me to stay?"

"I am. I want to hold you while you sleep, and I want to see your beautiful face when I wake up."

"Aww. Well, since you're turning out to be a bit of a sweet talker yourself, I will. I'll need to text Elle, though."

"Do you want me to fetch your purse?"

"Aww, thanks." She glanced at the bathroom. "I'll go brush my teeth."

Chapter Fourteen

"Good morning!" Elle called the moment Teresa stepped into the salon. She already had a client in her chair.

Teresa tried to hide her smile, but knew she wasn't doing a very good job of it.

"Morning."

"There's coffee in the back."

"Thanks. Do you want one?" At least she didn't have to worry about her daughter's disapproval; Elle was beaming.

"I'll be right in."

Teresa went into the breakroom and set her purse on the table before she poured herself a mug of coffee. She still had ten minutes before Izzy was due to arrive.

Elle came in just as she was sitting down. "Before you give me a hard time, remember that I'm too magical." She grinned and held up her mug. It had a cute little unicorn on the front with '*I'm too magical for your bullshit*' emblazoned beside it.

Elle laughed. "I promise I won't give you a hard time." She grasped her hands together and held them to her chest with a big silly grin on her face. "I'm bursting here. But I know I shouldn't ask, and I don't know what to say but … ?"

Teresa had to laugh. "I'm just happy that you're not mad at me. I would have let you know I wasn't coming earlier if I'd known myself. I didn't like sending you a text in the middle of the night like that."

Elle waved a hand at her. "It's fine. I wouldn't have been worried even if you hadn't texted at all. I knew you were safe. You were with Cal!"

"You like him, don't you?"

"He's wonderful, Mom! He's the best guy you've ever been out with. And he's a million times better than Dad."

"Elle! You shouldn't say that."

"My momma taught me to never tell a lie."

Teresa made a face. She didn't think it was right for a girl to talk about her father like that, but she could hardly deny that she agreed.

"Anyway, let's stick with the good stuff. Did you have a good time?" Elle waggled her eyebrows.

Teresa had to laugh. "I had a very good time."

"The best time ever?"

She laughed again. "Honestly? Yes! But I really don't think this is a conversation that we should be having."

"Neither do I, but I can't help it. I'm thrilled for you, Mom. I really am. I think he's great and I hope this goes somewhere."

Teresa nodded.

"Is it going somewhere?"

She smiled.

"Tell me! Did he ask you out? Like to be his girlfriend? Is that even a thing at your age?"

She had to laugh. "I think that would be weird at our age."

"So, he didn't? I guess you don't need that, do you? It's not like you need that to make it official."

It dawned on Teresa that Cal, being who he was, had needed to make it official in his own way. "He asked if he could be my man."

Elle put both hands over her heart and sighed. "Aww! He's awesome! You'd better be good to him, Mom. You've got yourself a real catch there. He'll have women lining up to get their hands on him if you let him get away."

Teresa made a face. "He is wonderful, but he thinks I'm a catch, too."

"You are! I didn't mean it like that."

"I know." Teresa knew she meant well, but for the first time it occurred to her that Elle was right. Cal could have any woman he snapped his fingers at—not that he was a finger snapper, but … No. She wasn't going down that road. He could no doubt have his choice of the ladies, but he hadn't chosen one in years by the sound of it. Now, he'd chosen her, and she wasn't going to second-guess it. She was just going to choose him right back.

They both turned at the sound of the doorbell. "That'll be Izzy; we'd better get out there."

~ ~ ~

"What time do you call this?"

Cal stopped dead in the doorway to his office. Ryan was sitting in his chair with his hands folded behind his head and his feet up on the desk.

He turned at the sound of a laugh from the corner. Manny was sitting in the easy chair with his feet up on the coffee table.

Cal scowled at both of them. "Haven't you asked me every day since I've been here to work fewer hours? This is the first day I come in at nine-thirty, and you're waiting to ambush me the second I arrive. What's your problem?"

Ryan pushed back from the desk and got up with a grin. "Don't go all badass on us. It's called teasing. You remember how that works?"

Cal didn't succeed at hiding his smile. Teresa liked to tease him, too. She'd teased him while he made her breakfast this morning—about cleaning up after himself as he went.

Manny got up, too, and came to stand beside him. "You need to get used to how small towns work, old friend. News of you dropping Teresa off at her house this morning arrived here about fifteen minutes before you did."

Cal blew out a sigh. "I should have known."

"You should, boss," said Ryan. "You're the one who taught me that you can't expect to keep your private life secret."

Cal frowned. "I'm not trying to keep it a secret. I have nothing to hide."

Ryan raised an eyebrow at Manny. "You were right, then?"

"About what?" Cal knew better than to let them draw him in, but he couldn't help it.

"I might have mentioned a hunch I have."

"What hunch? What are you predicting now?" Cal was surprised to feel his pulse quicken. They were only teasing him, but he knew Manny's hunches usually panned out with uncanny accuracy. He was hoping that this one would line up with his own hopes—hopes that if he were honest, he planned to keep secret for a while yet. He didn't want to scare Teresa off, and he didn't want Ryan and Manny to ... to what? They'd both gone down this road. They'd both fallen in love and had plans to marry soon. Perhaps they'd be more inclined to help him out than ridicule him?

Manny was smiling at him. "Are you sure you want to know?"

"No. I'm not sure I do."

"It's a good one," Ryan assured him. "You might like it."

Cal laughed. "I might. But if you don't mind, since I'm already getting a late start on my day, I'd like to get to work. Do you guys ever do anything? Dan works his ass off. Leanne does too," he smirked at Ryan, "and Donovan. But I don't think I've ever seen either of you do any actual work yet."

Ryan made a face at him. "I did a lot of the set up before you ever arrived. Now, we're waiting to go live and for the contracts to start coming in."

"Excuse me, guys."

They all turned to see Donovan standing in the doorway. Cal liked him. He'd come up to the lake as Leanne's assistant to work on the legal side, but whenever Cal talked to him, he was eager to learn every aspect of the business he could. He already knew enough to be useful on the cyber side and if Cal had to pick a civilian to help out in the field, Donovan would be his first choice of the guys available.

"Come on in." Cal narrowed his eyes at Ryan. "These guys were just leaving. They have work to do, apparently."

Donovan stood aside to let Manny and Ryan out before he came in. He looked nervous.

"Take a seat. What can I do for you?"

"I …" He hovered by the doorway. "I finally found myself a place to rent and I want to invite everyone over on Sunday afternoon. It's nothing big or fancy or anything. But I thought it'd be good. You know, to get everyone together outside of work for once? I mean some of us guys hang out sometimes, but sometimes it feels like there's a divide."

"A divide?" Cal sensed he was trying to get at something, but he didn't know what.

Donovan came in and sat down suddenly. "Do you mind if I just come straight out with it?"

"Go ahead. I'd prefer it."

"Some of the cyber guys are scared of you. Ryan and Manny, too, a little. But mostly you. I think if this place is going to work the way we all want it to, then we need to be one big team who all trust each other and pull together."

Cal pursed his lips. "Hm."

Donovan raised an eyebrow. "Is that *hm, interesting idea?* Or *hm, will anyone notice if I tear this minion limb from limb and dispose of him?*"

Cal laughed out loud at that. "Damn. Is that the impression I give? That I'd do that?"

Donovan nodded emphatically. "You have to remember that you're dealing with mere mortals here. Ryan and Manny already know you. Of course, the ladies all think you're God's gift, but to lowly programmers and lawyers you're … intimidating."

Cal had to smile. "I'm sorry. I don't often think about what impression I give."

Donovan nodded. "I sure as hell wouldn't bring it up if I didn't see it possibly becoming a hindrance when we get up and running around here. I can see it being an issue if one of the guys keeps quiet about something because they're too scared to come and talk to you."

"That's a good point. I'm glad you're raising it. Thanks, Donovan."

Donovan smiled. "Thank you. I don't mind telling you that I was scared to come talk to you. But I believe it's important—important enough for me to man up and do it."

"Well, I appreciate it. And I appreciate the invitation, too. Are you sure you want to use your housewarming as the occasion to do it, though? We could arrange something else."

"I'll be honest, I also want to do it for selfish reasons. I want to make this place my home—Summer Lake and the house. I like the idea of having everyone over."

"Okay, then. Let's do it." Cal thought about it. "You say you all go out together on the weekends sometimes?"

"Yeah."

"Well, why don't you see about getting the guys to the Boathouse on Saturday night? I'm going with Manny and Ryan, and it might be a way to break the ice first in a more neutral environment before cramming them all into your place?"

"That's a good idea. I'll talk to them about it." Donovan got to his feet. "Thanks, Mr. Callahan."

Damn. Cal realized how little notice he'd taken of how the guys who worked here saw him. "Call me Cal. Hearing you say Mr. Callahan makes me want to look over my shoulder for my dad."

Donovan smiled. "I'll try but forgive me if it slips out now and then?"

"We'll work on it."

Once he'd gone, Cal fired up his computer and stared at the screen. He felt the same way Donovan did; he wanted to make this place his home. He wanted to bring the guys he worked with together as a team, and most of all, he wanted Teresa—he smiled, Terry—to share his life, and his home.

He took his cell phone out of his back pocket and set it on the desk. It was too soon to call her; he'd only dropped her off at home a little while ago. She'd be at work now. He smiled as he pictured her in the salon, remembering the first time he'd laid eyes on her in there.

He picked his phone back up. A quick text wouldn't hurt.

Cal: I'll come for you at five.

Want to have dinner with me afterward?

He stared at the screen wondering if she'd answer or if she'd be busy cutting hair.

Teresa: I'd love to.

He smiled as he looked at the screen. When he'd asked the question, he'd been thinking that they could have dinner at Four Mile Creek while they were over there, but he'd rather take her back to his place again. They could get takeout, or he could cook for her. He wasn't so interested in dinner as he was in getting to spend the evening with her again—and the night. He pursed his lips. He wouldn't know unless he asked.

Cal: The purple toothbrush is officially yours.

He smiled as he waited for her reply. Perhaps he should have just asked if she wanted to stay over but …

Teresa: Are you suggesting that I might want to use it again tomorrow morning?

He chuckled.

Cal: I'm hoping

Teresa: Oh, good! I was, too ;0)

Cal: I'll see you at five then.

Teresa: See you later.

He set his phone back down with a big smile on his face, then grabbed it again when it beeped.

Teresa: There was still a green toothbrush left in the pack.

You could bring it with you tomorrow—if you want.

He grinned. He hadn't expected that. She'd invited him to go over tomorrow night so that Elle could go out with her friends. He was looking forward to it and looking forward to seeing little Skye again. It hadn't occurred to him that she might want him to stay, not with her daughter and her granddaughter there, but he didn't have a problem with it if she didn't.

Cal: I want.

He looked at the words before he hit send and as soon as he had, he knew he wanted to add more.

Cal: And I don't just mean the toothbrush.

I want you. I want this. I want us.

He hit send before he had the chance to second guess himself. Then he held his breath while he waited. It took a couple minutes before her reply came in.

Teresa: Wow! Well, we did say we're going to be honest with each other.

So, you should know that I want you. I want this. I want us, too.

He grinned as he read it. They'd both said what they needed to, but he didn't want to leave her wondering what he thought of her reply. He'd never used one of those smiley face things in a message before, but he found them and scrolled through them. They were hardly his style. But he found one that wasn't a face, just a heart. He glanced at the door before he hit send and then had to laugh at himself. He needed to get over the paranoia. Although he was thinking about Ryan and Manny teasing him, they weren't, they weren't the ones judging him— he was the only one doing that, and there was no need.

He laughed when her reply came back. He knew what the wink was about.

Teresa: Aww. And I wasn't sure there was anything soft about you. ;0)

See you at 5.

Chapter Fifteen

"Where is this place?" Teresa asked.

"It's down on the water—just a few houses down from Manny and Nina's. Open the glovebox, the brochure's in there."

She opened it and took the brochure out but froze when she saw what was underneath it.

Cal glanced over at her. "Everything okay?"

"Err, yeah." Her heart was hammering in her chest.

"What's wrong?"

"What's that for?"

"What?"

She pointed at the glovebox. "That. The gun. What ... why?"

He blew out a sigh. "Sorry. I didn't think. It's ... I've always carried. It was part of the job."

"But you're retired."

"I am, but ... Does it bother you?"

She thought about it. "Maybe not. It took me by surprise, that's all. I don't suppose it should have. I know you used to do dangerous work. I suppose I never really thought about it."

He reached across and took hold of her hand. "It's safe. I'm safe. I promise you."

She laughed. "I don't think you're going to shoot me."

He chuckled and shook his head. "That's good to know, but I didn't mean that. I meant I'm responsible. It wouldn't be in the glovebox if Skye were going to be in here. I keep it in a safe in the house."

"There's a safe in there?" It probably wasn't the most pertinent question, but she was thrown off seeing that thing in there. She didn't think she had a problem with it, but it did make her think about him differently. Not in a bad way. It just made her more aware of who he really was. What his life might have been like.

"There isn't one in the rental where I'm living, but I have my own."

She nodded as if she understood, but she didn't really.

He squeezed her hand. "Is it a problem?"

"No." She looked over at him. "I trust you. I know you're responsible. I just ... I need to wrap my head around it I suppose. It's not something that's ever been part of my experience. I mean ... this is Summer Lake."

He nodded but kept his eyes on the road ahead. "Think about it then ask me anything you want to know. It's never been part of your experience, but it's always been part of mine."

"Okay. Anyway ..." she held up the brochure and took a look. "Oh, my God! I love this place." She laughed, wanting to lighten things back up. "I have to say Blake Callahan, you have the best taste."

He chuckled. "I like to think so. I love the house. I love—" He stopped abruptly. "I found the most beautiful woman in town."

Teresa's heart pounded. It had sounded as though he was going to say he loved her, too. But no. He was hardly likely to say that. They were still just getting to know each other. He made it obvious that he liked her and that he wanted to explore a relationship with her, but it was a little too early to be talking about love. She wasn't sure that he was that kind of guy anyway. She batted her eyelashes at him, "Why, thank you."

He squeezed her hand. "It's true." He smiled. "I didn't know what retirement was going to look like. But I'd never have guessed that it would be this good—that I'd get to live in a great little town like this, hopefully in a great house, with a wonderful woman."

She swallowed. That sounded like he was saying that he wanted to live with her—that he wanted her to live with him, in this house he was thinking about buying. Nah. She was just getting carried away.

He glanced over at her, but she just smiled. What could she say? When his eyebrows knit together instead of smiling back at her, she knew she needed to say something.

"Well, if you manage to get this place," she waved the brochure, "you'll definitely have one of the best houses in town."

"You like it?"

"I love it. I thought about buying it, but it's a bit of a reach for me with all my other commitments, and then the Marshall place came up for sale. It's a better fit for me."

"You're moving?"

She laughed. "No. I'll rent it out."

"Ah, I see. You're quite the businesswoman."

"Yep." She knew she shouldn't feel defensive, but she couldn't help it. Steve had always given her a hard time about the way she scraped and schemed, as he'd called it. She preferred to think of it as saving and investing.

Cal blew out a sigh and she turned to look at him. "I feel as though I'm screwing up here. First the pistol, then ... I've upset you somehow, but I don't even know how. Forgive me?"

She leaned across the console and landed a kiss on his cheek. "You haven't messed up at all. I'm the one who should be apologizing, I get a little touchy, I guess, about the properties. It's ... Steve was ... Oh, you know what? Forget that. The gun isn't a problem. I was just surprised, that's all. And I love the house. I hope that you'll love living there," she smiled, "and that you'll invite me over sometimes."

"More than sometimes."

She loved the way he said that. "Well, I'll come whenever you invite me to."

He waggled his eyebrows. "I should warn you; I plan to invite you later."

She laughed, loving that he was being more playful. "Ooh. And I have no doubt that I will."

"I plan to make sure of it."

A shiver of anticipation ran down her spine.

He pulled off East Shore Road onto Lakeside Drive and drove all the way to the end. Dallas's Jeep was already parked in the driveway when they reached the house.

"Hey, Mrs. Clarke, Mr. Callahan." Dallas greeted them with a smile. "I've opened everywhere up for you. All the lights are on. I can wait out here till you have any questions if you like?"

Cal nodded. That suited him much better than having Dallas traipse around inside with them. "That's great, thanks." He turned to Teresa and gestured for her to go ahead of him.

She smiled at Dallas. "Play your cards right and you'll get a sale out of this no matter what."

She laughed when they both gave her puzzled looks. "I'm already in love! Even if Cal doesn't want it, I'll take it."

Cal's heart thudded to a halt. It took him a moment to process the rest of what she'd said. She was talking about the house. Not about him. What was he thinking? She was hardly going to tell Dallas that she was in love with him before she'd even told him. He needed to slow down. She was hardly going to say it at all when the thought had probably never even crossed her mind. He met her gaze. Or maybe it had? She looked as though she realized what she'd said, but she didn't look horrified. She looked ... apprehensive? Did she think she'd given too much away?

He didn't know, but he planned to find out just as soon as he could, and he couldn't do it standing on the front steps with Dallas watching them.

"I want it," he said, hoping that she might understand that he wasn't just talking about the house. She turned to open the front door, leaving him wondering if she had any clue what he was getting at or if he'd simply imagined the whole thing. Was he reading too much into her words because he wanted to?

He took a deep breath as he followed her inside. No. He wasn't and he knew it. He might be out of his depth when it came to women and relationships, but he knew how to read people. He'd spent his whole career doing it. It was one of his strengths and he wasn't going to start questioning himself now. If he had to bet on it—and he was planning to bet his whole future—he'd say that she was feeling the same way he was, and the thought made him happier than he'd ever been.

"Oh, my God!"

He hurried after her to where she stood in front of the wall of windows.

"This is amazing! It feels like we're on the water. Like, in a boat, not just next to the water." She turned back and looked around. "And the inside is just as good as the view outside. It's so clean and modern and …" She grinned at him. "Okay. You win. It's very you, isn't it? It's all straight lines and right angles and clean cut, no-nonsense."

He chuckled. "Is that how you see me?"

She came to him and slid her arms around his waist. He closed his around her as if it were the most natural thing in the world—which over the last few weeks, it had become. He dropped a kiss on her lips.

"I do see you that way." She shrugged. "You're straightforward and strong, no frills."

He leaned back so he could see into her eyes. "Is that a good thing?"

She laughed. "No frills? Yeah, that's a good thing, for a guy especially. What you see is what you get." She ran her hand up his arm. "And I like what I see."

He laughed with her. "That's good, because I intend to make sure you get it."

"Ooh." She looked around. "It's a pity it's not furnished. We could christen the place."

He held her closer, needing her to know the effect she had on him. "Want to go explore upstairs? I don't need a bed, there are walls."

Her eyes widened and she grinned at him. "You're more adventurous than I was giving you credit for, Mr. Callahan."

He swatted her backside as he followed her up the stairs. "You have no idea, Ms. Clarke."

She looked back over her shoulder and waggled her eyebrows. "It would seem not. But I look forward to finding out."

He took her hand when they reached the landing and she looked up at him.

"I was only kidding, you know. I don't think ... Not with Dallas down there waiting."

He laughed. "Relax. So was I. We can come back and christen it after the sale goes through."

"You're going to make an offer then?"

"I'm going to buy it."

She laughed. "Of course, you are. None of this make an offer and see what happens for you, right?"

"That's right. I want it. My decision is made. Now, I'll do whatever it takes to get it." He squeezed her hand, hoping again that she'd pick up on all the ways he meant that. Her eyes told him she did, but she didn't comment.

Instead, she tugged his hand, and led him into the master bedroom. "Oh, wow! The view's even better from up here."

"Isn't it? I'll share it with you as often as you want, since you like it so much."

She smiled up at him. "Thanks. I think I'll take you up on that." She let go of his hand and started opening doors. "Oh, look at this closet! I bet it'll be wasted on you, won't it?"

"Maybe." The closet was enormous. All the clothes he owned would only fill the rail along one wall. But he couldn't help hoping that she might fill the rest of it with her things. Was he crazy? It didn't feel crazy. It felt right. He was glad he'd asked her to come over with him. He didn't want this to be his home—he wanted it to be their home. All he had to do now was bide his time and hope that she might come to want that, too.

~ ~ ~

"So, Manny says you might be our neighbor?" Nina asked Cal.

Teresa turned to him to see what he'd say. They'd gone straight back to the office with Dallas after they looked at the house on Thursday and he'd written up the offer. She knew Cal was in a hurry, but he'd told Dallas to take his time and go over everything with Austin before he submitted it.

He smiled and nodded. "That's right. It should be soon, too." He took hold of her hand under the table and squeezed it. She squeezed right back.

They'd come to the Boathouse with everyone tonight and she was having a great time. She hadn't been sure how he'd be. She'd been fascinated to see him with Ted and Diego as well as Manny and Ryan. Apparently, they were all friends of old. He laughed and joked with them all; they were clearly all good friends, and, in some ways, it seemed like he was the leader of the group which kind of surprised her, but at the same time it didn't.

This was the first time they'd been out with everyone and she hadn't known how he'd want to handle it. He'd surprised her with how openly affectionate he'd been. He certainly wasn't trying to hide that they were here together. If anything, it felt like he was trying to let people know that they were a couple—and she was loving it.

"Don't be in too much of a hurry," said Manny. "Not if our experience is anything to go by. We just had another delay on closing."

Nina made a face at Teresa. "Yeah. I didn't tell you, but the sellers have asked us to delay again so they can have more time to move out."

"Oh, no." Teresa felt bad for her. She'd been all packed up and ready to go for a while now.

"We're lucky, in that respect, with the place being empty," said Cal. "Dallas is checking into possession before closing, but Austin had already said he didn't think it'd be a problem."

Teresa glanced up at him wondering if he knew what he'd just said. She'd guess from the way Manny's expression changed that he'd picked up on it. It wasn't just her then. He'd said *We*. He didn't look at her, but he squeezed her hand again. He'd said a few things now that had felt like he was hinting at her staying there with him. She kept convincing herself that she was just getting carried away. But she looked at Manny. He was thinking the same thing she was; she could tell.

Nina tapped her arm. "Want to do the girly thing and come to the ladies' room with me?"

"Sure." It made her wonder if Nina had picked up on it as well. She got to her feet, and Cal winked at her before she left. Maybe she'd have to ask him when she got him by himself. She'd drive herself nuts otherwise.

Then again, maybe she needed to take the time to figure out if it was what she wanted first. She smiled. Who was she kidding? Not herself, that was for sure. She'd love to!

As soon as they were away from the table, Nina grinned at her. "And just when did you plan to tell me?"

"Tell you what?"

"That you're moving in with him?"

"I'm not!"

"But he just said …"

Teresa nodded. "I know. I heard him, too. And it was as much of a surprise to me as it was to you."

"Oh." Nina looked so disappointed it was almost comical. "I thought you were going to tell me that he'd asked, and you'd said yes and … but he hasn't?"

She shook her head.

"Would you want to, if he did?"

"Honestly?" She blew out a sigh. "I was thinking that I needed a minute. That perhaps this little trip to the ladies' room with you might help me work out my answer. But that's not true."

"No?"

She grinned. "No. My mind might want a minute to catch up, but my heart already knows that if he asked, I'd say yes."

"Oh, Terry! That's wonderful! I'm so happy. He's lovely! He seems a bit scary at first, but he's a sweetie, isn't he?"

"He is." Teresa's smile faded. "But don't get too carried away just yet, will you?"

"Why not? Is there a problem?"

She laughed. "Just the minor detail that he hasn't asked me—and he might not."

Nina waved a hand at her. "He will. I know it. Manny's been telling me these last few weeks that he's just waiting for Cal to crack open. He's never seen him like this before. He says Cal doesn't know how to handle it yet, but that when he does, he'll be all in like he is on everything he ever does."

Teresa had to smile. "I hope so."

"You should tell him that."

"No. I feel as though I've set the pace with everything that's happened between us. And I don't mind that. You know me. I'm not shy. I don't wait around for what I want, I go out and get it. But this …" She shook her head. "I want it, I'd love to think that he might ask me to move in with him. But I'm hardly going to invite myself into his life, you know? I want him to want it because he wants it. I don't want to lead him there."

"I can see that. You need him to be the man."

She laughed. "As if he could ever be anything else."

Nina laughed with her. "I didn't like to say, but you know what I mean."

"I do. You get it. If that's where he's going, he'll get there in his own time."

As she followed Nina back across the restaurant to their table, she hoped that he might get there soon. He was standing beside the table now, talking to a bunch of younger guys. She recognized Audrey's son, Brayden, who worked for Dan. They must be the tech guys by the looks of them. They might be twenty years younger than Cal, but he was undoubtedly fitter and stronger than all of them. He looked like a man surrounded by boys. She smiled as she got closer; he was her man.

Nina turned back to her with a grin. "Listen! Are you coming to dance?"

The band had just started onto their final set which they usually kicked off with a bunch of very danceable songs.

Teresa pursed her lips. Normally, there'd be no question—she'd be the one dragging Nina up there but ... She glanced at Cal. He was busy talking to Brayden and the others ... Donovan, she knew one of their names. He worked with Leanne.

"Come on, they're talking shop." Nina tugged her on her arm.

When they reached the dancefloor, she glanced back at Cal. He met her gaze and gave her a forlorn look that made her laugh. She hadn't abandoned him—he was busy. He did it again, so she waved for him to come over.

She had to laugh at the look of horror on his face and the way he shook his head rapidly.

Nina laughed with her. "I'm guessing he's not a dancer. That's a shame."

Teresa nodded. It was. She loved to dance.

"And sorry, but I'd guess Manny's about to join us."

Now, Manny *was* a dancer. Teresa pursed her lips as she watched him break away from the group of guys. Diego joined him, tugging Izzy along in his wake. Teresa rolled her eyes. It must be the Colombian thing; those guys never had a problem getting up to dance.

She looked back at Cal. He was watching the others, then he looked back at her. The look of resignation on his face as he nodded made her want to laugh and cry at the same time. She loved that he'd come out here for her, but it made her sad that he really didn't want to.

His pained expression when he reached her, had her taking his hand. She couldn't do it to him.

"Come on, we can go and sit down."

"No." He didn't move, instead tugging her hand and bringing her back to him. When she was close enough, he closed his arms around her.

"I don't dance."

She chuckled. "I gathered. That's why I said we should go and—"

He put his finger to her lips and started to sway from side to side, holding her close against him, so that she moved with him. "You don't want to sit down. You want to dance."

She looked up at him, and he raised an eyebrow. "Will this do? I'll take lessons." The expression on his face said he'd probably be more enthusiastic about taking arsenic.

She had to laugh as she relaxed and wrapped her arms around him. "This will do just fine. It's perfect. You don't need to take lessons. You don't have to dance at all if you don't want."

He dropped a kiss on her lips and continued to shuffle his feet and move her from side to side while people danced all around them. "You love to dance, don't you?"

She nodded. She'd always loved to dance. She wasn't going to deny it.

"Then I'll learn. I want to be able to share the things you love with you." He pulled her closer and lowered his mouth to her ear. "I want to become one of them."

She froze as she ran the words through her mind a couple more times to make sure she understood what he was saying. She leaned back so she could see his face.

"You want to become ..."

He nodded. "One of the things you love."

She cocked her head to one side. "What ... ?"

He closed his fingers around the back of her neck. "I thought I should wait, give you more time. And you can have all the time you need. But I can't wait anymore to tell you." His expression was so stern, so serious. But she knew him now. There was nothing intimidating about him, not to her. She knew him well enough that she understood that the fiercer he looked, the more vulnerable he felt.

She ran her hand over his back, wanting to help him relax, to let him know it was okay. She thought she knew what was coming, but she wasn't going to go there first. "Tell me what?"

"That I love you."

Even though she'd half expected it, she felt as though fireworks were exploding in her chest. His stern expression transformed into his killer smile as he watched her face—which she could feel was beaming back at him.

"You don't mind?"

She shook her head.

"Not too soon?"

She shook it again.

He lowered his lips to hers and the dancefloor and the Boathouse, everything that wasn't just the two of them melted away.

When he finally let her come up for air, he was smiling. He looked down into her eyes. "Now that I've told you, I might overdo it."

"Overdo it?"

He chuckled. "I feel like the floodgates might open. There's so much more I want to tell you, to ask you, to ... but I can wait. I can be patient." His eyes looked more serious now. "And I can hope."

She reached up and pressed a kiss to his lips. "Well, if you're hoping that I might feel the same way, I can tell you that I do."

"You do?"

She nodded happily. "I love you, Cal. How could I not?"

He chuckled and dropped another kiss on her lips before spinning her around. She laughed and clung to him, trusting him to keep her upright. She was too giddy to even try.

"I thought you didn't dance?"

He grinned. "I told you. For you, I'll learn."

Chapter Sixteen

"I don't want to hold you up. There's no need to wait." Elle looked stressed, and it made Cal feel bad.

He gave her a reassuring smile. "There's no rush. It's not a problem. We've got all afternoon."

She rolled her eyes. "Maybe. But you don't need to spend your afternoon waiting for me." She glanced at Teresa. "Sorry."

"It's fine, sweetheart. It's not a problem."

Skye came out of the living room where Elle had sat her with her book while she ran around getting all her things together. Cal had thought it would be a good idea for them all to go over to Donovan's house together. Elle had been invited anyway since she knew … he didn't totally follow the connection, but she was friends with one of the guys from work, or friends with a sister or a girlfriend.

Teresa had stayed the night with him after the Boathouse last night. She'd brought her clothes and things for today, so they'd hung at his place this morning and only come over to her house to collect Elle and Skye just now. He ran his hand over the back of his neck. What he'd thought might be a good idea had apparently become stressful for Elle and that hadn't been his intention at all.

"Grandpa!" Skye flung herself at his legs, making him laugh.

Teresa looked at him wide-eyed, but he just shrugged and scooped the kid up. "Skye!"

"Are we going now? Mommy said I get to ride in your car." She leaned precariously away from him to look out through the window, making both Elle and Teresa start toward him as if to catch her, but Cal had it. No way would he let her fall.

"That's right, sunshine. We're all going for a ride in my car."

"Where are we going?"

"To Donovan's house on the other side of the lake."

She smiled at him. "Can we go to the beach?"

"Not today, sunshine."

Her bottom lip slid out. "I want to go to the beach."

He raised an eyebrow at her. "Did I say we couldn't go?"

She scowled at him.

"I only said not today."

"But ..." her chin started to wobble, and he knew what came next.

He pressed his thumb against her nose, but even that didn't raise a giggle.

"When can we go to the beach?"

"Next weekend," Cal answered before he thought to check that it was okay.

Judging by the expression on Teresa's face, she didn't like that idea. "Are we ready?" she asked.

Elle hauled the strap of a big bag over her shoulder and blew out a sigh. "Yeah, finally. Sorry." She gave Cal a rueful smile. "I never feel like I can go anywhere unless I have supplies to cover any emergency in madam's bag here."

He smiled. He knew how it went; he remembered from Darla's kids. "Let me guess, a change of clothes, possibly two. Juice, a snack, a book, some toys, wet wipes, and a diaper just in case?"

Elle laughed. "Did you watch everything that went in there?"

"Nope. I just know the drill. At least, the drill for good moms who think of everything." He felt a touch of heat in his cheeks when both Elle and Teresa smiled at him.

"Are you sure you don't have a son?" asked Elle.

He chuckled. "I don't."

She blew out a sigh. "I don't mean is that how you learned how to be so amazing with kids. I mean if I'm ever going to find myself a man, I want you to give him lessons first on how to be one."

Cal dropped his gaze. He had the feeling that they could both see the heat in his cheeks this time.

~ ~ ~

When they got to Donovan's place, Teresa was glad to get out of the car. The whole way here she'd wanted to ask Cal and Elle why she was the only one who was shocked by Skye calling Cal Grandpa. But the little madam had joined in on the conversation the whole way.

It wasn't that she minded so much. If she was honest, she loved it. But she wanted to know how it had happened. Something must have been said at some point or she wouldn't be the only one who'd been so shocked.

As she watched Cal get Skye's stroller out the back of his SUV—and unfold it and set it up, she had to smile. She wasn't denying that he'd make a wonderful grandpa.

There were cars parked all along the side of the road. She guessed they all belonged to people who were at Donovan's place. She hoped the neighbors wouldn't mind. This was only one street over from her rental house, which she now knew would be vacant again in a few weeks. She wanted to believe that rowdy neighbors wouldn't be a concern for her new tenants.

Cal wrapped his arm around her shoulders as they walked beside Elle who pushed Skye's stroller. "Are you okay?"

"I'm fine." She smiled. "I might have a few questions for you later, though, *Grandpa.*"

His smile faded, and she'd guess that was the first time it'd occurred to him that there was anything to question about Skye calling him that.

"Don't give him a hard time, Mom," said Elle from her other side. "That's all on me. Skye asked if she could call Cal Grandpa." She smiled at him. "And I explained that the title, and the position were his for the taking, if he wanted them."

~ ~ ~

Cal couldn't hide his smile when Teresa turned back to him. "Is that so?"

He nodded. "It is. And as you now know, I'm applying—for the position and the title."

He loved the way her eyes danced when she smiled.

"Do you think I might stand a chance?"

She laughed. "I think we all know that you got the job already."

His heart clenched in his chest. He couldn't say that he'd ever wanted a family of his own. He loved the role that he'd played in Darla's kids' lives, but they were and always would be his sister's family. Now, walking along the street like this, looking at Teresa, and Elle walking beside her, and little Skye in her stroller, he knew that he'd made some kind of quantum leap and the three of them already were his family. His breath caught in his chest when it hit him that the next thing he wanted to do was to make it official.

He nodded. "I feel as though I should still be on probation."

She laughed. "As far as I'm concerned you've satisfied all the conditions of your probation."

"Mom!"

Teresa laughed and pushed Elle's arm. "Don't blame me, young lady. I was talking about reading Skye stories, and being patient with you. You're the one whose mind went elsewhere."

Cal was relieved when Donovan appeared around the side of the house and waved at them.

"Hey, Mr. Callahan … Cal! I'm glad you could make it. Come on around. Everyone's in the—" He stopped midsentence and stared at Elle.

Cal's jaw clenched and he stood stock still as he watched Donovan's gaze rove over her. Jesus! He took a step forward, before he knew what he was doing, but Teresa's hand on his arm stopped him. Her fingers dug in hard.

"Hi, Donovan. Have you met my daughter, Elle? And her daughter," she waved a hand at the stroller, "Skye."

Cal finally remembered to breathe. That should be enough, shouldn't it? The way Donovan had looked at Elle had been a little primal for Cal's liking. Surely, seeing Skye would be a reminder of where those primal urges could lead—and hopefully a deterrent from wanting to indulge in them.

Shit! Apparently, not.

Donovan came to meet them with a big smile on his face. He reached out to shake with Elle, and to Cal's dismay, she looked as smitten as Donovan. Shit, shit, shit! Coming here had been a mistake.

"It's nice to meet you."

"You, too." Elle was doing the whole fluttering eyelashes and flirty smile thing that young women did—and that young men lost their minds over.

Cal looked at Teresa. She was beaming. Couldn't she see it? He was going to have to warn her.

He could feel the muscle twitching in his jaw when Donovan squatted down in front of Skye. He held his hand out with a solemn expression on his face. "Hello, Skye. It's nice to meet you. I'm Donovan."

Cal's heart sank when she giggled and shook hands with him.

"Hello, Dondervan." She looked up at Elle. "He's nice!"

Elle and Teresa laughed as if the ice were somehow broken. Cal shook his head, wondering what he was supposed to do.

Skye looked up at him and held her little arms up. "Want out, Grandpa!"

Donovan's eyes were wide when he looked up at him. He got to his feet and stepped back when Cal came to unfasten Skye and get her out of her stroller. He swung her up onto his hip and was more grateful than was reasonable when she wrapped her little arms around his shoulder.

He could hardly warn Donovan off Elle, but he was grateful that through Skye he could show him that they were ... he let out a breath. What were they? What was he? He was acting like a protective father, but it was hardly his role to play.

Teresa was watching him with a puzzled look on her face. He gave her a sheepish smile. He had a feeling she knew what was going on. But at least she wasn't mad at him.

"Do you want a drink?" Donovan asked.

"Thanks, I'd love one."

Cal watched as Elle followed him around the side of the house.

Teresa caught hold of his hand. "Did you just do what I think you did?"

He cringed. "What did you think I did?"

"You got jealous—"

"No!" Jesus. How could she think that he was jealous … that he … that Elle …? He shook his head in disbelief.

She laughed. "I don't mean like that! Don't worry. I don't think you're after my daughter. I meant that you went all protective. Like …" She blinked a few times and swallowed. "Like her father."

He nodded. "I'm sorry. I know it's not my place. But I can't help it. Obviously, she's not my daughter, but she's your daughter, and you're my lady and …"

She reached up and kissed his cheek. "I love you."

He leaned down to kiss her but was stopped by a sloppy kiss on his other cheek. "I love you, too, Grandpa."

He had to swallow. Hard.

Teresa chuckled and linked her arm through his. "Come on, big guy. This is far too much emotion for you to have to deal with. Let's find you Manny and Ryan and you can drink beer and talk guns, huh?"

He had to laugh as he followed her. How could she know him so well—and still love him anyway?

~ ~ ~

It was dark by the time they got back to Teresa's place. Skye was fast asleep in her car seat, so Cal unfastened it and carried her inside in it.

Elle gave him a grateful smile when they got inside the house. "Thanks so much. I can take it from here. You guys should get going."

"Do you want me to bring her upstairs?"

Elle glanced at Teresa. "I can do it. We hogged your whole afternoon and evening."

Teresa went to her and put her hand on her arm. "You didn't hog it, sweetheart. We all had a good time—together."

She looked at Cal and he smiled and nodded. "We did." He started up the stairs. "And there's no point in you waking her up just to carry her up to bed."

Elle hung back and looked at Teresa. "You're staying at his place again tonight, aren't you?"

"Unless you want me to stay here. I don't mind if …"

"No. I don't need anything. I'm good. And I might be busy tomorrow, too."

Teresa raised an eyebrow. She had a feeling she might know who with. But Elle shook her head. "That's not what I'm talking about. What I'm saying is that you should go with Cal and get him to explain to you about why Skye's calling him Grandpa. And why I said it's okay."

Teresa frowned at that, but Elle just waved her hand. "Talk to him. I'd better get up there and rescue him from madam before she wakes up and wants to keep him."

Teresa chuckled. "She does seem to have a thing for the good-looking guys."

Elle dropped her gaze.

"It's true," said Teresa. "She's besotted with Cal, and she seemed to have quite a thing for Donovan today, too."

"Yeah."

"Would I be right if I guessed that she's not the only one?"

Elle shrugged.

"Come on, sweetheart. It was obvious. You're not going to admit it?"

"Sure, he's nice. He's a good-looking guy but ..."

"But what."

Elle rolled her eyes and blew out a sigh. "I have Skye and I need to get up there to her so you can have Cal back."

Teresa touched her arm as she started toward the stairs. "Donovan seemed as taken with Skye as she was with him. And as Cal is proving, not all men run scared from little kids."

Elle shook her head. "Yeah, Cal's awesome with her. But he only has to step up and be her grandpa. That's a bit different."

Teresa knew what she meant. Any guy who came into Elle's life would be stepping into the role of father to some extent, and that was a big ask. She was hopeful about Donovan, but ... She shrugged. "Sorry, sweetheart. I know."

Elle kissed her cheek. "I'll see you tomorrow. Love you, Mom."

"I love you too." She blew out a sigh and sat down at the island, wishing that life could be easier for her daughter, but not knowing how. Of course, life was more difficult as a single mom, but neither of them would ever wish that she weren't one. Skye was far too precious a gift to wish that things had gone differently.

She jumped and then relaxed when Cal's hands came down on her shoulders. He did that so well; for such a big guy it was amazing how he could move around without making a sound.

"Are you okay?"

"Yeah. I'm tired."

He closed his arms around her and rested his chin on top of her head. "Do you want me to go and leave you to get some sleep?"

She turned around and looked up at him. "If you want?" That hadn't been the plan, but if …

He gave her a stern look, one that she'd seen him use on the guys to great effect, but he'd never tried it on her before.

"What?"

He narrowed his eyes. She'd guess it was supposed to be intimidating, but it just made her laugh.

"Don't you try your bully tactics on me, Blake Callahan."

He chuckled. "Yeah. I should know better. You're made of stronger stuff than most men."

"Thank you."

"I just. I don't want to go home and leave you here. I want you to go with me. But you said you're tired. So, I wanted to give you the option."

She reached her arms up to him and closed her eyes when he wrapped his around her. She buried her face in his neck and understood why Skye did that whenever she got the chance. He felt so warm and reassuring, he felt like home, and he smelled wonderful. His big arms felt like a safe place, and she never wanted to leave them again.

He held her that way for a long time before he asked. "Is that your way of saying goodnight?"

She lifted her head. "No. It's my way of asking you to take me home."

There went that smile again. "Isn't this your home?"

She looked up into his eyes. She'd told Nina that she didn't want to lead him there, but she needed him to know that she was open to it. "The way it feels these days, Cal. Home is wherever you are."

A little sound escaped from his lips as he crushed her to his chest. His fingers found their way into her hair and closed around the back of her neck. Then his lips found hers in the best kiss yet. It made the rest of the world melt away, as if they were the only two people who existed in the universe, and even better than that, his mouth told her without words just how much he loved her. She hoped he could hear how much she loved him right back.

They only broke apart when Elle cleared her throat behind them. "Sorry, guys. I didn't know you were still here."

Teresa loved that Cal didn't look embarrassed, he didn't even let go of her as he smiled at Elle and said, "Neither did I."

Less than half an hour later, she snuggled back against him as he closed his arm around her in bed. He nuzzled his face into her neck and kissed her.

"I know you're tired. I'll see you in the morning."

She turned over to face him and pressed a kiss to his lips. "Not so fast, mister."

He raised an eyebrow. "Hey. I was trying to be a gentleman. You said you were tired." He drew her closer and the feel of him, hot and hard against her made her want to drop the question she'd been about to ask.

She pressed herself against him. "I'm never too tired for that. You wake me right up, but there's something I need to ask you first."

"What?"

She smiled. "Grandpa."

He shrugged. "Skye asked if she could call me that. Elle said it was okay." He closed his hand around her ass, making her close her eyes and almost give in.

"Elle said you'd explain it to me."

He sighed. "Okay. Elle told me about her father. About what he has Skye call him and his wife." He frowned and his arm tightened around her. It felt more protective now, it wasn't about sex anymore. "She also told me that he used to call you Grandma—that he was mean about it before you ever were a grandma. As if you were like an old lady."

Teresa hid her face in his shoulder.

"Hey." He tucked his fingers under her chin. "Look at me, Terry."

She had to. She loved it when he called her that.

When she met his gaze, he planted a peck on her lips. "I get what he was trying to do. I hope for his sake that I never have to meet him. But I wanted you to know, I need you to know, that I don't see you that way—not in the no fun way that he meant. And as for the Grandma and Grandpa thing. I want to be that with you. I want to be your … man. I want you to be my … family. And if you are then Elle and Skye are, too. And so … if I get my way, then I will be her Grandpa someday. You have no idea how much I love you."

He kissed her again, and she felt as though her heart might melt in her chest. When he lifted his head, she looked into his eyes. "You have no idea how much I love you right back. I told you that first night when you brought me home, that you had the most amazing smile I've ever seen. Now that I know you, I can tell you that you're the most amazing man I've ever met. And you are by far the best thing that's ever happened to me."

He closed his arms around her and rolled onto his back, taking her with him so that she straddled him. She reached down between them, grateful as she always was that he liked to sleep naked. His eyes closed when she curled her fingers around him.

"And as if all of that wasn't enough, you're also the best sex I've ever had."

His eyes opened and he grinned at her. "You mean that?"

She nodded happily as she lowered herself onto him. He grasped her hips and thrust up until he was seated deep inside her.

"Cal," she breathed.

He rocked his hips and she moved with him. Right from the very first time they'd matched each other's rhythm. They fit together as though he was made for her. And they moved together as if they'd always known how. He linked his fingers through hers and moved faster, thrusting deeper and harder.

"Cal!" He was taking her to the edge, and she wanted him to go with her. "I ... I ... I ..."

Stars exploded behind her eyes as waves of pleasure crashed through her. "I love you," she gasped. And her words triggered his release. He tensed and let go deep inside her, carrying her higher.

"I love you, Terry," he gasped as his hands closed around her hips, holding her to him as he gave her everything he had to give.

When they stilled, she buried her face in his neck. "I know making love to Grandma isn't exactly—"

She didn't get the chance to finish. His laughter cut her off. She lifted her head to look down at him.

"I was just thinking, *Ride 'em, Grandma!* but I didn't know if you'd appreciate it."

She laughed with him. "I do! I never thought I'd get horny for a grandpa, but ... phew!" She waggled her eyebrows.

She slid down to lie beside him and he wrapped her up in his arms. She laughed again. "I never thought I'd know a grandpa with arms like yours either."

He tightened them around her. "You'll only ever know this one."

She planted a kiss on his lips. "That's fine by me; you're the only one I want."

Chapter Seventeen

Cal pushed hard to get to the top of the rise, his breath coming out in clouds in the chill morning air.

Manny lengthened his stride and pulled ahead, making Cal dig deep to catch him. They pushed each other on and reached the top in a dead tie. Manny held his hand up and Cal high-fived him. That was all the celebrating he'd be able to do until he got his breath back; they slowed to a walk and Cal bent over to stretch out his lower back.

"Is it just me or is that hill getting steeper?" he asked when he straightened up.

Manny laughed. "It's not the hill. You're built for strength not for speed."

Cal rolled his eyes. "Yeah. Whatever. You were gasping for air as hard as I was by the end there."

"Yep, but I don't mind admitting it."

Cal checked his watch.

"You in a hurry to get to work? You know there's no point in that. They'll only give you a hard time when you get there."

Cal smiled. "No. I'm finally getting the hang of that. It's not work I'm worried about. I have an appointment with Dallas this morning before I go in."

"Yeah? What's going on? Are you making progress with the house?"

Cal smiled through pursed lips. "Well … I hate to tell you this, given all the delays you've had to deal with on your place, but the appointment is at the title office."

"Shit! You're closing already? It's only been a couple weeks!"

Cal grinned. "I know. And I thought it'd take longer than this. But the sellers are as eager to get this deal done as I am. I managed to get all the inspections done. Dallas has worked his ass off for me. And it's all set."

"Damn! Good for you." Manny made a face. "I mean, I envy you, of course. But I'm happy for you. So, what happens now?"

"I need to furnish the place and I need …" He trailed off at the look on Manny's face. "That's not what you mean is it? What do you mean?"

Manny smirked. "I mean Teresa. I didn't pull you up on it the other week when we were all at the Boathouse, but when you were talking about the house you kept saying *we*."

Call grinned. "So, you did pick up on it. I thought maybe you were getting rusty."

"Of course, I did. But I figured that maybe it was a Freudian thing—that maybe you didn't even know yourself yet."

"No. I knew. I know. It's what I want. And I'm ninety-nine percent certain that it's what she wants, too."

"So … what are you going to do?"

Cal blew out a sigh and looked out across the lake as they walked on. "Mind if I ask your advice?"

"Fire away. I'm not sure I'll know the right answers, but I'll give you my opinion."

"That's all I'm asking for. I want to ask her to move in with me. I think that's what she wants too, but …"

"But what?"

"But I don't want to ask her too soon and I don't want to ask her too late."

Manny chuckled. "That sounds like a riddle that I'm supposed to be able to work out. But I can't, so help me out. What would be too soon and what would be too late?"

"Well, you know her daughter, Elle, is living at home with her—and Skye."

Manny smiled. "Yeah. And do *you* know that everyone wants to know how you got to be Grandpa so fast, but no one wants to ask."

Cal chuckled. "Skye asked me to be." He shrugged. "You've met her. She's a cutie. How could I say no?"

"It's a good thing that no one ever knew how soft you were before now."

Cal held his hands up. "What can I say? Turns out I'm a sucker for a pretty little lady—whether she's three or fifty-three."

"It would seem so. Anyway, go on. How do Elle and Skye affect your timing?"

"Well, I know Teresa missed them when they were in the city. She's loved having them home with her again. Elle doesn't plan to stay much longer anyway. She wants to get a place of her own. She's going to rent over at Four Mile."

"That's good, isn't it? Since your place is over there. They'll still be close. You won't be moving Teresa away to the other side of the lake from them."

Cal nodded impatiently. "Yeah, but I don't think I should ask her to move away from them before they move away from her. If that makes sense?"

"It does. I get it. So, you wait?"

"Yeah, but if I move into the house and don't ask Terry to move in with me—that's what I mean about asking too late. I don't want her to think that I don't want her with me. And ..." He gave Manny a sheepish smile. "Call me soft if you like. You might have a point if you do. But I want that house to be our place, our new beginning. So, I want us to move into it together."

Manny frowned and held his gaze so long that it made him uncomfortable.

"What? You're making me feel like I'm missing something. Tell me already!"

Manny laughed. "You really don't see it?"

"See what?"

"The obvious solution."

"Apparently, not. Go on, put me out of my misery. What am I not seeing?"

"You wait. You wait until Elle and Skye have moved to their own place. And then you ask Teresa to ..."

"Yeah, but—"

Manny held his hand up. "And *you* don't move in till she's ready to either. Just because you can close on the place in a hurry, doesn't mean you have to move in in a hurry. You can take your time; decorate, furnish it, do whatever you like so that when you do move in—when the two of you move in, it'll be exactly how you want it."

Cal rubbed his hand over the back of his neck and shook his head. "Jesus! I guess I really am getting old, huh? I didn't even think …"

Manny grasped his shoulder. "Don't be too hard on yourself. They say love can make a man blind."

Cal smiled through pursed lips. "Okay. I owe you that much. Yes, I'm in love with her. Yes, I have told her that. And …" what the hell, he might as well tell him. "I want to marry her—but no, I haven't told her that yet."

Manny grasped his shoulder again with a big grin on his face. "That's great, Cal. That's … amazing! I was going to say unbelievable—and it would have been a couple months ago, but now I'm not surprised. I'm thrilled, but I'm not surprised."

Cal grinned back at him. "Neither am I. I never thought I wanted it. You know … you remember."

"We were different back then, living different lives. Kim and I had a fair shot. We at least thought we were in love. You …" He shook his head. "Andrea wasn't."

Cal shrugged. "Yeah. I tried, but you know I never loved her."

"Honestly? I was never sure about that. I knew she didn't love you."

"Well, don't go feeling sorry for me. I never wanted her to. It was a marriage that served a purpose. Anyway, I didn't mean to get caught up in that. My point was that it's taken me more than half my life to figure out what this love thing feels like, what I want marriage to be and to find the only woman … the woman I believe I can make that happen with." He glanced at Manny.

"Go on. Ask. I'm not promising I'll know the answer, but I'll try."

"I almost said that I've found the only woman for me. Do you think that's true? Do you think there's only one person in the world for each of us? That some people find them early and get to spend their whole lives together, and that some people never do? I've always thought it worked that way and that I'd never find my person—because I never really bothered looking."

Manny smiled. "I think it works that way if you believe it does. Like you say, you're never going to find someone if you're not looking. But I think even for people who lose love early in life, if they believe there's another person out there for them, they'll find them."

Cal nodded. "I guess."

"Either way. We'll never know the truth of how it works, so like with most things in life, we take our own experiences and draw conclusions from them and decide that that is the truth. So, for you, yeah. There's only one woman. Her name is Teresa and you've taken half your life to find her. I'd say that's good motivation to make the most of every single day that you get with her."

Cal grinned. He didn't even feel embarrassed anymore. "I intend to. I'm going to ask her to help me make the house into a home and then when she's ready, I'll ask her to move in with me. And then … when I figure it out, I'll ask her to marry me."

Teresa was tired by the time she got to Cal's place. It'd been a busy day in the salon and then she'd gone to the gym. It was tempting to skip her workouts these days. She smiled as she pulled into the driveway and got out of her car—Cal was working her out most nights in a different and much more enjoyable way.

Her heart soared when the front door opened, and he stood there smiling at her. How had she gotten so lucky? She hurried up the path to him and he opened his arms to her. She stepped inside them and let out a happy sigh.

"Are you okay?"

She nodded against his chest. "More than okay. I'm happy." She looked up at him. "In case I haven't told you yet, you make me very happy."

He dropped a kiss on her lips. "In case I haven't told you, you make me very happy, too. Happier than I've ever been."

He led her inside and helped her out of her coat. "Have you eaten? I made lasagna if you want some?"

"I'm good thanks."

"Drink then?"

"Now that, I won't say no to." She followed him into the kitchen and pulled up a seat at the island, thinking that he'd fix her a vodka, lime, and soda. She was surprised when he opened the fridge and pulled out a bottle of champagne.

"Ooh, bubbly? What are we celebrating?"

"I closed on the house this morning."

"Oh! That's right! I forgot. I'm sorry." She frowned. She'd forgotten all about it. She'd been so busy all day. "I feel awful."

He made a face while he worked the cork out. "There's no need. Signing the papers doesn't mean much. This is the part that matters." The cork came out with a pop, and he filled two flutes and handed one to her. "I've been looking forward to celebrating with you."

She raised her glass. "Well, congratulations."

He nodded and they both took a drink. His eyes never left hers. She could tell he had something to say for himself.

"Well?"

"What?"

She laughed. "Tell me what you're thinking."

He shrugged. "I … Hmm. I can't lie and say nothing. I never want to lie to you. I'm too good at it."

She gave him a puzzled look.

"That was my life. That whole career was about being a liar, working and living in the shadows and never telling anyone the whole truth."

"I guess. I never thought of it that way."

"I enjoyed it, but it's behind me now. And I don't want to bring those ways into this life." He met her gaze, "Into our life."

"I'm glad. So, if you don't want to tell me what you were thinking, tell me something else instead?"

"Thanks. I will tell you at some point. It's something important and something that I hope will make you happy. I just want to get my timing right. Is that okay?"

"It sounds good to me."

"I hope it will. And in a swift change of subject, what do you want to do this weekend? I know you have to work on Saturday, but I keep thinking about little Skye wanting to go to the beach. What do you think, should we take her on Sunday? Give Elle a few hours to herself?"

"Aww. You really are the sweetest thing."

He scowled and folded his arms across his chest, making her laugh.

"I'm sure you scare most people off when you do that, but I know better. You don't fool me."

The furrows in his brow deepened, and if she didn't already know in her heart that he loved her, if she didn't already trust him one hundred percent, she'd be wary of that look. She shook her head at him. "Nope. You can give me all the hard ass looks you want to. But I know better. You're a big softie."

"Only when it comes to you."

She smiled. "And Skye, and Elle, too."

He rolled his eyes. "Because they're your family, and I want you to be my family. So …"

Her smile faded. He already felt like family to her. She loved the way he fit so well into their lives, and she still hadn't gotten over the way he'd gone all protective over Elle last weekend. But he wasn't her father and … She blew out a sigh. How had she forgotten?

Cal's frown was back, and it looked more genuine this time. "What's wrong?"

She made a face. "We can't take Skye this weekend."

"Why not?"

"Because I have to go out of town. Do you want to come?"

"Where are you going?"

She shrugged. "I have no idea."

"So, why are you going?"

"Because Steve's coming."

"And that means you have to leave town?"

"I said I would."

"Why?"

"It just makes life easier."

Cal didn't look happy.

"It's okay. I don't mind."

"What if I do?"

She raised an eyebrow. He was usually so agreeable, but his expression wasn't very agreeable right now.

"You don't have to come."

"I don't want you to go."

"Why not?"

He came to her and closed his arms around her. "I just closed on the house. I thought ... I wanted to ask you to come over there with me. I want to ask you if you'll help me decorate it and furnish it. I don't want to move into it until you—" He frowned. "Until it's ready, but I was hoping that you might ..." He shrugged. "It doesn't matter. I'm sorry. I'll go wherever you want to go. The house can wait. I was being selfish."

"Aww." She pressed a kiss to his lips. "You're not selfish. I don't think you have a selfish bone in your body. You're right. I shouldn't let him run me out of town. I can stay out of his way. You're more important to me." She ran her hand up his arm. "What do you want to do at the house?" She smiled as an idea struck her. "We could camp out over there. We can get started working on the place—whatever you want to do to it— and we can stay there." She waggled her eyebrows. "I can bring an airbed. We can christen the place. And if we stay over at Four Mile and tell Elle to stay over this side of the lake, we won't run into them and it'll all be good."

Cal smiled. "I like the idea of christening the place. I'm not sure I want you working on it. I want your ideas and your input, not your labor."

She laughed. "You don't know me as well as you think you do. Do you like my place?"

"You know I do."

"And who do you think decorated it?"

"I assumed it was all your doing, your taste, your design."

She nodded. "And my labor, too. I've done the work on the houses I rent out, too. I bring people in for jobs that are too heavy for me but there aren't many that I can't handle." She put her hand on his arm with a smile. "And now I have my own muscle-guy."

He pursed his lips.

"You don't want to? You want to bring professionals in instead?"

"No! It's not that. I love the idea of us doing it ourselves. I really do." He blew out a sigh. "I'm just wondering if it'd be better for us to go away for the weekend. There's no rush on the house. We have the rest of our lives for that."

Her heart pounded in her chest at that. She loved to think that he was going to be around for the rest of her life.

"And I have to be honest with you. I think it'll be best if there's no chance whatsoever of me running into your ex. Not even by accident."

She raised an eyebrow at him.

"You told me yourself that the man is an asshole. From everything I've heard about him, I couldn't agree more. And I'm not sure I'd be able to keep my mouth shut."

She was surprised to see his hands balled into fists at his sides. She rubbed her hand up his arm. "It's okay. We'll stay over that side of the lake and I'll tell Elle to keep him over this side. In fact, I'll tell him, too. I'll let him know that I'm not leaving town."

Cal's frown was back. "Does he know about me?"

"I haven't told him. I only spoke to him that one time we were in your car on the way to Four Mile." She had to laugh at his expression. "Will you stop that? I don't tell the man a damned thing about my life anymore. I barely speak to him. It's not as though I don't want him to find out."

"Maybe you should tell him."

"Why?"

He shrugged. "Forget it, I'm being … I don't know what." He tried to smile, but it didn't quite work. He was obviously rattled.

It finally hit Teresa. "You look the same way you did last weekend, when Elle met Donovan!"

He pursed his lips.

"You're not jealous. You're … what, protective?"

He shrugged. "Protective, yeah. But also …" He thought about it for a few moments. "I guess what I'm feeling is the desire for revenge."

"Revenge?" Teresa didn't get that. It didn't make sense. "What's he ever done to you?"

"He's hurt you. And that makes me want to …" He shook his head. "It makes me want revenge." He sucked in a big breath and slowly blew it out again, before he finally smiled. "And that surprises the hell out of me. I do cold, clinical, logical, and analytical. I don't do emotional or illogical. Or at least, I never have before. You," he dropped a kiss on her lips, "have turned me into a caveman, apparently. Don't worry. I won't act on it."

She waggled her eyebrows at him. "I'm kind of hoping that you will. I don't mean getting revenge on Steve somehow. I mean, don't cavemen drag their woman back to their cave and—" She didn't get a chance to finish. Before she knew what he was doing, he'd bent down and wrapped his arms around her legs, throwing her over his shoulder as if she weighed no more than Skye.

She laughed and beat at his ass with her fists. "I didn't mean right this minute. We have champagne to drink."

She watched the floor bounce by as he collected the bottle and two fresh glasses and headed for the stairs. When he reached the bedroom, he tossed her down on the bed. The look on his face surprised the hell out of her—and turned her on in a big way.

"And I thought you were such a gentleman."

His chuckle came out mixed with a growl. "I used to be, till you brought out my inner caveman."

All the muscles in her stomach and lower tightened as he stood over her, unbuckled his belt and pushed his pants down. Then he was down on the bed with her, pushing her skirt up around her waist, pulling her panties down and—oh God!

"Cal!" She grasped at his shoulders as he thrust deep and hard. They'd made a lot of love over the last few weeks, but he'd never been … he was always so considerate, so … "Cal!" she gasped his name again when he bit her neck. Her hands scrabbled at his back until he caught her arms and pinned them above her head.

He thrust deeper and harder, making her moan as he looked down into her eyes. "You're my lady, Terry."

She nodded, unable to speak. She linked her fingers through his and let him carry her away, driving her closer and closer to the edge and then pushing her over it, sending her soaring away.

"Mine!" He gasped as her orgasm triggered his, and she felt his release deep inside her. Their bodies melded into one. He was right, she became his in that moment in a way that went so much deeper than words ever could. And he became hers as she took all he had to give.

When he finally slumped down on her, she clung to him. If she expected one of his apologies, or any of his former uncertainty, she didn't get it. His smile and his eyes held total conviction as he nodded and dropped a kiss on her lips before rolling to the side and crushing her to his chest. "You're mine."

She nodded happily. "I know."

"And I'm yours."

She pressed a kiss to his lips. "I know that, too."

He smiled. "Forever. Did you know that?"

She had to smile back at him. "I think you just showed me."

Chapter Eighteen

"What's up, boss?"

Cal started and turned to scowl at Ryan.

"Whoa!" Ryan held his hands up and backed away. He'd made it into the office and almost to the desk before Cal had even realized he was there.

"Sorry. I was thinking."

"It looked more like you were trying to bore a hole into your screen with the death glare."

He gave Ryan a wry smile. "Sorry."

"Would you stop apologizing? It's freaking me out. What's going on with you?"

He had to laugh. "I'm wound up."

"I gathered that much. Want to tell me about it? Or should I go?"

Cal stared at him for a long moment. "Take a seat."

Ryan pulled up the chair on the other side of the desk. "Fire away. I'll be good. I promise. All joking aside. What's eating you?"

"What's eating me is that Terry's ex, Steve, is coming this weekend."

"And that's a problem for her?"

"Not for her, no."

Ryan raised an eyebrow. "It's a problem for you?"

"Yeah. It is. It shouldn't be. But …" He pursed his lips. "I'm not jealous."

Ryan nodded but wisely kept his mouth shut.

"I'm … I'm angry at him. I'm angry at the way he treated—treats her. Angry at the way he treated Elle. Angry that … honestly? I'm angry that he's still in the way. That he's still in their lives. You know little Skye calls me Grandpa?"

Ryan didn't manage to hide his smile as he nodded.

"Yeah." Cal shrugged. "I'm not going to deny it. I love it. She's a great little kid. But I want it to be real, you know? And it's not. I've only been in their lives for five minutes. He shared most of it. However much I want it, they're not my family. They're his. He's been a part of her life in a way I can never be. I'm in it now, and I plan to be there for the rest of it but …" He shrugged. He wasn't even sure he knew what he meant. "I'll only ever be an afterthought."

"No!" Ryan shook his head. "That isn't true. This guy was part of her life. He's Elle's father, and Skye's grandfather. But he's history. You're the one they want. You're the one Teresa loves—and I'd guess Elle and Skye do, too. I saw the way you were with them out at Donovan's place. You already are a family. Sure, it's new, but that doesn't make it any less real. This is the first time this Steve guy has shown his face since you've known her, right?"

Cal nodded.

"And she doesn't talk to him?"

"Only the once that I know of."

"And he's coming to see Elle and the kid?"

"Yeah. He used to see them when they lived in the city, but he hasn't since they came back up here."

"And that's been a few months now."

"Yeah."

"So, he'll come, and he'll stay a few days. Then he'll be gone again. He doesn't see them every day, he's not part of their lives in the way that you are. He doesn't get to bring the little one out so all his friends can fall for her. He doesn't get to scare away guys who start sniffing around Elle."

Cal frowned, and Ryan held his hands up. "Just saying. I like Donovan."

"So, do I. What can I say? I went all protective. I don't want ... But it's not even my place."

"Sure, it is. Did Teresa get mad at you about it?"

"No. She teased me about it, but she told me afterward that she liked knowing that I cared. Knowing that I've got her back."

"See? She likes having you as the man in her life."

"I know. I'm not questioning that. I just ... I don't even know what I'm whining about."

"You're not whining. You're processing your new situation and how you feel about it. And just when you were figuring out that you like it and you enjoy being the man of your new little family, the ex shows up. But you know what?"

"What?"

"If he'd been able to fill that role, if he'd been any good at it, he wouldn't *be* the ex, would he?"

"I guess not."

"Don't guess, know it. There are two ways of looking at this. Either he was the right guy and you're the afterthought who came along later, or you're the right guy and he was the failed attempt who came first. And this might help you: you can bet your ass that he'll see you as the afterthought. And if you keep thinking the way you are, you'll make him right. You'll be the secondary man in the family. What you need to do is make him wrong. You need to see yourself as the main man. He's just some clinger from the past who hasn't totally faded away yet."

Cal had to smile. "I like the sound of that."

"Then make it happen. I know you prefer to stay in the shadows, to pull the strings from behind the scenes. But I think this situation calls for you to step up and be the big man—well, you are the big man. But you need to believe it.

You can be the rock of your new family, not just some little pebble on the shore. Leave that to him and hopefully with time the tide will wash him away."

Cal laughed out loud. "I love it. Especially coming from you. I never knew you were so poetic."

Ryan grinned. "I'm not just a pretty face."

"I never said you were."

"Feel better?"

"I do."

"Want to buy me a drink as a thank you?"

Cal glanced at the clock on the wall. It was almost four. And on Friday afternoon that meant a mass exodus from the office. "I could. She's not finishing till five." He shook his head. "And when she does, we're going straight over to Four Mile—we're staying over there this weekend so that we don't run into him."

Ryan made a face.

"It's not my choice to make. Terry had already agreed to it. She says it'll make things easier."

"Well, you have to come then. Otherwise, I won't see you until Monday."

Cal chuckled. "What and you'd miss me?"

"Something like that."

~ ~ ~

Teresa finished sweeping around her chair and straightened her cart, ready for Tuesday. She wouldn't be back in here till then. She hadn't taken any new bookings for this Saturday since Steve had told her he was coming, and she'd canceled her few regulars. They didn't mind.

She looked over at Elle, who was just finishing putting color on a high-school girl who kept bouncing in the chair she was so excited. She'd talked non-stop since she came in.

Elle caught Teresa's eye and smiled.

"Are you going to be okay?"

"Yep. We'll be another hour here and then I'll go and get Skye. Dad said they'd be here by eight."

Teresa bit her lip. It wasn't her place to say anything.

Elle made a face. "I told him that's her bedtime and it'd be better to wait until tomorrow, but you know what he's like."

She nodded, not trusting herself to speak.

"They're going to come and get Skye from here in the morning and watch her till I get finished. I should be done by noon."

Teresa nodded again. Skye usually went to Jackie on Saturday mornings. But it made sense, she supposed. Steve and Maddie *were* coming to see her.

"Okay, well, I hope you have a nice time with them." She made herself smile for Elle's sake. "Call me when the coast's clear on Sunday night?"

"I will." Elle set the dye brush down in the bowl and wiped her hands before coming over.

To Teresa's surprise, she wrapped her in a hug and squeezed her tight. "I'm sorry, Mom."

"Oh, sweetheart. Don't be. There's no need. It's fine. He's your dad."

Elle squeezed her again before she let go. "I know. But I feel like I'm kicking you out of your home. And I'll miss you. And if I'm honest, I'm mad at myself."

"Why?"

"Because why would I take time off and arrange everything around them to be able to spend time with them when I don't even do that for you? And you know damned well I'd rather spend time with you and Cal, and Skye would too. I think she's going to be a handful. She keeps asking for her grandpa—and she doesn't mean Dad."

"Don't you give yourself a hard time! It's natural. I'm here all the time. I'm part of your everyday life now." She smiled. "And Cal is, too. It's only normal that you go out of your way for the people you don't see as much."

"It's not just that, though. It's because I know with you guys, you have my back. You're always going to be there. You, of course, but Cal, too. Just because of how he is. I'm mad at myself because I take you guys for granted because I know you love me. But I'm going out of my way for him just because he's my dad." She blew out a sigh. "This will probably sound awful, but if I was in a situation where I needed help, I'd call Cal before I called Dad."

Teresa rubbed her arm. "I don't think you should feel bad about that. I know I pull you up when you say things about him, and I believe that you should try to keep some kind of bond with him—if he deserves it. But if he weren't your father, you'd never choose him based on the person he is. I get that."

Elle smiled. "Thanks, Mom. That's exactly it. And if I got to choose whoever I wanted to be my dad, I'd choose Cal every time."

Teresa grinned back at her. "Me, too!"

"Eww!" Elle laughed. "But not to be your daddy!"

Teresa slapped her arm. "You know what I mean! I'm going. He's waiting for me. Call me if you need anything over the weekend, won't you? And don't bring them over to Four Mile. Cal's not thrilled about your father."

Elle raised an eyebrow.

"Just like you and Skye would choose him, he'd choose you. And from the little he knows, he doesn't think your dad deserves either of you."

"Aww. I wish you'd met him back then."

Teresa shrugged. "So, do I. But who's to say it would have worked? And whatever we think of him, your dad gave me you, and I wouldn't change that even for a lifetime with Cal. All we can do is be glad we have him now."

Elle pushed at her arm. "Go on. Get out of here before you make me cry."

Teresa pecked her cheek. "See you Monday. And tell my little sweet pea Grandma loves her."

~ ~ ~

Cal opened his eyes and looked up at the ceiling. Something wasn't right. He turned his head. Teresa was there, sleeping on beside him. He looked around the room. It was a good space. It'd be even better when it had some furniture. At least he'd managed to get a mattress delivered. He hadn't been looking forward to sleeping on an airbed this weekend. It might be luxury compared to some of the places he's slept in his life, but he was past that now. He'd earned the right to a comfortable bed—and he'd get one soon. He'd decided at around three this morning that this mattress would have to go in one of the spare bedrooms.

He looked around again. He still had the feeling that something wasn't right, but he didn't know what it was. He and Teresa had a busy weekend planned. It turned out that she was something of an expert when it came to remodeling and decorating. She'd brought a bunch of files and folders with her last night and while they'd sat out on the patio with takeout, she'd gone through them sharing ideas with him and telling him about all the suppliers she knew where he could get a good deal. He was looking forward to taking on this project with her. He had a feeling it would bond them in new ways. He smirked—it'd help them figure out who was boss for sure, and he had a feeling that they'd hand that title back and forth depending on what they were doing.

He wanted to get up. He needed coffee. And although his mind kept wandering, he really needed to figure out what it was that had him feeling so uneasy. Had he missed a detail? That was the kind of feeling he had. It had gone with the job when he was working. He was the guy who pulled all the threads of an op together, who kept an eye on all the moving pieces. And when something felt wrong it was because some detail had been overlooked. But there was no op. There were no challenges in his life at present. Everything was good—

better than good. Everything was great, he was happy. He couldn't resist moving a strand of hair off Terry's forehead. He was in love. Life was good and he expected it to keep getting better and better.

He slid out of bed. Since she hadn't even stirred when he touched her hair, he knew she must be tired. He'd let her sleep on. She liked it when the coffee was ready before she was anyway—and he'd made sure to bring the coffee pot and supplies over from the rental house.

Once he'd started the brew, he went to check his phone. He frowned when he saw a text from Elle.

Elle: Sorry to bother you. But Mom's not answering. Is she up?

Cal: No, but I'll wake her. Is everything okay? Can I do anything?

Elle: I'm so sorry. Would you guys mind having Skye this morning?

Dad didn't show. I'll explain later. I tried calling Mom, but it was late.

You guys must have gone to bed. But I have my first appointment in half

an hour. Dad and

The message ended there, and Cal understood why when the phone rang.

"Are you okay?" he answered.

"I'm fine—other than being pissed at that ... grr! I won't say it. They were supposed to arrive around eight last night. I tried calling at eight-thirty and nothing. I kept trying and leaving him messages. I was getting really worried. Then he sent me a text at one-thirty this morning; they'd been out last night, and he hadn't seen my messages. Apparently, they changed their minds about coming—he thought that was fine since he hadn't *actually confirmed*. He said that like it was my fault somehow. Or like I was dumb not to have known; well I suppose he's right there. I should have known! And get this …" She sounded madder than hell, and Cal held the phone a couple inches away from his ear. "They decided that it'd suit them better to come the weekend after next. Well! I told him—it might suit them, but it doesn't damn well suit me!"

It seemed she'd run out of steam, but Cal waited just in case. He'd already learned with Terry that the end of an outburst often came with a few final sputters.

"Are you still there?"

"I am. You want us to come and get Skye?"

"Would you mind? I'm supposed to take her to the salon with me and they were supposed to watch her this morning. Jackie's gone away this weekend and I … I'm sorry."

Cal smiled. "Don't be. I'm glad. I told her we'd take her to the beach this weekend and now I'll be able to keep my word. It was bothering me that I wouldn't be able to."

"Pft!"

Cal froze. He knew that sound. It was the same sound Teresa made when she was too angry to even attempt to form words. He had no clue what he'd done wrong, though. "I'm sorry. What …?"

He relaxed when he heard her laugh. "That wasn't at you! It was at the difference between you and Steve—that's all I'm going to call him now. You're worried about keeping your word to Skye about going to the beach and he doesn't give a shit about letting her down for the whole weekend!"

"Ah."

She laughed again. "See, and you're too nice to agree with me even, but we both know."

"Yeah." He didn't know what to say, so he didn't try. "Well, I'd better get moving. I'll see if your mom wants to come."

Elle laughed. "She will. Don't worry. Less than ten minutes from now, she'll be fully put together and walking out the door. As long as you give her coffee."

Cal laughed with her. "It's brewing now. Should we come to the house or the salon?"

"Call when you get to town? I should be at the salon by then, but just in case."

"Okay. We'll see you in around half an hour."

"Thanks Cal. You're the best."

He couldn't stop his smile but didn't know what to say.

"See you in a bit. Love you!"

She hung up, and he stood there staring at his phone. "Love you, too," he murmured. Then went to fix Teresa a cup of coffee.

Chapter Nineteen

"When do you plan to move in?" asked Teresa.

"I don't know yet." Cal didn't meet her gaze.

She gave him a puzzled look. "You keep saying that, and it's not like you."

He chuckled and came to sit down beside her. She'd taken a break from painting to run over to the café at the plaza. She'd set everything out on the island while he washed up. She handed him a plate with a sandwich and some chips and let her gaze run over him. Repainting the house was hard work but getting to watch him work in tank tops made it all worthwhile.

He chuckled and landed a kiss on her lips. "Do you even remember what you just asked me?"

She looked up into his eyes and laughed. "No clue! I got lost in admiring the view. Though, now I come to think of it, was I asking if it's bedtime yet?"

That smile! She let out a happy sigh. It really was the best smile she'd ever seen.

"I've been thinking about that."

"About bedtime?" She waggled her eyebrows.

"About you getting tired and needing sleep. You've been working your ass off in here with me for a couple weeks now. And you're on your feet in the salon all day, too."

Teresa pursed her lips. She had been feeling it, but she'd hoped that Cal hadn't noticed. It wouldn't be for long. They were nearly done. It wasn't as though the house needed much—it was only a couple of years old. They were only doing cosmetic stuff, paint and changing some tile but …

He was frowning at her. "Don't go all defensive on me."

"I didn't say a word!"

"You didn't need to. I can see it on your face."

She smiled. "Was that part of your training in your old job—you read people's minds?"

He shrugged. "Not exactly. And I wouldn't need any training to read you anyway. You're transparent."

"I am not!"

He chuckled. "You are to me—because I love you."

"Aww." She rested her head against his shoulder. "Sorry, go on. What have you been thinking?"

"I've been wondering if you want to do less."

She sat back up. "No! I want to help you finish this place. I love the thought that I helped you make this place your home. I know you've never really had one. And … well, I'm hoping that if I help you make it nice, you'll never move away."

He wrapped his arm around her shoulders and hugged her into his side. "I don't ever plan to move away—not unless you go with me."

"Aww! You say all the right things."

"You know it's not just words."

"I do."

"And I wasn't talking about you doing less here anyway. We're almost done now. I was thinking I could take Friday off. If I do, I can finish the smaller guest room and we'll be done."

"I thought we were going to do that together this weekend?"

"I thought it'd be nice if we did something fun over the weekend—or even if we did nothing. We could take a break. We have enough furniture now that we could just hang out and watch movies and …" He let his gaze travel over her, sending shivers racing all over as if he'd touched her with his hands not just his eyes. "Spend some time in bed."

"Ooh. Now you're talking."

He chuckled. "I thought that might persuade you. But you keep distracting me."

She rested her hand on his thigh and then started sliding it higher. "I'm trying."

He laughed. "And I'm not saying I don't want to. I'll take you up to bed soon enough. But what I'm trying to say is that thinking about taking Friday off made me wonder about taking Monday off."

"As well? What for?"

"I mean, regularly. Since that's your day off. And I know you talked about cutting back at the salon. I wondered how far back you're thinking."

Her heart was hammering in her chest. "What do you … what?"

"I'm trying to say that I'm only supposed to be working part-time and I wondered if you might consider doing the same—so that we get more time together. Skye keeps telling me that her grandma's a venture mouse, but we haven't had the time—or the energy left—to go on any adventures yet."

She grinned at him. "What kind of adventures are you interested in?"

"Anything, everything. Have you ever been sky-diving?"

"No! But it's on my list. Have you?"

He smiled. "Yeah."

"Don't tell me, you were an instructor or something?"

He laughed. "Okay. I won't. But if you're nervous we can do a tandem jump."

She made a face. "I don't like the idea of being strapped to some stranger."

"You wouldn't be."

She didn't get it.

"I mean you'd be strapped to me."

"Oh! In that case!" She grinned. "I think I will be nervous the first time—but I'll do it by myself the second time."

Cal laughed. "That's my girl."

The way he said that made her want to melt into him. She looked up at him. "How did I get so lucky?"

He dropped a kiss on her lips. "I don't think it's luck. I think we've earned this. I think everything else we've been through in life led us to where we are now, to each other."

"I don't feel as though I did enough to earn something this good. I screwed up."

Cal frowned. "You were young when you got married."

She had to laugh. "You didn't even hesitate for a second about what my screw up was, did you?"

He shook his head with a rueful smile. "Sorry. You know what I think about that."

"I do, and you're right. I chose poorly when I was younger, but you have to admit that my taste has improved as I've aged."

"I admit it. You chose the perfect guy this time around. And I got my perfect lady."

Her smile faded. "Talking about my screw up. Steve's supposed to be coming this weekend."

Cal made a face. "You thought I'd forget that? Why do you think I want to hang out here?"

"I'm sorry."

He shrugged. "It's not your fault."

"He might not even come."

"Has he not *confirmed* yet?"

"No." She knew Cal was still angry about the way Steve had let Elle down the last time he was supposed to visit. He'd been great about it. He'd driven her over to get Skye while Elle worked the morning in the salon. They'd taken her to the beach just like he'd told her they would, too. She blew out a sigh. "I have a feeling that he's going to change his mind at the last minute again."

"What makes you say that?"

"It just always seems to work that way with him. He'll have us all arranging our plans to accommodate him and then leave us blowing in the wind when he changes his."

Cal frowned. "Well, this is the last time I'm going to change things around to accommodate him."

"What do you mean?" Most of the time if he looked angry, she knew better. But when it came to talking about Steve, she wasn't so sure.

"I mean if he decides that he's not coming and that he wants to come the weekend after instead, he can't. He'll have to wait."

"Yeah."

Cal blew out a sigh. "And I apologize if I sound like a domineering asshole."

She laughed. "You couldn't be one of those. You're not like that."

He didn't laugh with her. "I know I'm not, but I also know that I might sound like one. But we're supposed to be moving Elle into the house next weekend."

"Yep."

"And I am not going to stay out of the way. We've made arrangements. I'm not …" He hugged her to him. "This isn't about me, you know. This is about you and Elle. If you or she asked me to, I'd have no problem changing the arrangements—waiting another week or another month or whatever you guys said. But I don't want him to make you change everything."

"I know." She rested her head against his shoulder. "Let's see what happens. It might not be an issue. He might come this weekend."

"He might." The look on his face told her that he didn't expect that any more than she did.

~ ~ ~

Cal had the second guestroom finished by lunchtime on Friday. He took his time cleaning the whole house. It'd been fun to work with Terry on getting it how they wanted it. They were still waiting on more furniture. He smiled as he remembered following her around the big furniture stores pretending that it mattered to him what she picked out. She'd pulled him up about agreeing with her even when she'd suggested a hideous ornate hutch for the dining room—apparently, that had been a test to see if he was even paying attention, and he'd failed.

She'd forgiven him when he explained that the furniture was important to him, but the only importance it held was how happy it made her. She'd made her aww noises and joked that he knew how to say all the right things. He wasn't sure whether she really believed that—believed that he thought he was saying the right things. He hoped she understood that all he was doing was telling the truth. Either way, she was happy and that was all that really mattered.

The rest of the furniture should be arriving next week. Of course, it was scheduled to come on three separate days. That irked him. It was inefficient, but a necessary evil, since it was the result of letting Terry visit what felt like every single furniture store in the county.

Even then, he was still going to have to go and collect the patio furniture that she'd ordered. It'd be worth it. He'd bought it from an old guy up near Stanton Falls who made one-of-a-kind pieces by hand. When Teresa had first said the word craftsman, he hadn't been keen on the idea—it brought to mind rustic, artsy stuff. Not that he disliked that style, but it wouldn't go with the house. Of course, he should have trusted her taste. There was nothing rustic about the modern teak and metal dining table and chairs she'd commissioned, or the lounge chairs that were all sleek, straight lines and right angles, just like the house.

He'd rented a small box van to move Elle next weekend. He hoped they'd have her and Skye settled into their new place on Saturday so that on Sunday morning he could take Terry for a drive up to Stanton to collect the furniture. He smiled, and by the time they got back here, Manny and Nina, and Ryan and Leanne, and whoever else Elle wanted to round up would be here—ostensibly to help unload the patio furniture. But he wanted them all to be here for something much more important than that.

He checked the clock. It was only three o'clock and he'd done everything he could find to do. Terry wasn't finishing work until five-thirty. He blew out a sigh, irritated not that she was working late but because she was only doing so because she was taking another Saturday off—to accommodate Steve again. As of this morning she didn't even know if he was definitely coming. If he didn't, he'd have to wait. He looked at his watch again. If he sat around here doing nothing, he'd get himself wound up. He reached for his phone and called Manny.

"Hey, Cal."

"Hey. What are you doing when you finish work?"

"Going to the Boathouse with Ryan. Nina's working at the gift shop. What are you up to? I thought you'd be hard at work getting the house finished."

"It's all done."

Manny chuckled. "And now you don't know what to do with yourself? Why don't you come over and meet us? Nina's supposed to come and meet me for dinner, and you know she'd love to see Teresa."

"I'm on my way."

He decided he'd call Terry on his way over. If Nina was coming to the Boathouse, she might want the four of them to have dinner together. He liked that idea. His smile faded when he realized that if Steve was coming, she might prefer to go back over to Four Mile.

He waited until he was out on East Shore Road before he called. She usually booked appointments to start on the hour or the half hour, so he was hoping he might catch her in between. He'd leave her a message to call him back if not.

"Hey, you."

"Hi."

"What can I do for you?"

He chuckled. "I was thinking more along the lines of what I can do for you. I'm all done at the house and I'm coming over to meet Manny and Ryan at the Boathouse. Manny said Nina's going straight there after she gets done at work, so I wondered if you want to have dinner with them."

"I'd love to. That'll be fun. And then we can go back to your place and just crash. I'm tired tonight."

"Great. I'll see you there whenever you get done. We can leave your car there until tomorrow if you like."

He had the feeling that her willingness to have dinner at the Boathouse meant that Steve wasn't coming. But if he were, she wouldn't want to have to go back for her car tomorrow.

"Okay. Sounds good."

That didn't help. Did that mean they were free to move around town? He pressed his lips together, wondering if she'd just forgotten.

"I'm going to have to go in a minute. My next one's just pulling up outside. Are you okay? You sound off."

"I'm sorry. I was trying to figure out without asking if Steve's coming."

"Oh!" She blew out a sigh. "No. He's not. It's like I expected. He called Elle this afternoon and said he can't come but he'll come next weekend instead."

Cal gripped the steering wheel tighter and felt the muscle start to twitch in his jaw. No way was he going to let the asshole mess next weekend up for him. He'd put off officially moving into the house until Elle moved out of Teresa's place. Teresa had stayed with him most nights anyway, but he'd dropped her home in the mornings so that she could help Elle get Skye ready and have some time together. Next weekend marked a new beginning in all of their lives as far as he was concerned, and he wasn't going to stand for her ex landing in the middle of it and spoiling things.

"Are you still there."

"Yeah. What did Elle tell him?"

"That she's moving and he'll have to wait. Don't be mad?"

"I'm not mad at you, Terry. Sorry." Damn. He didn't want to take it out on her. He needed to get his act together. "The only person I'm mad at is him. I'm sorry."

"It's okay. But I really have to go. She's here now. I'll see you just after five-thirty."

"Okay, I'll see you then. And I promise I'll be all smiles and no more Mr. Grouch."

She laughed. "I'll look forward to that. That smile …!"

He had to laugh with her. At first, he'd thought that she was teasing him about his smile, but he'd since figured out that whenever he used it, she was happy—and that was all he wanted. "I'll see you later. I love you."

"I love you, too. Bye."

Chapter Twenty

Cal was surprised to see Ben behind the bar when he walked into the Boathouse. He liked the guy, and he was easier company than Kenzie. He liked Kenzie, but her forthright manner threw him off. He was never sure how to handle it.

Ben greeted him with a smile. "Good to see you, Cal. How's it going?"

"Great thanks. How about you?"

"Doing well." Ben smiled. "Kenzie and Chase are closing on their house this afternoon. So, I'm afraid you're stuck with me."

Cal chuckled. "That's good—for them and for me."

Ben laughed. "I hope she hasn't—?"

Cal shook his head quickly. "That wasn't a complaint. She's awesome. Just a bit ..."

Ben laughed again. "It's okay. I know. She's a straight-shooter and she has no filters whatsoever, but she has a heart of gold and she's the best bartender I've ever had."

"I can see that."

"What can I get you? Are the rest of the guys coming? I wouldn't have expected you to be the first to leave the office. I heard that you're like me."

Cal raised an eyebrow.

"A workaholic."

"Ah. Yeah. I'm working on that. I've actually been at home today."

"At your new place?"

"Yeah. Finishing up with painting and getting everything how we want it."

Ben smiled but didn't comment.

"What? You have something to say—say it."

"When you said *we*. That's what made me smile. Is it official then; you and Teresa? I think she's awesome. I've known her my whole life. She's one of the best people in this town. She deserves to be with someone who makes her happy."

Cal smiled. It seemed that everyone knew her, and everyone loved her. He'd told her he didn't think it was luck, but he did feel lucky that he'd found her, and that she loved him the way she did. "It's almost official. I'm working on it. Ask me again after next weekend."

Ben grinned. "Are we talking the kind of official where she'll be changing her address or the kind where she'll be changing her name?"

"Both if I get my way." Cal's smile faded. "I never thought about it before, but is Clarke her name?"

"Yeah." Ben looked puzzled by the question.

"I mean, is it her maiden name?" The thought that she might still be using the asshole's name bothered him all of a sudden.

"Oh! Yes. It is." Ben made a face. "Her ex. Steve. His name's Crandall."

Cal nodded. He wanted to ask what Ben thought of him, but he didn't think he should.

Ben leaned on the bar. "I don't mind telling you that Teresa wasn't the only one glad to see the back of him when he left town."

That made Cal smile, he couldn't help it.

"I heard he was coming this weekend."

"Yeah. He was supposed to, but he changed his mind."

"That sounds about right with him. I never liked him."

"I've never even met him, but …"

"You wouldn't be inclined to like him even before you heard the stories, though, would you?"

"What stories?" he asked too quickly, and he knew it. He finally understood first-hand why some of the higher-ups at the agency only took single guys into their teams. It seemed that love took the edge off a guy's skills.

Ben made a face. "Sorry. I assumed you knew. I shouldn't be the one to tell you."

Cal scowled. "I know you shouldn't, but will you? I'm asking."

Ben shook his head. "I can't. If she wants you to know, she'll tell you when she's ready. I'm sorry."

Cal blew out a sigh. "That's okay. You're right. I'll have to ask her. But tell me one thing?"

"What?"

"I already dislike the guy. I hate the way he treats Terry and Elle. If I heard these stories would I hate him even more?"

Ben rubbed his hands over his face and blew out a sigh of his own. "Part of the reason I don't want to tell you is because I feel like it might make me an accessory to murder."

Cal could hear his pulse pounding in his temples. "Did he hit her?"

Ben shrugged, but the answer was written all over his face.

Cal spun around when a hand came down on his shoulder. Manny and Ryan both stepped back.

"Whoa! What's up boss?" asked Ryan.

Manny caught his gaze. "What happened? What do we need to do?"

Cal managed to get a grip. He took a deep breath to steady himself. "Nothing. I'm fine."

"Yeah, right," said Ryan. "And I'm the man on the freaking moon. What's wrong?"

"Nothing. I ... I just heard something about Terry's ex that ..." He glared at Manny. Did he know?

"What did you hear, and what did I do?"

Manny's expression told him that he didn't have a clue. He wouldn't be able to hide that kind of knowledge—he'd be as angry as Cal was.

"I thought you might already know, but you don't. And I heard ..." He knew they'd feel the same way he did if he told them. But he wasn't sure that he should. It was Terry's business, not his to share. He shook his head. "I heard something that makes me glad he's not coming this weekend."

Ryan gave him a wary look. "And the look on your face says that if he did come, he wouldn't be leaving again—except in a coffin."

Cal shrugged. "I'll calm down." He wasn't sure that was true, and the others didn't look like they believed it either.

"So, if he's not coming this weekend, does he plan to come next weekend? And will that affect your plans?" asked Manny.

"Apparently, he says he's coming. But there is no way I'm going to let him affect my plans. I've waited longer than I wanted to already. No way am I going to delay asking her because of him."

"That's right." Ryan smiled. "You should just forget all about him. He can't affect you. He can't mess them around anymore. Elle can tell him she's busy moving and that she's coming to your housewarming."

Cal nodded. "I know that. But it doesn't feel right to make her choose, you know?"

To his surprise, Ryan laughed. "She's already chosen. She wants to see her mom happy; you make her mom happy. She wants to know that someone has her back when she can't handle everything by herself; she knows you have her back."

Cal frowned. "How do you know all that? You don't even know her."

Ryan shrugged and looked at Manny, who put his hand on Cal's shoulder. "You look like you're about to explode anyway. I'm not sure you need—"

Cal scowled at Ryan. "Donovan? She told Donovan all that?"

Ryan shrugged again. "It's not like he's been telling everyone her secrets. He came to me to ask for advice—because I know you, and she's worried about her dad spoiling your big weekend."

Cal blew out a sigh. "Jesus! Life as a loner is so much fucking easier!"

Manny smiled and grasped his shoulder. "Easier, maybe. But much less enjoyable and you know it. This is the stuff that comes with being with a woman, being part of a family. You'll get used to it."

Cal let out a short laugh. "I'll try, but it'd be so much easier if I could eliminate this Steve."

Ryan gave him a stern look. "We're not allowed to do that anymore, remember?"

Cal laughed. "I meant from the equation, not ..." He shook his head.

"Yeah. Sure, you did, boss."

"Come on," said Manny. "You need something stronger than water by the look of you. Let's get you a beer, at least."

"I have to drive back to Four Mile later."

"We'll put you in a taxi if we need to."

"Okay." Cal let them get the drinks and lead him over to a booth. He had a lot to process before Terry arrived.

~ ~ ~

Teresa smiled when she pulled up in the square at the resort and spotted Nina coming in just behind her. She waited for her and grinned when she caught up. "This is a nice surprise, isn't it?"

"It is! Manny said that Cal was off work today, so I didn't expect to see you here."

Teresa held the door open for Nina to go in ahead of her when they reached the restaurant. "Is Leanne coming, too?" she asked.

"Manny said she might come later. It sounds as though she's been working all the hours God sends since she arrived. I like her, she's a tough cookie, but she's a sweetheart underneath the hard outer shell." Nina grinned. "Which sounds a lot like someone else we know."

Teresa smiled as she followed Nina's gaze to where Cal was sitting with Manny and Ryan in a booth. "Don't let all those muscles fool you; he's a big softy."

Nina laughed. "He is when it comes to you and the girls. It doesn't sound like he's soft on the guys, though."

"No, probably not."

"And God help Steve if he ever meets him."

Teresa blew out a sigh. "That might happen next weekend."

Nina stopped dead. "Next weekend? No! He can't come then!"

"I know. We're helping Elle move into the house at Four Mile and Cal's determined that Steve's not going to mess that up. But I've been thinking I might … oh, I don't know. I don't know what to do."

Nina patted her arm. "Next weekend is too important to let him mess it up for you."

Teresa wasn't sure it was such a big deal as Nina and Cal both seemed to think. But she just shrugged. She was too tired tonight to figure it all out. She'd just have to cross that puddle when it rained.

She smiled at Cal as they reached the table. He got to his feet and greeted her with a hug, but his killer smile was noticeably absent. She didn't want him to still be mad about Steve. She wanted to relax and have fun with their friends. She reached up and pressed a kiss to his lips, then turned to greet the others. "Hey, guys. It's good to see you. Are we eating or are we waiting for Leanne?"

Ryan and Manny both looked shifty, to say the least. "Sorry," said Manny. "Change of plan. We need to go." He took hold of Nina's hand. She looked puzzled but not upset. She shrugged at Teresa. "See you soon, I guess."

Teresa nodded and watched them go while Ryan shook Cal's hand. Then to her surprise, he leaned down and kissed her cheek. "See you soon, Terry."

She looked up at Cal as he walked away. "What's going on?"

He shrugged and put his hand on the small of her back as he guided her out of there. "It just turned out this way."

She blew out a sigh. She'd been looking forward to chatting with everyone, but she was hardly going to complain about a night in relaxing—and not painting—with Cal.

His index finger traced a circle on her back as they walked. It reminded her of the first night she'd met him. She smiled when he stopped to open the door for her. "Do we get a peaceful night in then?"

He nodded, but tension rolled off him in waves.

"What's wrong?"

He shrugged again and kept walking until they reached his Suburban. He opened the door for her, but she didn't get in.

"Would you please talk to me? If you're not going to talk, I might as well drive my car home."

The corner of his lips quirked up making her feel a little better. But she needed to know what was going on. "I'm not joking, Cal. I'm not getting in until you tell me what's going on."

He slid his arms around her waist and pressed her back against the side of the SUV. He surprised the hell of her when he leaned his weight against her and rested his forehead against hers to look into her eyes.

"I love you, Terry."

"I love you, too. But you said you weren't going to be Mr. Grouch and you haven't smiled once since I arrived."

He rewarded her with one of his smiles, but it wasn't a convincing one.

"Tell me."

"You know I'm wound up about Steve."

"I do, but I'm disappointed that you'd let that spoil our evening."

"I'm not! Okay, so I am spoiling our evening, and that's the last thing I want to do. But it's not about this weekend, or even next weekend."

"What then? It feels like you're angry. It almost feels like you're angry at me." Her shoulders sagged. "And that makes me uncomfortable."

A little growl escaped from his lips, but he lowered his head to kiss her before she could question it.

She smiled when he leaned back, hoping she could lighten things up. "I love the public display of caveman, but I really need you to tell me what you're angry about."

"I'm sorry. I don't mean to make you uncomfortable. I'm screwing this up because I don't know how to handle it."

"Try telling me!"

"Okay! Does me being angry scare you?"

"No." She ran her hands up his arms. "It probably should. I mean if you wanted to ..." She looked up at him. "What are you getting at?"

"I'm getting at the fact that I believe no man should ever hurt a woman."

Her heart sank. She had no idea how he knew, but somehow, he did. "I'd have to agree with you." She glared at him.

"Are you going to tell me?" he asked.

"Doesn't seem like I need to. Are you going to tell me?"

"I can't because I don't know. I just have an idea. And if that bastard ever laid a finger on you—"

She put a finger to his lips to stop him. She didn't want to hear it. "Stop. Stop it now. It's the past. It's gone and done. I'm not some weak little thing who needs you to ... to anything, okay? I wasn't a weak little thing back then either. Yeah, he pushed me around a couple times near the end. He hit me once, and if it helps, I punched him right back." She stopped and swallowed. Nina was the only person on Earth she'd admitted that to until now.

"Why didn't you tell me?"

"Because why would I? Why should I? It's the past, like I said. Have you told me everything that ever happened in your previous relationships? Would you want me to know? Or are there things that happened that hurt you, that you're not proud of and that you'd rather just let lie?" She glared up at him. He might mean well, but ...

He shook his head. "I'm sorry."

"Don't be. It's okay. I understand your reaction. A part of me even appreciates it. But while it's new information to you and you need to process it, for me it's ancient history and I don't particularly want to revisit it."

He hugged her to him, and she burrowed her face into his warm chest.

"I'm sorry."

She chuckled. "You keep saying that."

"I don't know what else to say."

"So, say you'll take me home now and that we can stop at the plaza for something to eat? I'm starving."

When they got in the car, he reached across and took hold of her hand, bringing it up to his lips to kiss it. "I love you, Terry.

I love you with all my heart and soul. That's not an excuse. I just want you to understand."

"I do. And I love you for it. But …"

"I know. You've dealt with it in your own way and you don't need me dragging you back there while I deal with it."

"Exactly." She smiled at him. "Even when you're acting like a caveman, you're very reasonable and understanding."

He chuckled. "At least, in front of you I am."

She gave him a stern look. "Then I'm guessing I'd better keep you in front of me at all times if Steve ever does come to town."

His scowl was very real—and very intimidating—as he nodded. "Yeah. I can't even joke about that. If he does show up next weekend, you'd probably better not leave my side. Because I can't make any promises."

She blew out a sigh. "I'll see what I can do."

"About sticking by my side?"

"About putting him off."

"That'd probably be for the best."

Chapter Twenty-One

"I can't believe another week's rolled by," said Manny as they made their way out of the office on Friday afternoon.

Cal nodded. "It's been a busy one, too."

"It has for you," said Ryan. "You've been bouncing back and forth around the lake like a crazy man. Have you taken care of all your deliveries now?"

He smiled. "All except the outdoor furniture. And we'll go for that on Sunday."

Manny grinned at him. "And you will keep me informed of your progress all morning and call when you're twenty minutes out."

Ryan laughed. "Yeah, and God help you if you don't have everyone at the house and on time. I'm glad you're in charge of that. I wouldn't want to screw up."

"It's okay. It'll all work out. Even if everyone's not there when we get back, we can act like it's just a housewarming thing until they arrive."

"True. You don't have to ask her the minute you get there," said Ryan. "And the ring? You have the ring in a safe place?"

Cal tried to hide his smile as he took the box out of his pocket.

They both laughed. "I thought you were going to keep it in the safe?"

"So did I. But I like having it with me." He shrugged.

They'd reached Manny's car now and all stopped. Cal was going straight to Teresa's house since she and Elle were closing the salon early to finish packing Elle's things. He wanted to get going, but he decided he needed to get over himself and ask the guys a question that had been bothering him all week.

"Can I ask you something? Something personal?"

They exchanged a glance before they both nodded.

"Whatever it is," said Manny. "Don't feel too bad about it. I'm guessing we've both already been there."

"Thanks. I do feel kind of ..." He shrugged again. "Dumb? I don't know. Embarrassed? It's not dumb. It's just so far outside my comfort zone that I don't even have words."

Ryan chuckled. "It's okay. Like he said. We've both been there. Women will do that to you."

"Thanks. So ... the thing is ... you know how I plan to ask her on Sunday, with everyone there?"

They nodded.

"Well, I keep wondering if that's right. I thought it had to be a public declaration, you know, tell the world and all that? But now, I'm not so sure. I keep wondering if I should ... if it'd mean more to her if I ask her when it's just the two of us. I'd probably be able to say more if I did it that way. If it's not too personal a question. What did you guys do?"

Ryan chuckled. "I won't go into the ... err, intimate ... details. But I can tell you that we were alone."

Manny laughed before he spoke. "We were alone, too. It didn't occur to me to ask her with people around. It was about the two of us. And I had something I wanted to share with her while I asked." He smirked at Ryan. "Not the same kind of thing you're talking about."

Ryan laughed and punched his arm. "I didn't think so. You wouldn't have the stamina for that at your age."

Cal laughed as Manny clipped the back of Ryan's head. He was relieved to have a minute to think while they joked around.

"To tell you the truth, I was surprised that you wanted people there when you asked her," said Manny. "It doesn't seem like your style."

"It isn't. But I thought … I thought it might be hers."

"If I had to guess, I'd say not," said Ryan.

"You don't think so?"

"Nah. I mean, she's outgoing and the life and soul of the party, but she's kind of private, too. She doesn't talk about herself much, she gets other people talking. I don't know, maybe I'm wrong. I don't know her that well, but I'd guess that it'd mean more to her if it were just the two of you."

Cal nodded. "Thanks, guys. I think that's what I'm going to do."

Manny grinned at him. "When?"

He laughed. "I don't know, sometime between now and Sunday afternoon. That way we can share our good news with everyone who's expecting to see me ask." He nodded. "Yeah. I like that better."

Teresa went to open the front door when the doorbell rang. She knew it was Cal, she'd just seen him pull up outside. It struck her as odd that despite all the time they'd spent together over the last few months, he had to ring the doorbell. He didn't have a key, he couldn't just come on in. She frowned. She was the same at his place. Even though he talked as though they both lived there—and they kind of had while they were working on it—and she even called it home sometimes, she didn't have a key. She blew out a sigh. He hadn't moved in himself yet. She didn't need to start getting caught up on details that didn't matter. He loved her, that was all she needed to know. She loved him, too. However they decided to live their lives was fine by her; as long as he was in hers, she'd be happy with whatever form it took—even if she did hope for more.

She opened the door and sucked in a deep breath at the sight of his gorgeous smile.

"Hey."

"Grandpa!" Little Skye flew past her and wrapped herself around his legs. "I missed you, Grandpa!"

He swung her up in the air and then kissed her cheek as he brought her down to sit on his hip. "I've missed you, too, Skye. Are you all ready to move to your new house?"

She nodded eagerly. "Yes! I have a new bedroom. And my new house is only five minutes from your house!" She grinned. "And only two minutes from Dondervan."

Teresa brought her hand up to cover her smile at Cal's reaction. He didn't understand at first.

"Donder …?" Then he scowled. "Donovan?"

"Yes! Dondervan! He's nice, Grandpa. He's your friend."

Cal narrowed his eyes at Teresa. But she shrugged innocently. "Come on in. We're nearly finished. Elle got most of it done during the week."

Cal followed her through to the living room where there was a stack of boxes and suitcases.

Elle looked up at him with a smile. "Hey, Cal! Thanks so much for helping with all of this."

"Of course. I'm picking the van up at nine in the morning." He looked at the boxes. "Is this everything?"

"Yep. I don't have much. It's mostly Skye's things. And the house is furnished anyway."

"And we can refurnish it as soon as you're ready." Teresa kept offering. She wished that Elle would just accept that the house could be hers now. But she wasn't having any of it.

"Thanks, Mom. I've told you, though. It's fine."

Cal chuckled. "Good luck holding out, Elle. Your mom's finished with our place now. I'd guess that you're her next project."

Elle gave her an inquiring look. She'd picked up on the way he'd said *our* place, too, then. Teresa smiled. It seemed to be a habit he'd gotten into. She just wished it were true.

"I thought we could order from Giuseppe's tonight." That seemed the safest route to go—change the subject to food before things got awkward.

Elle made a face. "I didn't realize you guys were sticking around. I thought you'd be heading back over to Four Mile."

"Well, I thought you'd still have more packing to do. I didn't realize that you were almost done."

"Yep. We've been busy every night this week."

"With Dondervan."

Teresa did her best not to laugh at the way Cal scowled.

Skye smiled up at him. "He helped! He's your friend!"

Teresa stepped through to the kitchen before she burst out laughing. She'd have to have a word with Cal. Donovan was lovely. Cal shouldn't have a problem with it, even though she kind of loved that he did. Elle might keep insisting that he was just a friend, but even if that *were* still true, she doubted it would be for long.

When she went back through to the living room, they were making arrangements for the morning. Apparently, Elle was kicking them out. Teresa guessed Donovan was coming over, and that was fine by her.

Cal reached for her hand as they drove back up the East Shore. "Are you okay about the way tonight worked out?"

"Yeah. It's all good. Part of me wishes that Elle and I could have one last evening in the house together, just the two of us with Skye. But life's already moved on from there." She lifted his hand to her lips and kissed it. "And it's taking us to better places."

He pursed his lips but kept his gaze on the road ahead.

She knew what was bothering him. "It is. You're part of our lives now. And Elle's moving over to Four Mile."

He glanced over at her and squeezed her hand.

"What?"

He smiled. "Can I tell you when we get home? I don't want to say it while I'm driving."

"Okay, but I hope you're not mad about Donovan? He strikes me as a good guy."

He let out a short laugh. "I'm not mad. I'm … concerned. But that's a caveman thing. He strikes me as a good guy, too. But that doesn't mean I won't be keeping a close eye on him."

"Keeping an eye on him is fine, but only from a distance and not interfering."

He chuckled. "I'll do my best."

"You'd better. I'm serious. It's the hardest part of being a parent. You have to let them make their own mistakes. And I'm not saying I think Donovan would be a mistake. But it's up to Elle. All we get to offer is guidance and support."

"You know I want to support Elle and little Skye. I—"

She had to laugh. "Of course, I do. What I meant was Donovan. Guidance and support are all you get to give him, too. No bullying."

He smiled through pursed lips. "I'm not a bully."

"I know. I couldn't even joke about it if I thought you were. But you know damned well what I mean."

"Okay. I do. I'll be good."

She had to laugh. She loved that he cared enough for it to bother him, that he was smart enough to understand that he didn't get to control anything, and that she trusted him enough that they could laugh about it.

~ ~ ~

When they got back to the house, Cal pulled into the garage next to Teresa's car. He'd driven her into work this morning so that they could drive home together. He was hoping that as time went by, they'd be able to match up their hours more. He liked coming and going with her.

"What do you want to do about dinner?" she asked once they were in the kitchen.

He pushed his hands into his pockets and smiled when he touched the little box. He knew he wanted to ask her one thing tonight, but he wasn't sure that he wanted to ask her the big question.

She came to him and put her hands on his chest as she reached up to kiss him. "Keep smiling at me like that and I could be persuaded to forget dinner."

He laughed. "We'll get to that. But do you want to go over to the lodge to eat?" Perhaps he should take her out for a nice dinner and ask her there?

She shook her head. "I don't really feel like going over there." She went to the fridge and looked inside. "How many people have you asked to come over on Sunday? I thought it was just going to be Elle and a few of your guys from work. You've got enough supplies to feed a whole houseful."

He didn't want to tell her yet that the numbers for their housewarming were growing rapidly. She knew about Manny and Nina and Ryan and Leanne, but she didn't know that he'd also invited Ted and Diego and their ladies—he'd had to. They'd been a part of his life for a long time, and even though he hadn't seen them in years until recently, he wanted them to be a part of his future. He smiled at her; she was his future.

He went to stand beside her at the fridge. "I may have overdone it." He reached inside. "We could have one of the quiches and a salad without leaving people starving."

She laughed. "That sounds perfect."

They sat at the dining table to eat and got to enjoy an amazing sunset. Teresa smiled at him as she set her fork down. "This place is perfect, and that view … It's something else."

"It is. It's beautiful, but not as beautiful as you are."

"Aww. There you go sweet talking again." She waggled her eyebrows. "Are you trying to get me into bed?"

He laughed. "I am, and I will—later. First, there's something I want to do." He got up and cleared the plates. She started to help but he wanted her to wait here. "Sit back down. You've been on your feet all day. I'll take care of these, and I'll be back."

He looked at the champagne in the fridge. He could bring it back with him. But he changed his mind. It felt too presumptuous. He didn't think that she'd say no, but … He closed his hand around the little box again. How about that? He was nervous! He could just ask her about moving in here with him. That was all he'd originally planned to do. He'd thought he'd ask her about moving in as soon as she was free to—as soon as Elle was taken care of, and then he'd ask her to marry him on Sunday. He didn't have to ask the big question right now. He could … He smiled to himself. He couldn't wait. It was time.

He went back to the dining room and sat down beside her. He took hold of her hand and she smiled at him, but it faded as she looked into his eyes. "What's wrong, Cal?"

He remembered to smile, and her eyes danced in reply.

"Phew! You looked really scary there for a minute. Is everything okay?"

"Everything's great, Terry. Everything. This place, my life, me, everything. And it's all because of you. I love this house because of the way you've made it—because of what you've done with it but mostly because of the way you make it feel by being here. I love my life because I have you in it. I'm happy because of you—because of the way you make me feel. Because I love you and I know you love me."

"Aww." She leaned in to kiss him. "I love you right back. I don't think you know how much."

"I think I do. I hope I do. And I'm hoping you're about to prove that I'm right."

She waggled her eyebrows. "What did you have in mind—I'll prove it to you any way you like."

He had to laugh. "We'll get to that, but I'm hoping that you'll prove I'm right by saying that you'll stay here with me."

"I thought I was. I'm not …" She gave him a puzzled look. "You don't just mean tonight, do you? Do you mean even though we're done with the house now? You still want me to stay sometimes?

He shook his head. "More than sometimes." He kept hold of her hand as he slid down from his chair and got on one knee.

Her eyes were wider than he'd ever seen them, and the gold flecks shimmered with tears.

"I'm hoping that you love me enough to marry me. I've told you before that I see you as my family—I want to make it official. I've asked you to be my lady, what I really want you to be is my wife. I didn't know I was capable of loving someone the way I love you." He smiled. "I don't think I would be capable of loving someone who wasn't you. You've taught me what love is. Will you marry me and let me spend the rest of my life loving you?" He looked up into her eyes. She was nodding, and the tears were spilling down her cheeks.

"Yes! Oh my God, Cal! Yes! I didn't expect that!"

He chuckled. "But you like the idea?"

She took his face between her hands and leaned down to kiss him. "Do I like the idea of you being my husband? Of getting to see your beautiful smile every day for the rest of my life? Err, hell yeah, I do!"

He held up the ring box which so far, she didn't seem to have noticed. "Do you want this then?"

She looked down at it and then up at him as her hand came up to cover her mouth. "Cal! It's gorgeous!"

"You like it? We can change it if you don't."

She shook her head rapidly. "I love it! It's perfect. It's beautiful." She held her hand out. "Are you going to put it on me?"

He laughed and took it out of the box. "Seriously, I've never picked out jewelry before. So, if my taste isn't great—"

She put a finger to his lips and smiled. "I'd say you have exquisite taste. You chose me, didn't you?"

He nodded as he slipped it onto her finger.

"I'm not just saying it, Cal. It's the most beautiful ring I've ever seen."

He got to his feet and took her hand, pulling her up to join him and closing his arms around her. Soon they were lost in one of those kisses that made the rest of the world disappear.

~ ~ ~

When they finally came up for air, Teresa looked up at him and then down at the ring. She couldn't quite believe it. "I love you, Cal."

"I love you, Terry. More than you know." His arms tightened around her and he leaned back so he could look into her eyes. "How would you feel about a short engagement?"

She raised an eyebrow; her heart was still pounding happily in her chest. "Are you in a hurry?"

He chuckled. "I am. It's taken me more than half my life to find you. I don't want to waste any more time."

"When are you thinking?"

"As soon as you want to. Talking to all the guys they have plans in the works but they're all taking their time." He frowned. "If that's a woman thing, I'll accept it. I'll go along with whatever you want but ..."

She laughed. "I don't need a big wedding. I never thought I'd get married again." She stopped when a shadow crossed his face. Why had she said that? The last thing she wanted to do was make him think about Steve right now. "Let's come up with something we can do soon—very soon."

His smile was back at that. "You decide what you want, and I'll make it happen as soon as possible."

She had to laugh. She knew that if it were up to him, her whole life would be that way from now on. "We'll decide. Did I see champagne in the fridge?"

"You did, but I didn't want to bring it out until you said yes."

"Did you doubt for a minute that I would?"

He dropped a kiss on her lips. "Not a whole minute."

Chapter Twenty-Two

As soon as they arrived back at Teresa's place on Saturday morning, Elle spotted the ring on her mom's hand. Her head jerked to look at Cal, and he smiled. He'd asked her before he bought the ring how she felt about it—she'd been thrilled. But he hadn't had the chance to tell her that he wasn't going to wait until Sunday anymore. He shrugged. He knew Terry wanted to be the one to tell her.

"Come in!" Elle grinned. "Do you want coffee first?" She took hold of Terry's hand and held it up. "Is there anything you want to tell me?"

Terry's smile was so big, it made his heart happy—and it hadn't left her face ever since he'd asked her last night. Even when he woke up before she did this morning, she still had that smile on her face while she slept. He had a feeling that his matched it.

She wrapped her daughter in a hug, while Skye held her arms up to Cal, and he scooped her up.

"Well ..." Terry began. "Cal—"

"Cal's my grandpa!" Skye declared.

"That's right." Terry laughed. "And now he's going to be your official grandpa, too."

Skye's little eyebrows knit together as she looked up at him. "What's a fishal?"

He laughed. "It means that your grandma and I are going to be getting married soon."

"How soon?" Elle looked thrilled. "Tell me you mean like, real soon?"

"We do." Terry smiled at him. "Just as soon as we can."

Elle came and hugged him. "Well, congratulations to you both. I'm so happy for you. I'm happy for us, too. We get a Cal out of this deal as well."

Cal smiled. He was thrilled that she was so pleased.

Skye grabbed his nose. "When you marry Grandma, you'll be my real grandpa."

He nodded, not quite sure that he should say yes.

Skye looked at Elle and then back at him. "Will you be my mommy's daddy?"

He frowned, hoping that Terry or Elle might take over here. Of course, he'd be happy for Elle to see him as a father figure, but ...

Elle surprised him when she laughed. "Well, I'm a bit old to be calling him Daddy. But if Cal doesn't mind, I'll think of him that way." She looked at Terry. "He's already proved he's better at it than the other one."

Terry smiled and nodded. None of them wanted the subject of Elle's father brought up but it felt as though that conversation had laid it to rest anyway. The names they used didn't matter—they all knew what they meant to each other.

"Anyway, coffee." Elle led them to the kitchen, and before long they were loading up the van.

Donovan showed up fifteen minutes after they started, and Cal did his best to be upbeat and friendly. He was here to help after all, and it was good to have him to help move the few heavy items.

They finished loading the last few things and went back into the kitchen. Cal frowned when he saw Terry's face; she didn't look happy, and Elle was agitated.

"What's wrong?"

Elle scowled and rolled her eyes. "Apparently, Steve's here."

Cal sucked in a deep breath to stop himself from cursing. Terry came and touched his arm. "It's okay. We're done here anyway."

Elle shook her head. "It's not okay, Mom. I told him no and I meant it. I won't let him spoil this weekend for you guys."

"Nothing could spoil this weekend, sweetheart. Not even your father."

Cal loved her for saying it, but he wasn't sure that she was right. He wanted Elle and Skye there tomorrow to celebrate with them and all their friends. He could feel the muscle twitching in his jaw.

Terry rubbed her hand up and down his arm. "It's okay. Relax."

He nodded, not trusting himself to speak.

Donovan was the first to break the awkward silence that had descended. "What did you tell him, Elle?"

"That I was busy, as I'd told him I would be. And that you guys were helping, so I didn't want him around." She blew out a sigh. "He said he and Maddie could come over this afternoon and help."

Donovan looked at Cal. "So, how about we get all the stuff moved now. We can just unload it. I'll put it away later. Then you guys can have your afternoon free, and Elle can see Steve."

Cal stared at him. He didn't know which was more difficult to process—the fact that he was taking charge, or the fact that they both kept referring to Elle's father as Steve.

Terry spoke before he managed to pull himself together. "I think that's the perfect plan. Thanks, Donovan. Let's get going." She looked up at Cal. "It's not a big deal. It's not much of a change to what we'd planned."

He frowned. "We were going to get everything moved in and set up."

"I can take care of it," said Donovan.

"And what about tomorrow?" Cal knew he should keep his mouth shut and let things work out, but he didn't want the asshole ruining the party he had planned for Terry.

Elle met his gaze. "Don't worry. We'll be there. I'll get rid of him by lunchtime and we'll be at your place just like we planned."

"See." Terry smiled at him. "It doesn't have to be a problem."

She was right. He smiled back at her and it turned into a laugh as he realized what she was saying. "As long as I don't make it one?"

She nodded emphatically.

Cal seemed relaxed and happy as they drove back from Stanton on Sunday. He loved the patio furniture, as she'd known he would. It was the final touch for the house. She couldn't help smiling—their house! She looked down at the ring and her heart swelled with happiness.

She reached across and took hold of Cal's hand. "Have I told you today how much I love you, Blake Callahan?"

He smiled and lifted her hand to his lips. "You have now. And I know I've told you at least three times, but I'll tell you again if you don't think I'm overdoing it."

She laughed. "I'll never get tired of hearing that."

"Good, because I never plan to stop telling you."

They rode on in silence for a little while before he spoke again. "Are you looking forward to this afternoon?"

"I am. I think it'll be lovely to have everyone over— especially now that we can share our news with them."

He chuckled.

"What's funny about that?"

"It will be news to them. They're the ones in for a surprise, but they think that you are. They're expecting to see me ask you. I thought that was how I wanted to do it; with everyone there. They don't know that I've already asked."

She laughed. "Wow. I had no idea."

"That was the plan. It was all going to be a big surprise. But then ... I couldn't wait and more than that I wanted it to be about you and me, just us. Not for show."

"Aww. I love that. I love the way you asked me. And I'm glad you did it that way. I would have loved it with everyone there too, but not as much. It's between you and me. I'm glad we get to share with everyone, but even happier that they weren't a part of it."

He squeezed her hand. "That's how I feel. I'm glad you see it that way, too."

"I do—" Her phone rang, and she reached for it, but stopped and made a face when she saw the name on the display.

"Is that him?"

She nodded. She so did not want Steve to spoil today. She understood now why Cal had been so adamant that he didn't want him here this weekend.

"You should take it."

"I don't want to." She waited for it to stop ringing, but it only started again a few seconds later. She blew out a sigh and looked at Cal. "I'm sorry."

"It's not your fault." He smiled, but it didn't reach his eyes.

"What do you want, Steve?"

"Hello, Terry. It's nice to talk to you, too."

She rolled her eyes. "I'm busy."

"So I heard. I was calling to congratulate you."

She sucked in a deep breath, surprised that Elle had told him. "Thank you."

"Grandma finally found herself a grandpa." He laughed.

"Excuse me?"

There was a hard edge to his voice. "Skye told me that she has a grandpa now. So, I'm guessing you went and found yourself some old fart."

She had to laugh. If he only knew.

"Well, you should let him know that we'll be coming up here more often now that Elle's decided she's staying. Skye might call this old man of yours Grandpa. But I'm her grandfather. And you should tell him that. My daughter. My granddaughter. My sloppy seconds."

Teresa's mouth fell open before she recovered. "What did you just say?"

"You heard me."

"You bastard! That's a horrible thing to say."

"I imagine it's a horrible thing to be. Anyway, I just wanted to congratulate you on getting your claws into an old fart. Maddie and I will stop by your party before we leave."

"You'll do no such thing!" She glanced at Cal. He'd kill him if he showed his face at the house, and right now she wasn't sure that she'd want to stop him.

"I'll do whatever I like, Teresa. Elle says she's taking Skye over there no matter what. And I'll want to say goodbye to them before I leave. You should warn your man."

She glanced at Cal again. He was scowling—looking more intimidating than she'd ever seen him. She should probably let him know now what was coming—though she doubted he'd calm down before Steve showed his face.

"So, you're telling me that I should warn my old fart, Cal, that you plan to come by the house this afternoon so that you can set him straight?"

Cal looked fit to explode. "Put him on speaker."

She did, just in time for Cal to hear, "That's right. And tell him I'll understand if he wants to stay out of the way while I see my girls."

Teresa's heart pounded when Cal spoke. He put the fear of God into her.

"We're having a private celebration this afternoon. Consider this your warning that you're not welcome. If you come anyway, I will consider you to be trespassing on my property."

Steve's laugh sounded a little less cocky this time. "And what are you going to do, call the police?"

"No." Cal didn't elaborate, but the threat contained in that one syllable was enough to make Teresa's blood run cold.

"I'll see you later." Steve hung up.

Teresa's breath came out in a rush. Cal's jaw was set, and he was scowling at the road ahead.

"I'm sorry." She felt terrible.

His expression softened. "It's okay. It's not your fault. It might turn out to be a good thing."

"How? I can't lose you now. You can't get sent to jail for murder just after you ask me to marry you."

He chuckled and the sound of it washed over her and made her relax a little. "Don't worry. I won't."

"What murder him, or get caught?"

He laughed again. "Either."

~ ~ ~

When they got back, the whole of Lakeside Drive was lined with parked cars.

Teresa shook her head. "Did you invite the whole town?"

"Just your good friends." He smiled. "And it seems that at least half the town thinks of you as one."

He pulled into the garage and cut the engine. His heart was still pounding, and all his senses were on high alert. He couldn't get over the gall of the guy. He took a deep breath and turned to Terry. No matter how angry he might be, she was all that mattered. He leaned across the console and closed his fingers around the back of her neck. "Don't worry."

"How can I not?" She looked panicked.

He claimed her mouth in a deep kiss before letting her go. "I intend to make your life better now that I'm in it. I give you my word that I won't do anything that would disappoint you."

She let out a shrill laugh. "Yeah, but you know that I'd happily castrate him myself!"

He chuckled. "I do. But we're better than that, you and me. We won't stoop to his level. But I will put a stop to him."

"What …?"

"Do you trust me?"

He relaxed a little when she nodded. She didn't hesitate even for a second.

"Thank you. I won't disappoint you. Now, let's go in there and have fun with our friends."

She pursed her lips.

"Okay, so let's just get through it until he's gone, and after that we'll have fun with our friends, how about that?"

She chuckled. "That at least, sounds possible."

"Will you do me a favor and give me two minutes to have a word with Manny and Ryan?"

"What are you going to do?"

"Nothing bad. I promise."

"Okay."

"As soon as I've talked to them, I'll find you and we can make our announcement, okay?"

She nodded.

"Do you want to tell them or shall I?"

She looked down at the ring on her hand. "If you take more than a couple of minutes, I think someone will notice."

"Ah."

"I don't want to take it off."

He leaned across and kissed her again. "I don't want you to—ever."

She smiled. "You'd better be quick then."

Nina greeted them at the door that led into the kitchen. "We saw you coming. Manny's over—" She didn't get a chance to finish before Cal headed over to him.

Teresa scanned the room for Elle. It was crowded. It looked like maybe three quarters of the town was here.

"Are you okay?" asked Nina.

Teresa smiled. "I'm wonderful. I've never been happier. But Steve's trying to spoil it."

She held her hand out a little way and looked down. Nina beamed when she saw the ring. "He asked you already! Oh, Terry!"

"Shh! We want to tell everyone together, but I had to tell you."

"Of course. But what do you mean about Steve?"

She blew out a sigh. "Skye told him that she has a grandpa—who's going to marry Grandma. And he's pissed, but he thinks I've found myself some old fart!"

Nina laughed. "He has no idea!"

"No, but he's going to find out. He said he's going to come over to see Elle and Skye before he leaves. He's got it in his head that I'm with some old man who'll be scared of him."

Nina's eyes grew wide. "Cal would squish him like a bug!"

She had to laugh, but she was worried that it might be true. "He's assured me that he won't, and I trust him not to do anything stupid. But Steve's … oh, shit!"

Her hand came up to cover her mouth. She could see Steve and Maddie coming up the path to the front door. She looked around and spotted Elle standing with Donovan, who was holding Skye.

"I'd better get over there."

Nina scurried after her.

Teresa didn't get to Elle before Izzy opened the front door. Her heart started to pound as she looked for Cal. She couldn't see him, but now Steve was heading for Elle. Teresa just reached her first.

"Mom! I'm so sorry. I don't know if he'd really do it but ..." she turned and followed Teresa's gaze. "Steve! I told you not to come here!"

Steve smiled at Teresa. "And I told you I'd see you here."

"Get out, Steve."

She had to wonder what had happened to him. He hadn't always been this bad, she didn't think.

Maddie appeared beside him and gave Teresa an apologetic look. "Come on, Steve. Let's just say goodbye to the girls and we can go."

He shook her hand off. "I want to meet this Cal before we leave." He made a face at Teresa. "I need to set him straight about a few things."

"What things?"

They all turned to see Cal scowling down at Steve. He was flanked by Manny on one side and Ryan on the other—as if he needed them!

"That's none of your business." Steve looked nervous when he spoke.

Cal glared at him. "You said you want to set me straight."

Teresa watched Steve's adam's apple bob up and down—it was funny the little details you noticed in moments of stress.

"You're Cal?"

He nodded.

"Well, I err ..."

"I'm Cal. This is my house." He looked at Teresa. "*Our* house. I told you that if you came here, I would consider that to be trespassing."

Teresa's throat went dry as she wondered if it was legal to shoot trespassers.

"Grandpa!"

Skye wriggled to get out of Donovan's arms and ran to Cal. He glared at Steve one more time before he scooped her up and sat her on his hip.

Teresa's breath caught in her chest when she spotted a holster on his other hip. Steve saw it at the same time she did. He turned white.

"I don't want any trouble. I just want to say bye to my girls. Skye …"

Teresa wanted to kiss her when she rested her little head on Cal's shoulder and snuggled against him. "Grandpa, that's Steve. Do you know Steve?"

"I don't, sunshine. And I don't think I'm going to either." His smile for Skye disappeared as he looked over her head at Steve. "Am I?"

Steve shook his head.

"They have to leave now," Cal told Skye.

She lifted her head and gave a little wave before turning back to Cal. "Can we go down to the beach now, Grandpa?"

He planted a kiss on her forehead. "In a little while, sunshine. Will you keep an eye on Donovan for me while I take care of something?"

Teresa watched, fascinated and terrified at the same time as he handed her back to Donovan. It felt as though he was establishing the hierarchy of male figures in her life and there was no room left for Steve.

"You were just leaving." Cal put his hands on his hips.

"Elle?" said Steve.

Teresa felt bad for her, but she didn't seem upset in the least. "Yeah. See you, Steve. I told you not to come here." She turned away from him, and Donovan put his arm around her shoulders and led her away.

Cal took a step toward Steve and he scurried for the door. Nina put her hand on Terry's arm as they watched him go, closely followed by Cal, Manny and Ryan.

"Wow!" Nina shook her head. "I think you've seen the last of him."

She let out a shaky laugh. "I think you're right. He looked like he was going to pee his pants when he saw the gun."

Nina laughed. "That was clever."

"You weren't scared? You don't think it was dangerous?"

"It was empty!"

"It was?"

Nina laughed and hugged her. "I'd put money on it. Manny's told me about that trick before. He says you don't need to carry a loaded gun, that people see it and their imagination—their fear—fills in the rest."

"Pft! Well, I don't mind telling you that I was scared."

"Not of Cal?"

"No, but of what I thought might happen."

Nina smiled. "My guess is that nothing bad will ever happen in your life again—he'll make sure of it."

She nodded and looked at the door, hoping that he'd come back before anything bad happened out there.

Her heart and her eyes filled up when he came back inside and immediately found her gaze. He held it every step of the way until he was back in front of her.

"It isn't loaded," he assured her before he wrapped his arms around her and kissed her.

"Wow!" she breathed when he lifted his head.

He smiled. "I told you I wouldn't let you down."

"I never for a minute thought you would." She winked at him. "I did have momentary doubt about whether you might take him down."

He chuckled. "So did I, but it was only momentary. This was the best way to deal with it."

"What did you do out there?"

"We had a little chat."

She raised an eyebrow at him.

~ ~ ~

But even if he'd wanted to—and he didn't—Cal didn't get the chance to explain. The sound of metal tapping on glass made them both turn to see Manny and Ryan standing on the bottom stair. They were both tapping spoons against their glasses.

The whole room went quiet as everyone turned to look at them.

Manny grinned. "Don't look at me! I'm just getting your attention. I believe that our host and hostess have something they'd like to tell us."

Cal took hold of her hand and led her to the stairs. Her hand felt so small inside of his. He knew she was capable and strong. Like she'd told him, she wasn't weak or helpless in any way. But she was his lady. And he planned to do everything in his power to protect her—and her two little ladies—from anyone and anything that could hurt them in any way.

When they reached the stairs, she got up on the first one and laughed when she turned and looked him in the eye. "You stay there. You don't need to get any bigger."

He chuckled and stayed where he was.

He looked around at all the faces turned toward them. "First, I want to thank you all for being here today. It means a lot. So many old friends and new ones. You all know that we wanted to invite you to see our new home. And we have some news to share with you."

The room went quiet and he tightened his arm around Terry's shoulders. "This beautiful lady has agreed to do me the honor of becoming my wife."

A cheer went up and it sent goosebumps racing over his skin. He'd never imagined himself in this situation, never thought he'd wanted it before, but now she was the most important thing in the world to him.

They got lost in a sea of hugs and backslaps and handshakes. Cal enjoyed all of it—even the people he didn't know but who'd known Terry all her life. They loved her, so he liked them.

When he finally made it back to her, she planted a kiss on his lips. "I love you."

He kissed her back. "I love you. I give you my word I will love you and honor and protect you till the day I die."

"You're big on the protecting thing, aren't you?"

He gave her a wry smile. "Maybe sometimes."

She laughed. "More than sometimes."

"I'm big on the loving you thing, too."

She tightened her arms around his waist and pressed herself against him. "Oh, I know it, Mr. Callahan. Very big."

He chuckled. "I meant on loving you, loving you. Not …"
He held her closer so she could feel what he meant. "*Loving*
you."

"I meant both. I know you love me and I sure as hell know it
when you *love* me."

He pressed a kiss to her forehead. "I'll love you forever,
Terry."

He knew it was true as she looked up into his eyes. "And I'll
be right here," she snuggled closer against him, "loving you
right back.";

;

~ ~ ~

I hope you enjoyed Cal and Teresa's story. I love them.
You'll get to see some more of them in my next book, too.
You may have guessed that Elle and Donovan—and Skye—
are up next. Their story is called Please Don't Say Goodbye
and you can check out their page on my website for updates.

A Note from SJ

I hope you enjoyed Cal and Teresa's story. Please let your friends know about the books if you feel they would enjoy them as well. It would be wonderful if you would leave me a review, I'd very much appreciate it.

Check out the "Also By" page to see if any of my other series appeal to you – You'll find a list of all my books – complete with reading order on my website www.SJMcCoy.com/reading-order.html.

There are a few options to keep up with me and my imaginary friends:

The best way is to Sign up for my Newsletter at my website www.SJMcCoy.com. Don't worry I won't bombard you! I'll let you know about upcoming releases, share a sneak peek or two and keep you in the loop for a couple of fun giveaways I have coming up :0)

You can join my readers group to chat about the books or like my Facebook Page www.facebook.com/authorsjmccoy
I occasionally attempt to say something in 140 characters or less(!) on Twitter

And I'm in the process of building a shiny new website at www.SJMcCoy.com

I love to hear from readers, so feel free to email me at SJ@SJMcCoy.com if you'd like. I'm better at that! :0)

I hope our paths will cross again soon. Until then, take care, and thanks for your support—you are the reason I write!

Love

SJ

PS Project Semicolon

You may have noticed that the final sentence of the story closed with a semi-colon. It isn't a typo. Project Semi Colon is a non-profit movement dedicated to presenting hope and love to those who are struggling with depression, suicide, addiction and self-injury. Project Semicolon exists to encourage, love and inspire. It's a movement I support with all my heart.

"A semicolon represents a sentence the author could have ended, but chose not to. The sentence is your life and the author is you." - Project Semicolon

This author started writing after her son was killed in a car crash. At the time I wanted my own story to be over, instead I chose to honour a promise to my son to write my 'silly stories' someday. I chose to escape into my fictional world. I know for many who struggle with depression, suicide can appear to be the only escape. The semicolon has become a symbol of support, and hopefully a reminder – Your story isn't over yet

Also by SJ McCoy

Summer Lake Silver
Clay and Marianne in Like Some Old Country Song
Seymour and Chris in A Dream Too Far
Ted and Audrey in A Little Rain Must Fall
Izzy and Diego in Where the Rainbow Ends
Manny and Nina in Silhouettes Shadows and Sunsets
Teresa and Cal in More than Sometimes

Summer Lake Seasons
Angel and Luke in Take These Broken Wings
Zack and Maria in Too Much Love to Hide
Logan and Roxy in Sunshine Over Snow
Ivan and Abbie in Chase the Blues Away
Colt and Cassie in Forever Takes a While

Summer Lake Series
Love Like You've Never Been Hurt
Work Like You Don't Need the Money
Dance Like Nobody's Watching
Fly Like You've Never Been Grounded
Laugh Like You've Never Cried
Sing Like Nobody's Listening
Smile Like You Mean It
The Wedding Dance
Chasing Tomorrow
Dream Like Nothing's Impossible
Ride Like You've Never Fallen
Live Like There's No Tomorrow
The Wedding Flight

Fight Like You've Never Lost

Remington Ranch Series
Mason and also available as Audio

Shane

Carter

Beau
Four Weddings and a Vendetta

A Chance and a Hope
Chance is a guy with a whole lot of story to tell. He's part of
the fabric of both Summer Lake and Remington Ranch. He
needed three whole books to tell his own story.

Chance Encounter

Finding Hope

Give Hope a Chance

Love in Nashville
Autumn and Matt in Bring on the Night

The Davenports
Oscar

TJ

Reid

The Hamiltons
Cameron and Piper in Red wine and Roses

Chelsea and Grant in Champagne and Daisies

Mary Ellen and Antonio in Marsala and Magnolias

Marcos and Molly in Prosecco and Peonies

About the Author

I'm SJ, a coffee addict, lover of chocolate and drinker of good red wines. I'm a lost soul and a hopeless romantic. Reading and writing are necessary parts of who I am. Though perhaps not as necessary as coffee! I can drink coffee without writing, but I can't write without coffee.

I grew up loving romance novels, my first boyfriends were book boyfriends, but life intervened, as it tends to do, and I wandered down the paths of non-fiction for many years. My life changed completely a few years ago and I returned to Romance to find my escape.

I write 'Sweet n Steamy' stories because to me there is enough angst and darkness in real life. My favorite romances are happy escapes with a focus on fun, friendships and happily-ever-afters, just like the ones I write.

These days I live in beautiful Montana, the last best place. If I'm not reading or writing, you'll find me just down the road in the park - Yellowstone. I have deer, eagles and the occasional bear for company, and I like it that way :0)